HANGMAN'S CORNER

HANGMAN'S CORNER

PETER KING

FIVE STAR

A part of Gale, Cengage Learning

GALE
CENGAGE Learning™

Detroit • New York • San Francisco • New Haven, Conn • Waterville, Maine • London

GALE
CENGAGE Learning™

Set in 11 pt. Plantin
Printed on permanent paper.

LIBRARY OF CONGRESS CATALOGING-IN-PUBLICATION DATA

King, Peter.
 Hangman's corner / by Peter King. — 1st ed.
  p. cm.
 "Published in 2008 in conjunction with Tekno Books and Ed Gorman."—T.p. verso
  ISBN-13: 978-1-59414-645-9 (alk. paper)
  ISBN-10: 1-59414-645-4 (alk. paper)
  1. Taxicab drivers—Fiction. 2. London (England)—History—19th century—Fiction. I. Title.
 PS3561.I4822H36 2008
 813'.54—dc22   2007041780

First Edition. First Printing: April 2008.

Published in 2008 in conjunction with Tekno Books and Ed Gorman.

My thanks are due to Tom Harris, London, England, for his exhaustive efforts in research on many matters related to London in the late nineteenth century.

CHAPTER 1

He was an unusual looking bloke. I can say that because I notice my fares—what they wear, how they carry themselves, what they do for a living, where they've come from and where they're going, as well as why. What I can't tell, I guess at, and I'm not often wrong.

I'm a hansom cab driver, and I like my work for that reason—all the interesting people I see in the course of a day. "A student of human nature." That's what Smiling Sid calls me, though I don't think of what I do as much studying as it is what Sid calls "speculating." Thousands of people I've had in my cab, taking them from one part of London to another, and there's hardly one of them I haven't "speculated" about. Not everybody is like Sid though. Most people say I just don't know how to mind my own business, but Sid used to teach at Oxford until he—but I'm not a tattletale.

Nobody's really ordinary; we're all different. The thing that made this chap noticeable, first of all, was his clothes. They puzzled me at first. He wore black trousers, a black waistcoat and a coat that didn't quite fit him. He kept pulling at the collar of his gray shirt as if it was tight, and it wasn't. Well, lots of folks are making do with what they can get in these hard times, but this bloke wasn't one of those. His clothes had been cut from some other clothes, the cutting being the best somebody could do without spending much time on the job.

In appearance, he was medium height, had dark hair, no

beard or mustache, not old but with a face that said he was carrying most of the cares in the world. It was when he got out that I noticed his shoes. They were black shoes, not boots like most men wear, and as soon as I spotted them, it all fitted together.

I picked him up at the Fulham end of the King's Road.

When I dropped him in the middle of Vauxhall Road as he asked, he paid the fare and gave me a halfpenny tip. It's not much for that sort of ride, but I thanked him. I always try to be civil. It was what happened afterwards that stuck in my mind.

He disappeared.

He didn't go up in a puff of smoke like the Demon King in a pantomime. There was none of the trickery you might see in the Musick Hall. It was just that simple—one second he was there, and when I looked again, he was gone.

It's true that I wasn't watching him that careful. After pocketing the coins, I looked up and down Vauxhall Road to see if there was another fare in the offing. It was quiet, not many people about and no other vehicles. On the side where he had got out was a high brick wall covered with ivy, and on the other side was a row of two-story houses. I had thought it a bit unusual that he had asked to be dropped in the middle of Vauxhall Road and not at any particular address, but then people have different reasons for doing things like that.

The most likely answer was that he had gone into one of the houses, but he couldn't have in that short a time. I would have seen him, and I hadn't. I don't miss much as a rule, *but you have this time, Ned Parker,* I told myself. Must be getting old.

I was born the year Queen Victoria came to the throne, 1837, and I was thirty-two now. Maybe that was getting old. Better not let on, I thought, or the other cabbies'll get a big laugh out of it if I say anything about a bloke disappearing. They pull my leg anyway about seeing and noticing everything, about poking my nose into everybody's business, wanting to know everything that's going on and why.

The chap hadn't really disappeared. I knew that. Well, I mean, people just don't. There had to be an explanation. I just hadn't thought of it yet. I kept thinking about the happening though for the rest of the day and the next day, I was still puzzling over it. I kept running the scene through my memory, trying to remember any little detail that might help me make sense of the whole business. It was later in the morning that it really came back into my mind, and then it was only because I found myself staring at the chap who'd disappeared.

He was lying flat on his back, naked, and as dead as any man would be with all those stab wounds in him.

It was one of those rare cab trips that took me past the little room that I call home—and there was Jacko on the doorstep waiting for me. I call him Jacko, though not to his face. Detective Rollo Jackson's his proper name, and he's not a bad chap— for a copper. I know him fairly well.

He's had me in custody a couple of times—well, perhaps three or four. He's always had to let me go, as he didn't have enough evidence, or they found out that somebody else had done the crime. He was fair, was Jacko, fairer than a lot of them on the Metropolitan force who didn't need evidence to put somebody away.

If you saw him and didn't know him, you wouldn't think he was a copper, and when you found out he was one, you wouldn't expect him to be fair. He had a thin face, a bit like a ferret. He had lanky hair and big ears, and his manner was often snarly, like a cat whose tail you had stepped on. But speak as you find, I always say, and he was fair with me, and I never heard anybody say different. He was a bit short with me this morning, though.

"Whip up that broken-down horse of yours, Parker," he

snapped. "You're taking me for a ride."

When he's in one of those moods, it's best not to argue with him. I made a few comments about Perseus not being broken down, but being one of the best cab horses in London, then asked him where he wanted to go.

"I'll direct you," he said—as if I didn't know my own way around town, blindfolded and half-drunk. From my room over the butcher shop in Pimlico, it wasn't very far, although I was still trying to guess where we were going when we turned off just before Blackfriars Bridge and on to Carlisle Street.

I knew then, because he told me to stop—right in front of the Carlisle Street Police Station.

Jackson gave me a wave to follow him, and after looping the reins around one of the cast-iron bollards, I did. We went through several grim rooms, some with miserable looking blokes in them, most of them villains. Uniforms were there, too, and we went on through into the police hospital at the back. A door swung open as we walked past, and I got a horrifying eyeful that told me I'd better take good care of myself. Cries and moans came out and were thankfully cut off as the door slammed. I hurried after Jacko so fast I almost knocked him over.

He led me into a room with rough brick walls that had been whitewashed, and a low ceiling. There was a hospital smell that I've never liked. An oil lamp burned, sputtering cheap oil and throwing flickering shadows into the corners.

I could see how they didn't need much light in here. All the people in the place were dead.

Wooden tables had sheets over them, and the shapes underneath made me queasy. Jacko jerked the sheet off one of the tables.

"Know this man?"

It had been a man. Now it was a body, a dead body, its naked flesh a grayish white. I'd seen bodies before that had been fished out of the Thames, but this one was particularly revolting with all those ugly knife slashes. I glanced quickly then looked away.

"No," I said.

Well, it's the natural answer, isn't it, to anything the police ask you? And specially if they show you a body and ask if you know him, naturally, you say "no."

"Look again," growled Jackson.

I did, and as I turned away, he grabbed my chin and forced me to take another look. When he let go, I tried not to heave.

"No," I said and my voice must have been husky. "No, I don't know him."

"Cast your mind back. Yesterday, starting from the Fulham end of the King's Road."

It was the bloke I'd taken to Vauxhall. I knew that. I also knew that I'd been fingered. Jackson had brought in cabbies from various parts of London, and one of them had remembered seeing the man and seeing me. Every cabby knows me.

I changed my expression. "Wait a minute," I said and snapped my fingers. Jacko watched me with a wicked smile.

"Let's go next door. You can tell me all about it."

"Next door" was a tiny, chilly room with water dripping off the ceiling in one corner. It wasn't a lot better than the one we had just left. It had a little table, two old chairs, and a big picture of Queen Victoria.

Some papers lay on the table in front of Jacko. He shuffled them, and one slid out of the pile. Jacko didn't seem to notice, but I did. It was an artist's drawing. Gawd love me! It was a drawing of me!

Well, I say "me." I knew my short cut black hair was tidier than that. My nose isn't that long, even if folks do talk about me poking my long nose into everything. The mouth was more or less right, but the chin was wrong. Mine is more determined, this one looked a little short. At the bottom, it said, "Height 5 feet 10, Weight 10 stone, Cabby." Jacko had been shuffling the other papers when he noticed this one and quick-like, pulled it back.

"When was that made?" I asked him.

"When was what made?" He was all innocence.

"That drawing of me."

"Oh, saw that, did you? Oh, after that bank job in Islington."

"I had nothing to do with that."

"You drove a man from the scene of the crime."

"How did I know he was a look-out? He was just a fare to me."

"Lucky you didn't get booked," he grunted.

"You've no right to make drawings of me," I protested.

He gave me that grin of his. It's creepy. "Protecting your rights, that's what we're doing. It makes sure you don't get wrongfully arrested."

I opened my mouth to argue, but he was first.

"Talk!" he ordered.

I told him everything. Well, everything except that the bloke had been wearing clothes that had been cut down from a clergyman's outfit, that he had worn shoes sold only to clergymen, that he kept pulling at his neck where he was used to wearing a clerical collar—and that he had disappeared. Naturally, I didn't tell him any of that, particularly the last bit.

Jacko sat watching me like a hungry cat eyeing a fat mouse. "The cabby who saw you picking him up in front of the White Lion on the King's Road said he was dressed strange."

"Strange?" I said.

"You've got a reputation, Parker, for being curious. You notice details about people, all kinds of details, some that other people might not notice at all. Not only that, but you can put 'em together, make sense out of 'em. Now make some sense out of this bloke for me. What was he wearing when you picked him up?"

I rubbed my jaw. Some do that, natural-like, when they're thinking. I don't; I think too fast. It looks good though, and I've learned to do it when I want an extra second or two to think. Jacko was about to snarl at me when I said, quick-like, "Yes, I remember. He looked like his clothes had been cut from a suit to make it look different."

"Come on, come on," Jacko said, impatient. "You noticed more than that."

"It was what I didn't notice that struck me as funny," I said, and I waited till Jacko had his mouth open again and I went on, "I didn't notice where he went."

He took an angry step toward me and I shuffled back. He's not a bully though, even if I was goading him a bit.

"No, straight up," I protested, "it's the truth!" His expression changed at that word, but before he could make anything of it, I was going on. "He got out of the cab, paid me and sort of walked off. Well, Vauxhall Road's not the best place to pick up fares, but I glanced round—just on the off chance. There wasn't many people, and none of 'em looked like fares. It was then that I noticed the bloke had gone."

Jacko gave me one of his nastier looks. "He went into one of the houses."

"I'd have seen him cross the street."

"Where else could he have gone?"

"Dunno. The wall is too high on the other side. He couldn't have jumped it."

Jacko kept up his nasty look. He does it when he's mad, and though it's frightening when you see it for the first time, after that he looks as if he's trying to go cross-eyed, and then you just have to laugh. Well, you want to laugh but you don't, of course. I was trying not to laugh now, and he mistook the look on my screwed-up face for fear.

"Come on now, Parker. Just tell me the truth and you have nothing to be afraid of. People don't vanish. Where did he go?"

"I honestly don't know—honest."

"Guess," he invited me.

"I can't. It's all too impossible."

"And you didn't tell anybody about this?"

" 'Course not. They'd think I was crazy."

I said that on the spur of the moment and, funny enough, it seemed to convince him that I was telling the truth. Well, most of it anyway; he knows me too well. He kept on at me, but I stuck to my story. I'd helped the police enough. Now it was their turn to do their job.

"Pity we stopped sending evil-doers to Australia a few years ago," he said, almost as if he was talking to himself, but he was making sure I could hear him. "Still, keeping 'em here means we can keep a closer eye on 'em."

He fixed me with that nasty look again. "We can jerk your license as easy as kiss-your-hand. You know that, don't you?"

I nodded. Last year, control of London's cabs had passed from the Foreign Office to the Metropolitan Police. Within the first twelve months, more than a thousand licenses had been pulled. I hope that doesn't mean there was a thousand bad 'uns, I don't think it could be that many.

Jacko tossed out a few more reminders of all the things he could do to me, but I reasoned that if he was only talking about taking away my license, he couldn't be thinking seriously that I had had anything to do with this bloke's death. Finally, he said, very reluctantly, "All right, you can go," and I was halfway to the door when he added, "I'll have my eye on you. When I talk to you again, maybe you'll remember."

"Remember what?" I asked innocently.

"What you haven't told me."

I got a few steps nearer the door when he said, "Word is that the new commissioner is going to come down real heavy on this case."

Edward Bradford was the name of the new Commissioner of Metropolitan Police—I keep up on these things. My old mum taught me to read and sent me to the Catholic School, where the nuns paddled any kid who didn't pay attention. They never had much trouble with me because I liked reading, so I got real good at it.

Result was, every day, I read the papers that fares left in my cab. I knew that after starting as a cadet with the East India Company, Edward Bradford had served with a Madras cavalry regiment, then gone back to India with the Dragoons. He was in the Sepoy Mutiny then helped put down Tantia Topee's rebellion. He only had one arm—the other had been so badly mauled by a tiger that he had to have it cut off at the shoulder—and they did it without putting him into the twilight sleep. A few weeks later, he was out hunting lions with a spear, holding the horses' reins in his teeth. Millie, my girl friend, knew all about him too, due to the fact that she's a great reader of books and he married the niece of one of her favorite writers, a woman called Jane Austen.

"He's been on the job four weeks already," I said brightly. "He's got to get results fast, hasn't he? They say he's a hard man, too. You're going to like working under him, Jacko."

He jerked an angry finger at the door, and I decided to push him just a little bit further.

"Who is the stiff, Jacko?"

He was about to growl at me, then must have thought it better to keep me on his side. "Don't know yet—but we will."

"Stabbed before he was dropped into the river, was he?"

He scowled but answered. "Yes. Any of the stab wounds might have done it. Whoever killed him was no amateur."

15

The smell of the place was making me want to heave again. It was a relief to have him tell me, "Get out of here!"

Later on, I had a fare wanted to go to the Old Kent Road, and after I dropped him off, I turned Perseus toward the river. Vauxhall Road wasn't that far, and that curiosity of mine just wouldn't let go. It was crisp and dry, and Perseus was feeling frisky for a trot. I slowed him down when we came to the place where I had dropped off the poor bloke the day before. The houses looked normal; nothing to notice there, and on the other side, only the brick wall that went on and on. When I got to the end of the road, I turned around and came back. Then I saw it.

I should have spotted it before, but it was hard to see. A small door let into the wall, but it was painted the same color as the wall, and the ivy covered it so that it was nearly invisible. I hopped out and ran to it. A black iron handle turned, but the door was bolted on the inside. I got back in the cab and followed the wall down to the river.

This was one of those places where you get the great views of the Houses of Parliament and Big Ben over on the other bank. Where I was stood a big house with iron gates and a big brass plate, fresh polished, that said:

VAUXHALL PALACE
RESIDENCE OF THE BISHOP OF VAUXHALL

Well, this was a turn-up for the book, and no mistake! A bishop's palace! My fare must have been expected, nipped in the side door, left unbolted to let him in, and then the next thing, he's cruelly murdered!

I looked at the building. I'd passed it dozens of times, but naturally I'd never been in it. Small for a palace, but the stone looked hundreds of years old, and the leaded windows and the great big oak door behind the iron gates made it look important.

Well, that was one mystery solved. I was just flicking the whip at Perseus to get him moving, when the front door opened and who should come out but what could be no other than the bishop himself. From the carefully laced gaiters and polished boots, to the short cloak and the black four-cornered hat, he looked every inch the part. He was elderly, but lively, despite a stomach from too much good food and red-faced from too much port.

A servant came bustling out after him, a pinch-faced chap, skinny as a poker. He opened one of the gates and stepped out into the road, waving at me. Well, I thought, I can get a fare out of this, at least, and drew up to him.

"Take His Grace to Mildenhall Mansions in Belgravia," the servant ordered and opened the door of my cab.

I knew the address well. It was one of the posher addresses in London and near enough to Buckingham Palace that, as I went past, I could see their big Union Jack flying, meaning the Royal Family was in residence. Mildenhall Mansions is a big spread, four stories high and in five separate buildings. Each building had its own entrance up a flight of wide stone steps.

The bishop rapped on the roof of the cab. "The far end."

He gave me a shilling and a nod that meant "Keep the change." I watched him climb the steps and knock on one of the doors with a fancy trim. It opened at once, and I got just a glimpse of the woman inside.

A real knockout, she was. Golden hair piled high, a lovely face with a wide mouth painted red, tall, and wearing a gown of blue and white lace. She pulled him in and was putting her arms around him as the door closed.

Well, I thought, you old rascal. Still, you wouldn't believe some of the sights us cabbies see. If all we know was to be printed in the *Daily Mail* on Sunday, London would be half-empty on Monday morning.

17

CHAPTER 2

In Battersea Park near the Albert Bridge is an area not many people know about. It's one of a few cabby hideouts that are scattered all over London. Driving a cab fourteen or fifteen hours a day is a thankless job, really, and who could deny the poor cabby a place where he could have a smoke, a jaw with his friends and a short rest away from the hurly-burly?

Hangman's Corner, they call it, and the old gallows is still there, right on the banks of the Thames. It's not that many years ago that big crowds gathered to hold their breath until the trapdoor dropped, and then they'd shout and cheer as the body jerked and danced in midair. The newspapers got all holy though, and said that watching hangings was as bad as watching the Romans and their animals chewing up Christians. Finally, they got it closed, but the wooden gallows is still there.

We try to ignore it, the gallows, as much as we can. The city council says they're going to take it down, but none of us cabbies hold our breath about anything they say.

One end of the park is screened off by big piles of rubbish that people have been dumping there since they closed down the Tivoli Tea Gardens, and a fence on the river side means that the hideout can't be seen from any of the roads round it. A hansom cab trotting through the park is a common enough sight, and people never notice when one turns off down a track you can hardly see.

I had just done a delivery job for a bookie in Earls' Court—

well, even a cabby has to make a living, and dodging the rules of the Jockey Club was a game that everybody joins in. Earls' Court has become a very busy spot since the big new underground railway station opened there last year, and as I was near the Battersea hideout, I thought I'd stop in. I do this once in a while to chat with my mates and get the latest skinny. A couple of dozen cabs must have been there this time, horses thirstily guzzling water from the troughs, and some drivers standing about, some sitting on old tea chests, some eating, some smoking.

Paddy O'Flaherty, a grizzled old veteran of the cab trade, put on his thickest Irish accent when he saw me, just like he always does. "Faith and who is it coming toward us? 'Tis none but himself, Ned Parker, fresh from flogging candlesticks, is it?"

A laugh went up from the small group and Arthur Evans, another cabby of thirty years' or more experience, chipped in. "Gonna buy us a pint with yer ill-gotten gains, Ned?"

"I can name a dozen of you more likely to be flogging candlesticks than me," I told them, "and that's before I even pause to draw breath." There was another laugh. I knew what they were referring to. Last week's newspapers all had the story about a silver candlestick being stolen from a church in London, only to be followed two days later by the theft of another silver candlestick from another church.

"I'm an honest bloke," I reminded them. "Robbing churches is more your style than mine."

Tommy Thompson, red-haired, shiny faced and near my age, came up to me. "How's Millie then? She must have tossed you over by now! Tell her I'm available any time." Millie Sanders, my girl friend, is in the chorus at the Strand Musick Hall. She wants to get a job at the Gaiety Theatre, but I hope she doesn't. The blokes who hang around the stage door there are toffs with lots of money to throw about. Of course, Millie wouldn't have her head turned that easy but still . . . you never know.

"She's in the pink, Tommy," I told him. "And I won't give her your message. She's too good for the likes of you."

"Good, is she?" Tommy chuckled. "I've seen her showing her ankles—and very nice ones too. They say that new place in Camden Town has girls showing a lot more than that, and I hear Millie is having a try-out there."

"That kind of place isn't Millie's style," I told him, and he grinned as if he didn't believe me.

Toby, a veteran cabby, was telling some cronies about having his cab turned over in a clash between the Sabbatarians and the Sunday Defense League. "Fancy," he was saying, "risking the lives and limbs of innocent people, fighting over whether people should be allowed to do what they want on Sunday!"

A new lad, Alec, still wet behind the ears, was telling of his problems the day before. "This bloke got really ratty when I told him I didn't know where the Rhymers' Club was. 'I don't know where every club in London is,' I told him."

A couple of regulars laughed. "Better learn quick then," one of them said.

"All right," said Alec, "where is it then?" and there was no lack of voices to tell him that it was a group of writers and poets who met in a tavern called The Cheshire Cheese, which is in Wine Court just off Fleet Street.

A couple of cabbies had a fire going, and one was holding a sausage over it. He was known to one and all as Preacher, and he called me over. "Fancy a bite, Ned?"

I didn't, because I knew where he got the sausages. Any stray dogs in that neighborhood ended up in the sausages that Preacher's wife served up at her stand in Ludgate Circus, but I just thanked him and said I wasn't hungry.

"Got to keep your strength up," he warned me.

Bombardier spoke up. Limping from being wounded in the

war in Persia, he was straight and stiff-backed and had tried several jobs in Civvy Street before becoming a cabby.

"Anything on the grapevine about them candlesticks, Preacher?" he asked.

He isn't really a preacher and never has been, but he takes care of the graveyard at St. Michael's Church in Clerkenwell when he isn't cabbying, and that makes him an expert on all church matters among us.

"A reward's out," Preacher grunted, carefully turning the sausage so it didn't burn. "Bishop's offering it."

"They must be valuable," Bombardier said thoughtfully.

"They're silver," Preacher said.

If I hadn't had that experience with a bishop, it would never have occurred to me to ask my next question. It was just that curiosity of mine, the bit of my brain that wants to know everything, that made me say, "Which bishop's offering the reward, Preacher?"

"Bishop of Vauxhall, o' course. Both churches where the candlesticks were robbed from are in his parish."

It was only coincidence, nothing more. Yet as Preacher's sausage dripped bits of blazing fat—and it did smell a bit off—I was thinking. A man in clothes that had been cut down from a clergyman's outfit had disappeared in Vauxhall Road, and the only way he could have done that would have been by slipping through that hidden gate into the grounds of Vauxhall Palace, where the bishop lived.

The poor bloke had then been stabbed several times. The notion was scary. Then there was these thefts of silver candlesticks from two different churches—both in the parish of that same bishop. There couldn't be any connection. Could there?

"One coincidence is chance, two coincidences is suspicious, three coincidences isn't coincidence." That's what my old dad used to say. He was with the police, my old dad, and he saw a strange thing or two in his day. I wondered what he would have made of this.

"Come on, Ned," said Preacher, " 'ave one of these sausages. You look like you need one. I've got plenty more."

Maybe it didn't smell that bad after all, but I couldn't forget what it was made from. That might not have mattered so much if I hadn't had a little dog when I was a boy. "Thanks, Preacher, not at the moment. Where are the two churches the candlesticks was lifted from?"

"Saint Mary-in-the-Fields out Clapham way is one, the other's All Hallows in Brixton. Why you asking?" He took a bite and licked his lips. "Mmm, real tasty," he said, chewing and rolling his eyes.

"Just curious."

"Like always," said Preacher, his mouth still moving. "Always curious, ain't you, Ned? Ever hear what curiosity did to the cat?"

I had a sudden picture flash across my mind. It was a body, horrible gashes ripping the decaying flesh.

"Sure you don't want me to put a sausage on for you?"

"Go on then," I said. "Maybe you're right about building up my strength. I might be needing it."

It was Sunday next day. Day off? Not ruddy likely, everybody in London works seven days a week—well, except for the blokes in Government; they only work five. They must do hard work if they need two days off every weekend.

So, bright and early I was flicking Perseus into a trot over Chelsea Bridge and down Queenstown Road, then along Battersea Park Road to Clapham.

My sister, Cecilia, lives there, not far from the Royal Victoria Patriotic School, the one that was built for the kids of the soldiers killed in the Crimean War. That's how Cecilia describes it anyway. She's really nearer to Wandsworth Prison, but with over a thousand villains inside its walls, it's no wonder she doesn't want to mention it. Her husband Jack is a sailor, and as he is with the China Squadron, I knew she hadn't seen him for a long time and would be glad of a visit. Besides, I've always had a soft spot for Cecilia. She took care of me when our mum and dad died.

"Looking perky as ever, Ned!" she greeted me. "Still poking your nose into everybody's business?"

"Whenever I can," I told her.

We chatted for a while about young James, aged six and sleeping like a little angel, and about our sister Fanny, who lives in Hereford. She is married to a farmer, which none of the rest of us in the family can understand, all of us being city born and bred. We talked about the weather, then Cecilia came out with it.

"All right, Ned, to what do I owe the pleasure?"

"Come off it, sis," I said. "Can't a bloke visit his own sister without—"

"No, he can't, not when it's you. You only come to see me when you've got some good reason. What is it this time?"

"I'm really disappointed in you, Cecilia. Here I come all this way . . ."

We went on like this for some time, like we always do, good-natured joshing, until I said, "Get ready then. We're going to church."

She nearly fell off her chair. "Church! You!"

"I go to church. I went—"

"You haven't been since Christmas—and then it was only because Millie made you."

"She doesn't make me do anything. I can . . ."

Cecilia got ready though, putting on her best bonnet and saying she enjoyed a ride in a cab, and it was only when I came round that she got the chance to do that. She's four years older

23

than me, and a pretty thing with light brown hair and brown eyes. So off we went to St. Mary-in-the-Fields, after depositing young James with crippled Mrs. Harris next door.

The sermon wasn't bad at all. It was about five loaves and two fishes, though I didn't understand the bit about feeding five thousand people with them, and that, the parson said, was not including women and children. I couldn't tell whether they got anything to eat or not, and I thought I heard a sniff from Cecilia, which she often does when somebody suggests that women aren't people. She'll get into trouble one day if she isn't careful, probably join one of those women suffrage movements. The choir wasn't bad either, and the time went by quick enough; then we were outside, the congregation standing about, talking and greeting each other.

"Him over there," I said, nudging Cecilia. "Know him?"

An important looking bloke, all dressed up in his best Sunday clothes, was talking to some people. He raised his hat as they left, and I nudged Cecilia again.

"This is Mr. Meecham," she introduced us. "This is my brother, Ned." We shook hands, and I said, "Pleased to meet you. I always like to meet the man who takes my money." He smiled because he had taken the collection, and I didn't think he could have noticed I didn't put anything in.

"It was very generous of you," he said. I was right, he hadn't noticed.

"Mr. Meecham's one of the church deacons," Cecilia said.

"Ah, then you must be very upset about this terrible business," I said, eager to get my oar in before we got on to another topic.

He was heavy-set, some gray hair, and looked prosperous. He had been cheerful, but now he went serious.

"The silver candlestick, yes. Very disturbing. To think any man would commit such a crime against the church."

I was trying to avoid Cecilia's eye, I knew she would have a "so that's why you wanted to come" look on her face.

"Mr. Meecham's running for alderman," she said, trying to change the subject.

"Did the church have the candlestick a long time?" I asked innocently.

"That's the strange thing," Mr. Meecham said, having no objection to talking about the theft. "We had only had it about a month. It was a gift from one of our most generous benefactors."

"And who would that be?" I wanted to know, still avoiding Cecilia's eye.

"Sir George Willoughby."

I didn't know the name, but I said, "Well, at least that sort of thing doesn't happen every day."

"Hmm, still," he said, "unfortunately, it has happened at another church too."

I gave him a surprised stare. "What? Another candlestick?"

Cecilia was edging close to me. I suspected she was going to kick me in the ankle if she could get close enough to do it without being noticed.

"Yes," said Mr. Meecham, "an almost identical one. You see, Sir George bought two of them at an auction in Finchley. He most generously donated one to us, and the other to All Hallows in Brixton. A month later, they were both stolen."

"On the same night?"

"No, two nights later. The police think that the same thief took both of them."

"Remarkable," I said.

"Mr. Meecham's our local undertaker," Cecilia chipped in.

"Must be a good business," I said. "People dying to be your customers."

His smile was polite, even though he must have heard that

one a hundred times before. I let Cecilia chatter on and when we were going back to the cab, she hissed, "What was all that about? Is that why you wanted to come here?"

"One of my fares was found dead. It might have some connection with the candlesticks. The police are questioning me and—"

"Oh, Ned, say you didn't have anything to do with it!"

" 'Course I didn't! But I've got to protect myself, find out what I can."

She changed from worried frown to a bitter laugh. "Besides, you can't resist poking your nose into it, can you? You've got to find out what's going on. Why can't you leave it to the police? That's their job, not yours."

We'd had this argument for years, on and off. She never will understand. "You're going to tell me you got your curiosity from Dad again, aren't you? You always do."

That probably is where I get it. Dad couldn't let things alone either; he just had to know. It was how he made his living actually. I always say he was with the police and he was . . . well, in a way. He collected information for the police. He kept his eyes and his ears open and when he learned something useful, he tucked it away in his mind or else searched for some other facts that might fit with it. That way, when he did sell his information to the police, it was worth more. I learned a lot from him, and my old mum said I inherited his "inquiring mind."

I took over the business—the cabbying business, not the other kind—from him when he died at the age of forty-two. They said it was influenza. I saw him laid out. One side of his face was bashed in, and he had lost several teeth. You couldn't be in the police-informant line of work without getting somebody mad at you.

I'm too much of a coward. I didn't intend to be treated like that, so I stuck to cabbying. You might say that using my inquiring mind was a hobby.

CHAPTER 3

I had a spot of lunch back at Cecilia's—a nice slice of tongue with some lettuce and tomatoes from her next-door neighbor's allotment. She'd have cooked me a roast, she said tartly, if only I'd told her I was coming. Two cups of tea later, I was on my way back into London and another day's work. I'd have to rustle up a few fares on the way, I thought, and make up for the time in church. Still, I'd learned a bit and maybe even clocked up some good marks in heaven.

The church bells had finished their clanging for the day and the streets were fairly quiet, most people still eating their Sunday lunch, the big meal of the week. It was cloudy and bit nippy from the wind. As Perseus clip-clopped across Clapham Common, a few families were out, some kids flying kites and others kicking a football.

Sunday is a different day for cab drivers. The streets of the city are quiet, lorries and wagons don't deliver, buses and trains have reduced services. The only vehicle there's more of is bicycles—"the two-wheel menace," as cabbies call them.

As we came on to Long Road that cuts across the Common, a small group of blokes was unfurling banners, trying to fasten them on to poles despite the wind that was getting blustery. They looked like they were getting ready to go on a march. These protests were becoming more and more regular, out-of-work men wanting work and in-work men saying they were overworked and underpaid.

I could sympathize with some of these because I was on the cabbies' committee, trying to start a trade union of our own. "Trade Unions"; that's what they called them. The dockers were one of the trades that started it—a sort of revolution really. Leo Dempster—he's on the committee with me—knows all about this and says that ever since the Industrial Revolution began, the company bosses just got stronger and richer. As a result of all this power, they ground down the workers— "exploiting" is the word that Leo likes. They make more and more money out of us, but do working conditions and wages get better? Not on your nelly.

What can the workers do about it? we asked Leo when he first got us cabbies together to chew it over. "Strike!" said Leo, and when we argued that the bosses would get the police on us faster than you can say "Robert Peel," Leo said, "Not if we're organized." When we asked him what he meant, he explained trade unions and how they would make us sort of legal. We'd have rights, Leo said. We liked that idea and got to liking it more when Leo explained that the dockworkers had been one of the first labor groups to get a union. They were really big on strikes, and you saw their marches all the time. We were as important as them, said Leo and our committee grew out of that first meeting.

I turned on Elspeth Road, and we trotted past the town hall on Lavender Hill. I had an eye open for fares naturally, but I didn't expect much luck. We went over Battersea Bridge and into Chelsea, where some business was a bit more likely. Kings Road was quiet, but I slowed down as we came into Sloane Square. Construction blocked the road where the old Dissenters' Hall was being rebuilt.

The sign said they were going to build a theatre there and call it the Royal Court Theatre. I thought to myself, blimey, that'll make the old Dissenters turn in their graves. A cabstand was at the Cliveden Gate end of Sloane Square and four cabs stood there, so there was no point in making five.

From the nearest cab, Harry Farmer gave me a wave of his whip. There was no mistaking that head of thick gray hair. I waved back, then noticed that he was waving again, calling me over. I eased Perseus into the space next to him. "What's the matter, Harry?" I asked him. "Want to know the way to Saint Paul's Cathedral?"

His lined, crackly face folded into a few more creases as he smiled. "If I did, you'd be the last one I'd ask."

"What's up then? If it's money, forget it. If it's a fag, you know I don't smoke."

He pointed his whip at me. "The peelers are after you."

"After me?"

"What you been up to, Ned? Didn't reckon you for a rampsman."

"Violence? Me? You know better than that, Harry. I couldn't rough anybody up—not even if they said rotten things about Perseus."

"It's Jacko. He wants to see you."

So it was Detective Jackson. Must be something to do with that stiff he had showed me. Had the police actually been working and got hold of some new information? Had Jacko found out the name of the body? Why did he want to see me?

Harry smiled wider. "Got you worried, I can see. Don't worry, Ned, I'll come and visit you in Newgate."

I waved my whip back at him. "Don't talk so sappy. Jacko wants my advice, that's all. Can't make a move without talking to me first. Suppose I'd better go see what the poor bloke wants, I always like to help his career."

Harry didn't believe a word of it—but he wasn't real sure. "He wants to see you at the Nine Elms Station. Mind how you go, Ned. Don't tell him anything I wouldn't."

Detective Jackson was drinking a cup of tea when I finally got to see him after waiting for half an hour. He was busy, they had told me. I was ushered into an icy cold little room with nothing in it but a table and two chairs.

"You got here at last," Jacko snarled. "Took your time, didn't you?"

"Came the second I got the word. You know me, always ready to help Her Majesty."

He grunted and leaned back in the chair till it creaked. "What time of day did you pick up that bloke on the Kings Road to take him to Vauxhall?"

The cold room seemed to get colder. "About three," I said.

He grunted again. "You sure?"

"Give or take ten minutes."

He looked at his fingernails. They looked clean enough to me, as well they should when he never touched anything dirty except a stiff now and then. He didn't say anything. I knew he was waiting for me to get nervous. I tried not to oblige him.

His chair creaked again.

"Herbert Summers is in Cannon Street Station," he said in a conversational sort of tone.

Herbert is a cabby; been one for years. He's older than me, quite a bit. Quiet chap, not much upstairs but friendly in his own way. If Herbert was at Cannon Street, it was something serious but I wasn't going to ask. I just waited.

Jacko was waiting too. Then he said, "Friend of yours?"

"I know him. I know nearly all the cabbies."

"You wouldn't say you work together?"

"Work together? How can we? We've both got cabs of our own."

"Work together like partners. You know what I mean. Rolling

31

customers when you think you can get away with it."

I was getting uncomfortable now. This didn't sound good at all. Cooperating with the police was one thing. Now Jacko was getting insulting, and I didn't have to stand for it.

"I don't do anything like that and you know it. I don't believe that Herbert does either. He's a good bloke, never been in any trouble."

"Summers is in Cannon Street," Jacko said in a voice like wet velvet, "charged with murder."

"I don't believe it," I said promptly. "Anyway, he didn't do it."

"Didn't do what?"

"Didn't murder anybody."

"Like who?"

"I said. Anybody."

Jacko eased back in his chair. He'd already shaken me up. Now he was going to ease off, let me cool down then he'd be at me again. I know him.

He looked at his fingernails again. They were just as clean as they had been before.

"You know the victim," he said, sort of off-handed.

"Who?" I asked cautiously.

"The bloke you saw yesterday. The stiff."

"What's his name?"

Jacko ignored that. I guessed he hadn't found out yet and didn't want to admit it.

"The dead man was seen an hour later—after you had taken him to Vauxhall. He was seen getting into Summers' cab."

"That lets me off the hook then."

He shook his head. "No. The two of you were probably in cahoots."

I put on a laugh. It wasn't a good laugh, but it was the best I could do. Either way, Jacko ignored it.

"I never saw the man again after I dropped him in the Vauxhall Road," I insisted. "I never saw Herbert at all that day. And
Herbert and I have never been in cahoots over anything."

"You're sure about that?" Jacko was back to his growl. "You
didn't see the dead man again after you dropped him off, and
you didn't see Summers at all?"

"Swear it on a stack of Bibles," I said promptly.

Jacko sneered. "Bibles? You?"

"Just came from church."

That took him aback. I pressed home my advantage.

"Saint Mary's Church in Clapham. Ask Mr. Meecham. He's
one of the deacons there. Running for alderman, he is. His
undertaking parlor is the biggest in Clapham, and he—"

"All right, all right." Jacko knew when to change his tack.

"Don't need me any more then? If not, I'll get back to work."
I started to get up and he didn't look like he was going to object.
"Can I visit him? Herbert?" I asked hopefully.

It was natural that he would snap back, "No, you can't."

I put on my most reproachful stare—at least, that's what Millie calls it. "Has he been charged yet?"

"He's going to be."

"Well, if he hasn't, I should be able to visit him. The law says
that—"

"Don't you quote the law at me!" Jacko was beginning to get
shirty.

"Fifteen minutes, that's all. Just fifteen minutes? Poor chap.
His wife died last year, and there's nobody to visit him." I didn't
think there was much chance that Jacko knew Herbert's wife
was very much alive and nagging him to retire and move to
Somerset.

"I said no. You'd better get out of here while you still can."

"If I could talk to Herbert, I might find out something that
would help you."

"You wouldn't tell me if you did," Jacko snapped.

"To help Herbert? 'Course I would."

Jacko jerked a thumb. "Out! Before I throw you in a cell for obstructing justice."

I headed for the door, stopped halfway. "Ten minutes then. If Herbert knows anything, he'll tell me."

Jacko was on his feet. *"Out!"*

I shrugged, going as slow as I could. I was opening the door as he shouted after me, "Cannon Street. Ask for Sergeant Barton. Ten minutes. Not a second longer!"

The tiny windows with iron gratings always struck a bolt of fear in me whenever Perseus took me past Cannon Street Station. It's one of the grimmest stations in the city, and I couldn't help but think of the poor miserable creatures locked away inside those dismal cells. How much guilt and pain were inside these walls, I wondered. How many men were saying, "If only I hadn't . . ." How much shame and misery were in there, and how much violence and anger too? I even had the awful question cross my mind of how many innocent men were in there.

I spoke to Sergeant Barton at the desk and he called a constable, who took me through a heavy oak door, bound with iron, and down a narrow passage. Another uniformed man had me sign a large register, then I waited until I was taken down a flight of stone steps into a long sort of chamber with separate stalls. Each stall had a bench and seats on each side of it.

I sat down where I was told. Voices shouted from a room not far away. It sounded like an argument, but if it was, there was no doubt that the police were winning it.

A sharp yelp ended the noise, and the silence that followed it was even more unnerving than the argument had been.

Time passed. The door opened, and a uniformed man brought Herbert out. He shuffled in, blinking as if he had come from somewhere dim and gloomy. "Blimey, Herbert," I said, "what a funny place to pick for a holiday! Got sick of Clacton and the beach, did you?"

He was still wearing his cabby clothes. His hair was untidy, and there seemed to be more lines on his face than when I had seen him last. He slumped on to the bench opposite me and shook his head as if he was exhausted.

"Never get locked up, Ned," he said, and his voice wasn't too steady. "It ain't worth it. Whatever it is, it ain't worth it."

"Listen, Herbert," I told him, brisk and cheerful like, "we're going to get you out of here."

His face twisted up. "I don't know, Ned. It looks bad for me."

"Just tell me what happened," I urged him.

He looked like it was hard for him to remember, but he said, "I picked up this fare in Vauxhall. Funny-looking bloke somehow. He—"

"What was funny looking about him, Herbert?"

He scratched his chin. "Dunno, really." Herbert isn't the fastest thinker of all the cabbies in London, and I had to give him time. Besides, I suppose the numbing effect of being in jail slowed him down some more. He said slowly, "His clothes, I think." Then he nodded. "Yes, that was it. His clothes."

I listened to him describe them. He wasn't as sharp an observer as me, although I say it myself, but the description he gave left no doubt in my mind. He was describing the same man that I'd had disappear on me outside the bishop's palace.

"Where did you take him, Herbert?"

"He said he wanted to go to Chiswick. So I set off through Wandsworth, and the bloke kept looking out the back. Seemed real jumpy, frightened. Asked me if I couldn't go faster. Well, I did the best I could, but you know Daisy."

I did know Daisy. Getting on in years she was, and many a

cabby would have sold her to the knackers' yard by now and got another, younger horse, but Herbert was a sentimental soul. I could understand that she might have given Herbert an extra one mile an hour, but that would have been her limit, bless her willing heart.

"Why was the bloke looking behind, Herbert?" I asked. "Was somebody following you?"

"I looked. There was a cab back there, but when I turned on to York Road, it was gone. I thought I saw it again later, but it might have been another cab."

I had the feeling I wasn't going to get a lot of help here but I kept on. "So then what happened?"

"We was making a turn on to Armoury Way when a bloke steps out of another cab in front of us, sudden like. I reins in Daisy and the bloke looks in my cab and says something to my fare. He says something back, and the next thing I know this second bloke has jumped in and my fare calls to me, 'Drive on,' which I did."

"What did the second bloke look like?"

"Ordinary sort, not bad dressed, a hat and a cane—"

"That's all you noticed?" I never did understand why everybody wasn't as observant as me. I'd have had a full description of him from head to foot before you could say Prince Albert. "You've got more curiosity in you than any ten cats," Millie often said to me.

"Well, he surprised me, stepping out in front like that and then getting in," Herbert protested. "Anyway, I went on. They was talking, but I couldn't hear a word they said. Then they went quiet. We was passing the park when there's one of them parades, you know, out-of-works—"

"I know. There's a lot of them these days."

"They're crossing the road, big stream of 'em. They swarmed round us—I'd had to stop. Pressed against the cab, they did,

36

and we tilted over but bounced back. I pulled the blind—" I knew he meant the small wooden shutter that was the only connection between the driver and his fare. "—and blimey!" Herbert's eyes were big as saucers and nearly as shiny. "There's the fare laying across the seat, blood all across his front. I whipped up Daisy and we went charging towards Putney Bridge where there's always a copper on duty. But I didn't get there. Another one stopped me and was telling me I was going too fast for a crowded area. He looked in, saw this bloke's body. And here I am."

We chatted a bit more, but I could hear heavy footsteps approaching and I knew time was up. Herbert needed some good cheer. Proper down in the mouth he was. I only had a minute, so I had to make it good and make it fast.

"Herbert, I'm going to get every cabby in London to help," I told him. "Don't worry, we'll get you out of here. Six thousand pairs of eyes and ears will be working for you, Herbert! Remember that! Six thousand of 'em!"

The door banged open. "Time's up!"

Herbert's face showed the first glimmer of hope I had seen since I came in here. As I went out, I could hear him repeating the words in a whisper.

"Six thousand pair of eyes and ears—six thousand!"

CHAPTER 4

I was out bright and early the next morning—and that means seven a.m., on the street and looking for a fare. About half of London's six thousand cabbies are small masters, which means they own their own cabs. The others drive cabs for their owners, and a lot of owners have a dozen, twenty, some of them more, cabs. Most of these drivers are known as morning men, and they work days only—that's from seven in the morning till six at night. Not many work the night shift, just those who service the areas with the nightclubs, the gambling casinos and the bawdy houses.

I'm not mentioning the bucks—the unlicensed drivers. They hang about the cabstands and the public houses. They take a cab while the regular driver is having a meal or is maybe home sick or is taking a day off. A bad lot, those bucks. If they catch anybody asleep or drunk in a cab, they'll have a dive through his pockets. A lot of them used to have licenses but lost them, and a lot more are drunkards and thieves.

Me, I'm a small master. I inherited my cab from my dad. Dad worked real hard, he did, long hours too. I'm the envy of a lot of my mates because I'm younger than most of them, and they don't think it's right I should own my own cab while they have to work for a master. A lot of the masters aren't bad blokes, but a few are real slave drivers.

'Course, that's one of the things we're trying to change, the three of us on the committee. The other two are Sidney Morris, known to one and all as Smiling Sid, and Leo Dempster. Sid had given up teaching at Oxford for reasons he never told us. He had become an assistant to a lawyer, worked for him for years and knows a lot about the law. He had to leave when money from the petty cash in the office went missing. Nothing was proved—so Sid says—but he had to go anyway and took up cabbying. Leo worked in the county council offices and had a good job there until he had a row with his boss. That wouldn't have been so bad if Leo hadn't punched his boss in the nose when the man tried to get too friendly with Leo's wife.

The whole idea of the committee started when we were having a chinwag at Hangman's Corner, a lot of us, at the end of the day. One of the masters, a swell called Roger Sherrington, had told his drivers that he wasn't making enough money from his cabs and said from then on, the cabbies had to start at five in the morning and work till nine at night. Well, they objected to that, and Sherrington told them if they didn't like it, he would fire them. Plenty more waiting to get your job, he told them, and unfortunately he was right.

Sid got up and told the rest of us that a man called John Fielden was going around the country talking about "the freedom of contract" act and something called collective bargaining. The dockworkers had formed what was called a trade union, and they were refusing to work "excessive" long hours. What's more, they had demanded a minimum wage guarantee. Some nasty meetings had followed, and the bosses brought in some strong-arm men, but a couple of newspapers gave it plenty of coverage and even printed pictures of the hovels that some workers lived in because they couldn't afford homes of any kind.

The dockworkers have proper representation, Sid had said, and we're as important as they are. We should demand the same. Naturally, we had all liked the idea, and someone shouted to Sid, "Put up or shut up! How about you being the first on the committee?"

I promptly voted for that and everybody followed. How did he repay me? Do you think he was grateful? No, he wanted me on the committee with him. Leo Dempster was next to be proposed and with his experience, all were in favor. Leo liked the idea too, glad of the chance to get his own back on the county council.

The only cabbie coming away unhappy was Diddy Cartwright. His name was Didymus, which he told everybody was from the Bible, and what stuck up his craw was that he wasn't on the committee. We had decided that three members were enough and any more would be awkward. Diddy thought he was better qualified than me because he had been a teacher. Reason he wasn't any more was that another cabby'd had a little boy who was in one of Diddy's classes and his story was that Diddy liked little boys more than a teacher should. Some other parents came forward with the same story and complained to the head, with the result that Diddy's teaching career lasted less than two years.

We hadn't been able to do much yet, but we were going to have a big meeting and set an agenda, as Sid called it. All three of us were studying the Employers and Workmen Act that a fellow called Richard Cross had written. We had lots of ideas and we knew it was going to be difficult, but we were all determined and willing to take on the bosses.

The Hyde Park riots were still very much in the public, mind and we were sure we could get plenty of support.

All this was going through my mind as we rolled along Grosvenor Place. "Your mind's never still, is it?" Cecilia had said to me. "Don't you ever give it a rest?" Well, I don't and cracked my whip over Perseus to overtake a dray load of furniture piled so high I wanted to get past it before it all came tumbling. I never use the whip on Perseus, just over his head to remind him I was boss. A lot of cabbies whip their horses, but Perseus has a willing heart and will do anything I ask him, even though he is getting a bit old in the tooth.

I turned across Knightsbridge to go up Park Lane. When they build an underground station like they're talking about, it will be a popular stop, but in the meantime, I get plenty of fares there, mostly blokes going to the offices in Whitehall and Pall Mall. I like to drive slow past bus stops, especially at the busy times. Blokes who are going to be late to work will get impatient waiting for one of those buses that never comes. I had several fares in a row that way, then, with them all at their desks, I did some cruising near the railway stations. They have cab ranks there, of course, but some people come in who don't know the station and wander outside looking for a cab.

That brought me to the middle of the morning, *the lull,* as some call it. I headed across Waterloo Bridge to our own Hangman's Corner. Lots of cabbies were there already, and I lost no time in telling them about Herbert Summers. "If you pick up any gossip," I told them, "let me know. I've told Herbert that we're all working to get him out of jail," I said, "and that's what we've got to do." Most of them knew him, so they all agreed.

Next, I did a little digging for myself. My curiosity, as Cecilia always called it.

I had two or three cabbies in mind, but top of the list was Tommy Levitt. I was in luck, for there he was, smoking a cigarette and looking out across the Thames. I pulled in alongside, hitched up Perseus, who neighed a welcome to Tommy's nag.

"Thinking about the good old days, Tommy?" I asked cheerfully.

He turned and smiled. "Hullo, Ned. No, not really, it was

them good old days that got me into stir."

Us cabbies were a mixed bunch. Almost all of us had done three or four other jobs before turning to cabby work, and it was hard to find a job that somebody hadn't done at one time or another. We had former innkeepers, musicians, actors, shopkeepers, jewelers, carpenters, joiners, saddlers, jockeys, bartenders, grooms, sailors—the list went on. All hard-working professions and all honest ones, but it stands to reason that we had to have some of the others too. So we had our share of pickpockets, cracksmen, housebreakers, burglars, mobsmen and other villains. Most of them had served time in jail.

Tommy used to be a cracksman—and a good one by all accounts. See, there's two ways of cracking a safe—by busting and by screwing. Busting means using force to break it open, but the other way, screwing, is the delicate way to do it, and it means using picklocks or keys. Tommy was a master at screwing. Oh, I've heard he could pick a lock with a bit of bent wire as cleverly as any of them, but he told me once—when he'd had a drink or three—that the best way was getting hold of a key and copying it.

How did he do that? Tommy was a good-looking chap, despite the creases and lines in his face—got most of 'em from his time in jail, is my guess. He must have been a real charmer in his younger days; he must have swept many a serving girl off her feet. He once said to me, "See, Ned, one out of every six women in England is in service. A lot of those are in service in a house where there's something worth stealing. Well, me, I love girls, every last one of the darlings, so why not combine business with pleasure, that's what I say."

That's how he did it. Cooks, maids, tweenies, chambermaids, laundresses, seamstresses, personal secretaries—Tommy treated 'em all alike, as if they were special. If he had the time, he would get the loan of a key long enough to copy it. If he didn't have that much time, he always carried a wax blank, and he swore he could copy a key quicker than stealing a kiss.

"Bad news about poor old Herbert," Tommy said. "I'll tell you if I hear anything that'll help."

He was making it easy for me. "Thanks, Tommy," I said. "Yes, we've all got to do what we can for the poor old geezer." Like I'd just thought of it, I went on, "Matter of fact, there is something . . ."

Tommy put out his cigarette. "Anything," he told me, and I continued quickly, "You must have known a few fences in your day."

Tommy frowned. " 'ere, Ned, you're not thinking of trying that, are you? Believe me, it's a mug's game. John Law is too smart these days and—"

"No, no, it's not like that. Just want to help, that's all."

He knew I meant Herbert, and his face cleared. "That's all right then. What did you want to know?"

"Fences who would handle church valuables. Know any of those?"

"A couple," Tommy said cautiously.

"Who would they be and where can I find them?"

Tommy considered. "Any fence might handle them, but most don't like to. The two I know have made a bit of a specialty of it." He stopped and gave me a tight look. "This any connection to them silver candlesticks that disappeared unexpected-like?"

"Ask me no questions and I won't have to tell you no lies," I chirped, and he grinned.

"Fair enough. All right, one is Abe Hurwitz in Camberwell. The other is Swiveler Grimes up on the Finchley Road."

Hadn't Mr. Meecham at St. Mary-in-the-Field's Church in Clapham mentioned an auction house in Finchley?

"Swiveler?" I questioned.

"He's got a swivel eye. It's his left one, but looking at him

43

you can never be sure. Upsetting, it is, talking to him. You don't know where to look." Tommy was still looking at me with that tight expression on his face. "Thinking of talking to either of 'em?"

"Maybe."

"Forget Abe. He's out of the country for a while."

"Deported?" I gasped. "Australia?"

"They're not doing that any more. Not that they feel bad about it. Just got too expensive. No, Abe got mixed up in a hoop-de-doo and thought it safer to go abroad. The word is that he's in Italy, but I know a man who—well, never mind. All that matters to you is he has been . . . wherever he is . . . for a little while now. His nephew is minding the store, but he's acting as nervous as a cat on a hot stove. Probably isn't handling any merchandise unless it's got a certificate from the Archbishop of Canterbury."

"So Swiveler is the number one in the game right now?"

"Right. Makes it easier for you, does it?"

"Maybe," I said airily. "Probably won't do anything about it, really. Thanks for the word, though. Oh, by the way, where is Swiveler on the Finchley Road?"

While we had been talking, more cabs had come in and a bunch of cabbies came over to us. "What's all this about old Herbert then?" asked one of them, and I went through my story again. All agreed they'd do what they could to help, and I told them to pass on the word to any cabbies they ran into it who might not know about Herbert. It was important, I stressed, to spread the news of Herbert's plight as far as we could. Before I had finished talking, Tommy left, giving me a wave and a "Mind how you go," along with a warning look.

No time like the present, my old dad used to say. It wasn't advice he always followed himself, but he often said it. So I headed Perseus north across the river, through St. James' Park

44

and up on to Park Lane. I had to avoid the top end of it, near Marble Arch. One of the worst traffic blocks in London, that was, and every cabby knew to stay well clear of it, else he could lose a half hour. Up the Edgeware Road and by then it was noontime and I was getting hungry, so I went into Maida Vale and had a kidney pie and a cup of tea at Mabel's stand. Been there donkey's years, has Mabel, and she makes the best tea of any stand in London.

I was ready for anything after that—well, nearly anything. As a parting word of advice, Tommy Levitt had reminded me that fencing is a dangerous business and the men at the top end are ruthless. They wouldn't want to admit much to a stranger, and I'd have to be careful. I'd waited for Tommy to say he'd come with me, but he hadn't, and I didn't press him.

The Finchley Auction House was on Fountain Street. It didn't look like there'd ever been a fountain on it—not since Roman days anyway. The auction house was a big brick building, looked like it had been a warehouse. The neighborhood wasn't bad, sort of quiet, a row of shops up at the Finchley Road end and a pub down at the other corner.

I spent a few minutes driving slowly around. It was mostly residential, nothing fancy but not slummy. A few people were out shopping, and on my second time around, a wagon pulled out of an opened gateway that was part of the auction house, but the load was well covered.

The pub at the corner was called the Red Lion. It looked to be nearly full, and I decided it was a good place to leave Perseus. I pulled in a bit away from the place and tied the reins round a cast-iron bollard. I found my heart beating a bit harder than usual, and I took a few deep breaths to calm down. Then I sauntered down the street and went in to the auction rooms where the door was open . . .

CHAPTER 5

I was in a big room, and there wasn't enough light to see anything at first. A door was open on the far side, and that and the door to the street let in enough light that I could tell I was in a cloakroom. Going through the other doorway, I found I was in an auction room. It was half full of chairs stacked up, and crates and boxes of all sizes were piled high. I couldn't hear anybody so I walked cautiously through to another large room.

This one was full of furniture, a few nice pieces, but mostly pretty ordinary items.

I was looking for other rooms when a loud voice behind me shouted, "Hey, what are you doing in here?"

He was a beefy built, red-faced man in a tweedy suit. I put on a bit of a smile and said, "Looking for somebody. It was empty up front."

He didn't appear too friendly, but I tried to overlook that and asked, "You one of the auctioneers?"

"I'm Walter Greenfield. What can I do for you?"

"It's my old aunt in Epping. See, she died and had all this furniture in the house. We didn't know what to do with it, but a bloke mentioned this place, said you was always on the lookout for stuff—"

"What bloke?"

"Didn't catch his name—it was in a boozer on the Old Kent Road."

His attitude hadn't changed. I wondered if they treated all

customers like that. Still, I had wandered in off the street. He studied me for a minute. "We could send a man out, look the furniture over, tell you what it's worth. How much does she have?"

"It's a big house," I said, "lot of rooms."

That seemed to interest him a bit more "Where is it?" he asked.

I was thinking of a good answer to that when another voice called out, "Bring the gentleman in here, Walter."

Walter jerked his head for me to follow him and led the way. We went out and along a narrow corridor, and then into an office. It was the plushest one I'd ever seen. A thick carpet in reds and golds was on the floor. A big carved desk—looked like mahogany—had a leather top, while a huge pendulum clock stood against the wall ticking softly. A rack held blue and white china vases that I supposed were Chinese and that looked ancient. A couple of paintings and a tapestry all looked old and valuable. A chandelier of crystal glittered gently in the light of two golden wall-lamps that gave off a soft glow. I didn't need to be told that I was in the office of Swiveler Grimes.

He was skinny and old, with arms like pipe stems and bones sticking out all over his face like a skeleton's. His skin was an unhealthy color, almost yellow, and his eyes were like chips of marble. I was glad Tommy had warned me about those eyes though. They would have been really scary if he hadn't.

Swiveler sat behind the desk with his elbows on it and his claw-like hands on his scrawny neck. One eye was staring straight at me, but it seemed to be focused right through me. The other was to the side and might have been looking at the pendulum clock. Then suddenly, the two eyes switched, and the other one was looking at me.

I tell you, it would have turned my stomach if I hadn't been more or less expecting it. Even then, I felt a bit of a lurch.

The room was quiet except for the ticking of the big clock. Walter Greenfield nudged me toward the chair facing Swiveler. Walter himself remained standing, half behind me where I couldn't see him. He had closed the door.

"Your old aunt, you say?" Swiveler's voice was as cracked and ancient as any of his treasures.

"Yes, I—"

"Your dad's sister?"

"Yes, that's right," I managed to say.

"In Epping, you say?"

I didn't ask how he had heard the conversation between Walter and me. Nor did I like his tone. I liked it even less when he said, "We was good friends, your dad and me."

My mouth was dry. I'm not often at a loss for words but I was now. All I could say was a weak, "My dad?"

"You're Eddie Parker's boy. Saw you when you was a nipper, twelve or thirteen. Brought you to my house, your dad did."

I recollected it. My old dad had taken me a lot of places; he was real proud of me. I was good in school, could read and write and do arithmetic. I remembered a big house in St. John's Wood; it was somebody's birthday. Lots of goodies were spread out on large, white-clothed tables and I had eaten too many of them before going on the swings in the back garden. When my old dad had found me to take me home, he'd said, "You look a bit pale, son. Feeling all right?"

The eyes swiveled again and I was glad I'd only had a meat pie for lunch and not all those goodies I'd had before. "Call you Ned, don't they? O' course, you and your dad was both Edward. Your mum wanted to call you Eddie like your father, but he said, 'No, I want the boy to be independent. We'll call him Ned.' "

Considering that until today, our only acquaintance had been just over ten years ago and only an afternoon then, he knew an awful lot about me. That queasiness in my stomach had nothing to do with food. Swiveler was watching me with what might have been fondness if he had been anyone else. I didn't know what to say and decided to let him set the pace.

"Nice of you to come and see us." The crackly voice went on. "Still, you had to go around the building a couple of times before you made up your mind, didn't you?"

That did it. All my shakes went away. Swiveler Grimes knew a lot about me and had been keeping an eye on me. What did he know? What did he suspect?

"That's good," Swiveler said, "I like a young man who's careful. See, son, I know why you're here."

My confidence was coming back, but I cautioned myself to remain alert. This was a dangerous man. He knew more than he should, he'd been having me watched, and he had a large organization behind him.

"You do," I said, keeping any meaning out of my voice.

" 'Course I do. It's taken you a while, but you've decided at last that you're going to take after your old man. Who wants to drive a cab all their life? Not you. You're too smart, too ambitious. Besides, if you marry that Millie of yours, you'll need a lot more money than you can make cabbying."

I felt a little cold inside. Was there no limit to what this man knew about me?

The eyes swiveled again. I wasn't sure where they were looking now. Past me somewhere? "What do you think our young friend wants to bring us, Walter?"

Behind me, Walter coughed. I had forgotten he was there. "I dunno, Mr. Grimes. Something valuable that a fare left in his cab? Some crib he's spotted? One that's easy to knock over?"

That was a relief. So this old goat thought I wanted to flog some swag goods. Well, I could let him think that—even encourage him to think it. Better that than have him suspect that my

49

visit was about the stolen candlesticks and Herbert being in jail.

Swiveler's eyes were making circles round me. "Like father, like son, eh, Walter? Think he'll turn out as good as his dad?"

What was he talking about? He knew my father worked for the police, bringing them information on crooks and villains like him.

"Maybe even better, Mr. G." came the words from behind me. "Looks like a bright young feller. Could bring us a lot of business."

I tried to keep my voice steady. "I never knew anything about what my father did. Worked with you, did he?"

"Garn!" said Swiveler scornfully. "You must have guessed. One of the best pointers in London, your dad was."

He was saying my father scouted out likely premises for robbing and sold the information on them along with details on alarms and watchmen and what the burglars should look out for. If that was what Swiveler wanted to believe, it was all right with me. He evidently didn't realize it had really been the other way around. My dad had hobnobbed with criminals so he could learn what they were planning and then tell the police. I remembered him saying one time, "Always like to help the authorities and do my duty to the public." The best thing I could do was string Swiveler along. I'd have to tread carefully though. He wasn't going to be an easy man to fool.

"I don't have it clear in my mind yet," I said, trying to sound hesitant. "But it's like this. See, cabbies don't make much money. Now if I could make a bit extra on the side . . . I mean, I would like to get married one day and some extra longtails would come in handy."

Behind me, Walter chuckled. "Ambitious, ain't he, Mr. G?"

Some extra five-pound notes was perhaps a lot of money, but if they thought me an amateur and greedy to boot, well, let them; it would be to my favor.

Swiveler nodded. My approach was one he could understand. "But you've got your eye on a crib—that right?"

"It might be. It's—"

"Where is it?"

"Mayfair—well, Mayfair way."

"You pass it in your cab," said Swiveler with a nod. "All right. Tell you what you do. Look it over some more. Learn all about it you can. Find out what's in there, where it is, how many's in the house, when the coppers go by, what they've got in the way of alarms—all you can. Then come and tell me about it. I'll see you're taken care of."

I nodded, as much in relief as anything else. Feeling a little bolder, I said, "Er, it's not so much a house. That doesn't matter, does it?"

Swiveler shook his head. "We can handle any kind of swag. Don't matter what it is. Right, Walter?"

"Right enough. We get all kinds through here."

Including silver candlesticks? I would have liked to ask but that was too risky.

"One more word before you go, Ned."

"Yes, Mr. Grimes?"

"Watch your step." The crackly voice was deeper, harsher. "These are dangerous times, Ned. Men get greedy, overstep when a lot of money is concerned. Don't let it happen to you."

"I'll remember, Mr. Grimes." I hurried off.

CHAPTER 6

It was a humdrum day after that. Still, any kind of day would have been, wouldn't it? I hadn't been so scared since the day my dad took me to the fair in Stepney.

I wanted to go on the swings—the high ones—and he told me I wasn't old enough. I sulked until he let me, and that was a mistake on the part of both of us. The height, the motion, the terrifying sensation of flying through the air with all London spinning around me—well, the idea of being trapped in one of Swiveler's spider webs was as bad, and here I thought I was all grown up.

I got a few fares though, including a nice long one out to Hounslow and another on the way back. Late in the afternoon, I put Perseus in his stable next to where I lived and set about getting spruced up to take Millie to the music hall. I'd promised her last week, and I knew she was looking forward to it. The girls I'd gone out with before Millie liked the idea of riding in a cab, but Millie didn't. *People might see us,* she'd say. *What if they did?* I'd ask. *Well,* she'd say, *it's what you do for a living, isn't it?*

So we'd go to places on the bus. Strange girl in some ways, Millie. She loved the music hall though, and had the ambition of being a star in it herself. She'd had a few small parts—walk-ons, she called them—and was trying to get bigger parts. She'd get an audition now and then, but London was full of girls from all over the country trying to do the same thing. She was determined though. I'll give her that.

She was all ready when I picked her up at the house where she lived with her father and mother and two sisters. She didn't ask me in—I was on the outs with her parents. Rum pair, they were. Time was when they thought I wasn't a bad catch, having my own cab and all. Then Millie or one of her sisters, both older than her, would latch on to or at least talk about some swell with a job in a government office in Whitehall or in a bank or perhaps with one of the newspapers, and next thing I knew it was thumbs down on Ned.

She looked very nice in a blue dress with a white belt and shoes, and I told her so as we walked to the bus stop. Her fair hair and blue eyes seemed fairer and bluer than usual, and the dress fitted her nicely. I could see why she would think she had a good chance of getting a job on the stage. She was as good-looking as any of them, and her figure was better than most.

"Collins Theatre is getting a lot of the top artists now," she told me as we stood at the corner, waiting for the number thirty-two bus. That was where we were going, Collins Theatre on Islington Green.

"Who's on tonight?"

"Martindale's Merry Minstrels are on first." Millie's voice was light and lively and full of excitement, especially, like now, when she was talking about the theatre she loved so. She sensed rather than saw or heard my view on them "You don't like them, do you?"

"Don't really see any point in a white person blacking his face with burnt cork so he can go on the stage. I mean, if the theatre wants black people on the stage, they can hire them, can't they? There's enough of them in London."

"That's not the point." Millie's voice hissed when she was annoyed. It was hissing now. "In America, they have a lot of Negroes in the South. They're all good singers."

"But they don't sing good songs, do they?"

The line was getting longer behind us and we were all getting impatient. Where was that bus?

"Some people think they're good songs," Millie said tartly.

"But they're all about their home in Kentucky or somewhere. They miss their old mammy, the women complain about their husbands drinking too much and the husbands complain about having to work too hard."

"That's their life," said Millie forcefully, "and their life isn't easy."

I had my mouth open to remind her that life in London wasn't easy either, but she beat me to it. "Anyway, that's not the point. People like their singing and—"

"Here's the bus. Would you believe it? Standing here all this time waiting for a bus and here comes two of them!"

It took a bit of pushing and shoving, but we got on. "Take your time! Take your time!" the conductor said as we struggled up the stairs. "Plenty of room."

Millie liked to sit upstairs where she could see better.

We had to change at Charing Cross, near the station, but we were lucky there, as a number ninety-four bus was just filling up and we got two of the last seats. That got us to the theatre early because Millie liked to watch the performers come in. So I bought the tickets and we stood by the stage door in the alley with a few other people.

Oohs and aahs greeted the artists as they arrived and, "There's so-and-so," and, "Looks different in real life, doesn't she?" and, "He's older than I thought," rang out along with other comments. When we went round to the front of the theatre to take our seats, some buskers were out on the pavement with their hats on the ground, open and eager.

Next to them was a spare, sad-looking man, very poorly dressed, with some colored chalk drawings on the flagstones. We laughed at a pair of mimes, then applauded a juggler in a red jacket, and went inside.

"I suppose you're going to object about the price of the program," Millie said.

"I always do," I agreed, trying to avoid any more arguments. Funny how we liked each other so much, yet so many remarks turned into arguing. "I don't think it's right to pay money for seats then have to pay for a program that tells us what we already paid money to see."

"You always say that," Millie said.

I forked over a penny reluctantly and handed Millie the program.

I'm not a great theatre-goer—well, not like Millie is. She's what they call addicted. Still, I have to admit that there's something magic about the moment when the gaslights dim, the orchestra strikes up and the curtain slowly rises.

We were in the gallery. The seats there are only three pence each, and in the Collins Theatre, the gallery is enormous. It was full, too, and even the boxes were packed. I was very good, didn't say a word about the minstrels and I even clapped when they finished.

Some acrobats were next, a whole family of them, and they built a human pyramid with the father and his two older sons at the bottom, then building all the way up to a little chap of no more five years of age. He folded his arms and put on a big beaming smile as he sat high up there, happy as if he were on a high chair in the kitchen.

A man singer came on after them. "Raymond Walters," Millie whispered, looking at her program. "He's a tenor." He sang a song about a sailor who misses his girl back home, and a dozen girls danced onstage and surrounded him. Millie leaned forward, excited. "That's Edie Ellis, the end one. I know her." The girls did a dance, and Millie clapped real loud as they went off.

A comedian named Doug Docker was next. He made jokes about his mother-in-law and his next-door neighbors and even his milkman. Millie really liked the magician who followed. When he shut his girl assistant into a box and made her disappear, Millie clapped and so did I. I was about to say, "Wish I could learn how to do that," but I wasn't sure how Millie would take it, so I kept that to myself.

A girl singer came on then, a big girl with a powerful voice that Millie said was soprano. Her husband accompanied her on a French hurdy-gurdy, and she even sang a song that Millie said was in French. They ended up marching off stage to "The Bonaparte's Retreat."

It was the interval next, and I bought Millie a vanilla ice cream from a woman with a tray of them. A whistler was first on the bill after that. He could whistle anything and even did some birdcalls. The dancing girls came on again, nice looking girls, all of them.

"Good, aren't they?" asked Millie and I agreed.

An Indian juggler called Ramo Samee did his act, throwing colored balls into the air, first just from hand to hand, then from under one leg, then the other. After that, he got really fancy, catching them on his knees, his elbows and the back of his head. A comedian dressed like a tramp told sad stories that were sort of comic somehow, but then a family called MacTavish followed, four of them all dressed in kilts and tartan clothes and playing flutes and bagpipes, marching to and fro across the stage. A husband and wife comedy act came on, both complaining about each other, then the evening ended with a rousing number from the dancing girls.

It was dark when we went outside into the street. Millie grabbed my arm. "Let's go back here a minute." Before I had a chance to ask where and why, we were at the stage door. We stood there. "What are we waiting for?" I asked.

"You'll see," said Millie.

A couple of girls from the dancing group came out after a short while. Then one came out alone and Millie hurried forward. "Hello, Edie!"

The girl was about Millie's age, a little shorter, and dark haired. "Oh, Millie, it's you!"

They embraced and Millie introduced me. Then she asked, "Edie, when are you leaving?"

"Next week," was the reply, and Millie said to me, "Edie's getting married, then she's going to live in Portsmouth."

I congratulated the girl, who then turned to Millie. "I've talked to Max. He says it's all right."

I looked at Millie, puzzled.

She turned a radiant face to me. "I'm taking Edie's place."

"On the stage?" I asked in amazement.

"Of course on the stage! Don't you see? It's my big chance!" She was bubbling with excitement.

"Do your parents know about this?"

"No. You're the first to know. I'll tell them tomorrow. I know the routines. I can dance as well as any of those girls. I can sing too, I can—"

Edie saw my face. "Millie is very good," she said quickly. "Max said so. He's the stage manager."

I turned to Millie. "You've already auditioned for this job?"

"Yes, last week."

"And you didn't tell me?"

Millie pouted. "No point in it until I knew I'd got the job." She tossed her head. "A lot of other girls would have liked it too, you know."

We chatted a few minutes longer, but I didn't say much. On the bus back, Millie was quiet for a short time then she blurted out, "It's no good sulking. You know I've always wanted to go on the stage. Now I'm doing it. I didn't want to say so in front

57

of Edie but I'm not just as good as any of those girls. I'm better. I can dance better, I can sing better, and I can act—"

"But you've never—"

"It doesn't matter. I know I can. And this is just the beginning. I can get a part in a musical comedy. They're going to do 'Bertha of Bermondsey' at the Alhambra. I shall try out for that. They're talking about doing one of the shows that are on Broadway—that's in New York. I can get a part in that. Lillie Langtry may do a musical play at the Saint James. Oh, Ned, I'm going to be a star one day!"

We didn't say much on the bus home after that. At least I didn't, and I'm not often at a loss for words. Millie hardly stopped gabbing, and after thinking of asking, "What about us?" I gave up the idea and just listened to her go on.

CHAPTER 7

I was still worrying about Millie as I flicked the whip over Perseus' head next morning. She was a headstrong young woman, Millie, and I couldn't help but admire her ambition. I liked the way she looked for different angles, too, such as finding a girl who was leaving and getting herself in a position to replace her. Other girls would audition and then wait to be called.

But it was the life she was getting into that worried me. From what I had seen of people in the theatre, they were a hard, ruthless lot who would stop at nothing to get ahead, who drank a lot and had no respect for the laws of marriage and of decency. Was I an old stick-in-the-mud, behind the times? Well, maybe I was, but I felt that you had to have some guidelines to run your life on. Millie's family looked to me to be about as God-fearing and respectable as mine, so where did Millie get her ideas from? Her sisters were satisfied with normal lives.

I'd had two fares already. One bloke, well dressed he was, wanted to go to South Africa House. Then, riding slowly down Northumberland Avenue, I picked up another who wanted to go to Westminster Hospital. The weather helped my business, a faint drizzle and a chilly breeze off the river making a wait at a bus stop unpleasant. The journey to the hospital put me near Vauxhall Bridge, and a stop at Hangman's Corner for a chinwag with the other cabbies sounded like a good idea.

Tommy Thompson must have been there early, because he was just pulling out as I eased Perseus alongside Bombardier.

Tommy gave me a wave of his whip as his horse trotted away. A familiar smell and wisps of smoke told me that Preacher was already cooking sausages

"Hey, Ned, over here," called a familiar voice, and I saw Leo Dempster, one of the other committee members. He was sitting on one of the old benches we had sort of rescued from Battersea Park next to us. His thick white hair made him stand out; he wasn't that old, but his hair gave him a distinguished look. Perseus ambled over to the trough to get himself a drink. He always could take care of himself, so I joined Leo on the bench.

"Law's after you again, Ned. What have you been up to now?"

"They can't seem to run the Metropolitan Police Force without getting my advice all the time," I grumbled. "Who is it now? I told the commissioner to stop bothering me but—"

Leo chuckled, showing a fine set of white teeth. "No word from the commissioner for you today. No, it's your old friend, Jacko."

"One of these days, I'll have to make it clear to him to do his detecting stuff all by himself."

"He sent a copper over to tell you he wants to see you at the Brook Drive Station right away. Know where it is?"

" 'Course I know where it is," I said. "I'm a cabby, aren't I? Back of All Saints Hospital, going into Southwark. Jacko'll wait. Meanwhile I wanted to ask you, we need to have a meeting, the three of us, get ready for the big visit."

"Right. How about Friday afternoon? I think Sid's all right for then."

Diddy Cartwright strolled over to join us as he often did when he saw any of the committee members talking together. Since he hadn't got the place he wanted on the committee, he liked to tell us what we were doing wrong and chip in with his ideas.

"Heard you talking about a meeting Friday," he called out.

He was a skinny bloke, with a long neck and a beaky nose. "Hope you're going to see the City Council soon about getting their agreement to start a cabbies trade union. You've been talking about it long enough."

That was the way he was. He always managed to slip a needle in along with his words. Still, we had learned to put up with him, and while we were still feeling our way with this union notion, all three of us tried to be tolerant. That was a word Leo liked to use. "Be tolerant," he would remind us.

"Friday suits me," I said. "About five?"

Leo nodded and turned to Diddy. "Our presentation to the Council is next week. Our meeting Friday is to prepare for that."

It was going to be a battle. We all knew it, and we had to be ready.

"Good," said Diddy. "If you need any help, let me know."

He strolled off and Leo raised an eyebrow at me, but we waited until he was gone before we chatted about our ideas for a few minutes. Then I stood up and stretched. "I've got to go take care of the Metropolitan Police Department," I said.

"I'll go over to the War Office," Leo grinned. "Trouble brewing in India again. They'll be wanting to know what I think they—"

"Good idea," I said, and went to get Perseus before Leo could take the mickey out of me anymore.

A constable led me to a bare, desolate room in the back of the police station on Brook Drive. A rough wooden bench had stools around it; the room contained nothing else. The iron door could not keep out the smells of the bogs or the lye that was losing its struggle to hold those smells down. Glad I don't have to work in here, I decided, and I spared a thought for the coppers who had to.

Jacko came in with a rush, and the iron door clanged behind him. He didn't look too happy, so instead of the breezy greeting I was about give him, I changed at the last second to, "Good morning, Mr. Jackson."

He glared, and no wonder. He wasn't used to me being polite. He had some papers in his hand and he put them on the table and sat facing me. He looked as uncomfortable on his stool as I felt on mine, and I hoped discomfort would keep the meeting short.

He looked at the top paper, holding it so I couldn't see it. "Come with me," he snapped.

He bounced off the stool and went off, me trying to keep up with him. It wasn't far, just down the narrow stone corridor. The smells got stronger, the worst one being that antiseptic smell you get in hospital. We went past gates and gratings and steel doors with big locks. They all went a long way to make you think escape from this place would be impossible. Jacko yanked open a door, we went in and I saw why. We were in a hospital.

"The people at All Saints Hospital run this for us," Jacko said as we turned into a little room with nothing in it but a wooden table. It wasn't the table that bothered me though—it was the sheet and the shape under it.

"Look," I said desperately, "I've already been through this with that bloke—"

"Not this one you haven't," said Jacko nastily and whipped the sheet away.

He was an older man with a lot of lines on his face. His hair was going gray, but he had muscles in his arms and legs that were better developed than most men's. I guessed him to be a manual worker, and that he'd been doing it for years. His hands were big and gnarled, with cuts here and there that had healed over the years. His skin had a funny look. The body wounds were the worst part.

"I don't know him," I said, my throat a little dry. "Never saw him before."

"Keep looking!"

"I could look all day, and it wouldn't make any difference. I've never seen him—never."

Jacko often refused to believe me—or at least said he didn't—and kept on at me anyway. This time, he threw the sheet back over the man and led the way back to the other room. We sat down and he shuffled through the papers.

"The other bloke . . ." he said. "The one in the Carlisle Street Station . . ."

I waited.

"We've identified him," Jacko said. "His name is Paul Worth."

I waited some more.

"He was an unfrocked clergyman." He looked up at me. "But then you knew that, didn't you?"

I looked back at him, all innocence. "No," I said. "How could I know? I'd never seen him before, either," I added quickly. "Wait a minute, though . . ."

"Go on."

"Those clothes—if you remember, I did say that his clothes had been cut from a suit—cut to make them look different! That was why. It was clergyman's clothes!"

"And you didn't know," Jacko drawled, sarcastic like.

"How would I know? 'Course, now you tell me—yes, that's it."

He wasn't convinced, but he just glared some more. He said, "He vanished, you told me."

"I did."

"I didn't believe that, either."

"Well," I began to explain, "vanish is a funny word. He didn't vanish right before my very eyes. I had turned away after he left the cab, and when I looked back, he wasn't there. That's what I told you. I said he'd gone. Matter of fact, it was you who used the word vanished."

Jacko grunted. "Had any more thoughts about that?"

"Me? No. Got a living to make, I have. You're the one who does the detecting—and a very good job you do of it too," I added quickly. "You'll get to the bottom of this business in no time, I'll be bound."

"What business?" he asked sharply.

"These two blokes."

"Think they're connected?"

He was always trying to trap me, but I could usually stay a step ahead of him. I gave him my all-innocence look again. "Well, they must be, mustn't they? They're the only two bodies you've shown me."

I waited until he'd looked at his papers again, even though I could see he was just doing it to give him time to think. Then, I asked, "Pulled him out of the river, didn't you?"

"How'd you know that?" He leaped on me like a cat on a ball of thread.

"His skin. Dead giveaway."

After a second's pause, he said, "Yes, we did. That wasn't the cause of death though."

"Oh? What killed him?"

"What would your guess be?"

"The stab wounds. Come to think of it, they look a lot like the wounds on the other bloke."

"Maybe we should hire you."

"Not a chance. Couldn't live on a copper's pay."

He put the papers down. "Anything else you want to tell me?"

Well, I could have told him that I knew where the first bloke— Paul Worth, Jacko was saying his name was—had disappeared to, but if I told him it was the Bishop of Vauxhall's palace, he would have fallen on me like a ton of bricks. So I kept quiet on that and said, "There's nothing I can tell you, honest. If I think of anything, naturally I'll—"

"How are you involved with these two men you say you don't know?" His voice was grating a bit now, like it did when he was getting hot under the collar.

"I was only involved with the first bloke because he picked my cab to get into. He could have picked any cab out of the six thousand in London, now couldn't he? As for the second bloke, I never saw him before in my life—never. I don't have the faintest idea who he is."

Jacko fiddled with his papers again. He must have been making a decision. It was one that surprised me. "I'll tell you who he is. His name's Luke Marston. He died from stab wounds, and any one of them could have killed him."

Sharing police information with me—well, that wasn't like Jacko, and I wasn't sure whether to be delighted or suspicious. To keep him away from any further nasty thoughts about me and my involvement, I said, "Stabbed. Like the first bloke. Same knife, you reckon?"

"Maybe it was."

"There you are then. Couldn't have been Herbert Summers. He's in jail."

"Common sort of knife. We can't be absolutely sure."

"So you're not releasing Herbert?"

"No." He sounded definite. "Besides, we don't know how long Marston's been in the river."

"Not long," I said.

"I'll keep your expert opinion in mind," Jacko said with that heavy sarcasm he trotted out now and then. "But," he added, "if you do learn anything that might make a contribution to solving this case, you'd better be round to see me in a flash. Otherwise, you'll be in the next cell to your pal Summers."

"Detective Jackson," I said, summoning all the honesty into my voice that I could, "I don't hold with blokes being killed, for one thing. For another, when one of my fellow cabbies gets the blame for a killing, I want to help him all I can. I know old Herbert well enough to know that he'd never kill anybody, so I'll do whatever I can to help him, and the only way to do that is to find out who did it. So I'll tell you whatever I can."

It sounded real good, I thought, and naturally, I had to add in my own mind that I didn't mean every little tiny thing. How could I do that?

Jacko's narrow face hardly ever showed much emotion, well, not the friendly kind. So for a minute, I didn't know what he was going to say. When he did open his mouth, he surprised me again.

"The stab wounds on this bloke you just saw—well, they're not just stab wounds. That's because after the bloke had been stabbed, somebody worked on him with an axe."

I shuddered. "Why'd they do that?"

"So they wouldn't look like stab wounds any more. They looked more like injuries from some kind of machinery. We're lucky here in the Metropolitan Police Force. We've got one of the finest police surgeons in Europe. Even the Frenchies call on him from time to time when they're stuck. He's the one who spotted this."

"What kind of work did the bloke do?"

"Can't release any details at present," Jacko said, going all official on me. He seemed to weaken a bit and went on, "Want to keep some of them out of the press—so no squeaking to them, mind!"

"Not me," I said, and I meant that. I never talk to the press anyway.

"You can go now." He gathered up those precious papers of his. "Remember, anything you find out, I want to know!"

He went to the door, opened it and bellowed for the constable who took me out. We went back through the same corridor and to the front desk, where the constable handed me over to the desk sergeant, who looked up my name on his list. He put a check mark against it.

"You can go," he told me, and I was just heading for the door when a woman bumped into me. She wore a brown woolen dress and a shawl over her shoulders. She was sobbing so hard, she didn't even notice me.

"Sorry, missus," I said. She looked up at me with reddened eyes and stained cheeks. Through her sobs, she said, "It was my fault. It's my husband, you see. He's in here. I had to look at him and say who he was—" The sobs became too much for her.

I patted her on the shoulder. "I'm very sorry, really. Come on, let's go outside. You'll feel better in the fresh air. This place'd give anybody the creeps."

She nodded and I took her elbow and steered her out of the building. "Look," I said, "there's a stand at the corner. How about a nice cup o' tea? That's what you need."

A few sips of tea—and it was really hot—helped to steady her. "Thank you," she said gratefully. "That's better. It was such a shock though, seeing poor Luke like that."

Chapter 8

"Luke? That was his name?"

"Yes, Luke Marston. He's worked for them for years—" she was anxious to talk, and I encouraged her. At first, because it helped her get a grip on herself, then, as soon as I realized she was talking about the body I had just seen, I had even more reason.

"Who did he work for?"

"Greathead and Barlow—them what dig the big tunnels."

"Was your husband working on the new tunnel then?"

"Oh, yes, one of the company's best men he was . . ."

Like everybody else in London, I knew about the Greathead Shield. It had been invented by a chap called James Henry Greathead, and it was a gigantic digging machine.

His partner, Peter Barlow, and him had got the contract to dig a tunnel from Tower Hill to Tooley Street underneath the Thames River.

"This spectacular feat of engineering" had been one of the newspaper headlines, I remembered. Barlow had figured the engineering of the tunnel all out, but it had been Greathead's invention of this huge digger that had made it possible. "He was so proud of what he was doing, Luke was." Mentioning his name brought another sob, so I quickly asked her, "So your husband drove that huge machine, did he?"

"Yes, him and his mate, Dickie Drew—"

"That's the machine with those huge great blades . . ."

I wanted to bite off my tongue as soon as I said it. Her eyes welled with tears. "You think that's how he died?"

"No, I'm sure he didn't." I remembered that Jacko had told me of stab wounds, any of which could have killed him. "He probably died instantly, and there wouldn't have been any pain."

I half expected Mrs. Marston to ask me what I knew about all this, but she was too grief struck. I was thinking hard though. Who would want to kill a mechanic driving a big digger? And why?

"Do you have someone at home to stay with you?" I asked.

"My sister's coming over—I have to get back. Do you know where the bus stop is?"

"No need for that," I said, and took her to the stand where Perseus was waiting patiently. Her eyes widened. "My treat," I told her.

I kept Mrs. Marston talking all the way back to her home in Wandsworth. It held back her tears and gave her other subjects to occupy her mind. I gathered a few snippets of information that could be useful though.

After I had made sure that her sister was waiting for her at home, I headed Perseus up Lavender Hill. I picked up a fare on the way, a man and woman going to a birthday party in Kennington Lane and then, in a real stroke of luck, a man going to Waterloo Station. That put me right where I wanted to be.

I went to one cabstand after another along Union Street and Borough High Street. Four of them had only a cab I wasn't looking, for but at the fifth one, I saw Jeremy Watts.

He's another of our great characters, is Jeremy. Born and raised in Southwark, he knows every inch of this part of London. He's been driving a cab since he was a youngster and never done any other job.

I pulled in alongside him as he waited hopefully for fares

coming out of the Stretton Arms Hotel. Besides being a popular hotel, it has several bars, a ballroom, and is a big and busy place.

"Jeremy," I shouted. "Still starving the barbers?"

He has a lot of hair, has Jeremy. A big beard, mutton-chop whiskers and a lot on top of his head. A true Cockney sense of humor, too, like me.

"Blimey, Ned," he called back, "ain't you been able to grow even a couple of hairs yet? Chin's still smooth as a baby's bottom! I can let you have some of Doctor Everett's Patent Restorer—grow hair on a duck's egg, that will!"

After a few more exchanges like that, Jeremy climbed down from his seat. "Haven't seen you for ages, Ned. Come on in to the Stretton and let's down a beer."

Well, I'm not much of a drinker, but once in a while I don't mind a Burton special, so we went into the public bar. All Jeremy's old cronies were in there and a real cozy place it was, all glass over the bar, mugs hanging on hooks, the smells of different brands of cigarettes and the steady chatter of cheerful voices.

"So what brings you to the better part of London?" Jeremy wanted to know when we had settled into a corner booth with a full glass in front of each of us.

"You've heard about poor old Herbert Summers?"

Cabbies generally tend to work in certain areas. They'll go anywhere in London a fare wants to go, but mostly they operate in a district they know well. Jeremy had heard about Herbert's plight, but he hadn't been at Hangman's Corner for a long time so he'd had no chance to talk to any of us. Cabbies in this area had their own place under Blackfriars Bridge.

I told him. He drank some beer and nodded. "So you're trying to help old Herbert. Well, aught I can do, you know I will."

"I was hoping to hear you say that. What do you know about

the underground station they're building across from Tower Hill?"

He gave me a sharp look. "Lot of work going on there, Ned," he said in a quiet voice.

"I'm not surprised. Haven't been there myself. Now tell me something useful, Jeremy."

He smiled. "What exactly do you want to know?"

"Everything. Facts, rumor, gossip—all you've got."

"Any particular reason?"

"We can get to that later," I told him. "I thought if anybody knew all the scuttlebutt, it would be you."

He took a long swallow of his beer. "All right. Facts first. They're digging under the river, deep under. The tunnel is deeper than any tunnel that has ever been dug and when it's finished, the underground railway will run through it. You must have seen how bad the traffic is over London Bridge?"

"Horrible," I agreed. "Costs me money every time I get stuck on it."

"All of us," said Jeremy. "Well, this tunnel should help that. Besides, it'll link up all the traffic on the underground on the south side of the river with all that on the north side."

"Not all cabbies think that's a good thing," I said.

"They're wrong. This tunnel will bring us more business, not less. The underground will be used more, that's true enough, but that'll just mean more fares for cabs to take to and from the underground stations."

I knew I was talking to right man. "Go on, Jeremy."

"A lot of work is being done. Tooley Street gets blocked with traffic from time to time when they're hauling soil away or big new pieces of machinery are being brought in. The tunnel's supposed to be nearly finished, but it's behind. Work has stopped, and they're saying they don't when it will start again."

"Has this happened before?" I asked.

"A few times. It always does start again—it has to." Jeremy stopped.

"Keep on talking," I urged him.

"You said you wanted to know everything—"

"Yes."

"Even rumor and gossip, you said."

"Sometimes," I said, "rumor and gossip are more useful than facts."

Jeremy took another pull at his beer. "Is that an old Chinese proverb?"

"No, it's a new Parkerism."

"You believe in ghosts, Ned?"

"Don't be daft."

"No, I'm serious," he said and looked it. "See, there's been a lot of accidents. Cave-ins, floods, supports collapsing, roofs falling. Now and again, an accident stops work. Sometimes, the workers don't want to go back to work because they're afraid of the same accident happening again."

I drank some of my beer and had to move my chair a bit closer; the pub was filling up. "Big projects like this—must be accidents, stands to reason."

"Maybe—but this is different—"

"What's this about ghosts?"

"Voices. Blokes hear them echoing around and swear they're the voices of men who have died. Then there's the ghost trains."

"You're having me on!"

"No, honest and true. Sounds that are just like a train coming through the tunnel."

"But trains haven't started running yet," I protested.

"That's right," Jeremy said quietly. "You want to hear more?"

"I thought I did. Now I'm not so sure."

"Monsters," Jeremy said. "Horrible looking creatures—terrify all that sees them."

"You've heard these stories direct from men who saw them—and heard the voices, the trains—"

"Heard the stories direct. In here, in other pubs—"

"Oh, pub stories!"

"No, Ned, not pub stories. Blokes I believe, blokes you wouldn't expect to tell stories like these."

We had one more beer, and Jeremy convinced me that he wasn't pulling my leg. His stories were hair-raising and when I left, I didn't know what to make of them. Oh, I've heard folks talk of seeing and hearing ghosts, but I never saw or heard one. Never paid much attention to such stories. But now . . .

I was lucky after leaving Jeremy. I headed down towards the Elephant and Castle, where there's always a lot of people, and picked up a foreign bloke coming out of a hotel who wanted to go to one of the government offices in Horseferry Road. After dropping him off, I got another fare that took me to Harleyford Road, just across the river. We passed the Oval cricket ground—I always liked to tell fares that the home of England's national game was played on land donated by a Dutchman. Being so close, I just couldn't resist—I turned Perseus in the direction of Black Prince Road in Kennington.

The cabstand at the corner outside St. Agnes Hospital was empty, so I parked.

Mrs. Marston had told me that Dickie Drew, her husband's workmate, was in there and not expected to live long. I hated to disturb the poor bloke's last hours, but I wasn't going to stay, and he might have a few words of value for me if he could talk.

A starchy old biddy of a nursing sister didn't want to let me see him at first. "I'm afraid poor Mr. Drew isn't going to be with us long," she said, but I told a tale about being an old friend. After I agreed not stay more than a few minutes, she let me go in.

He was in a big ward, and most of the blokes in the other

beds looked to be in as bad shape as Dickie. It looked like a well-run hospital. The walls were freshly painted white, and all the white uniforms were clean and smart. Sister's even crackled a bit.

Dickie Drew looked to be about the same age as Luke Marston, but he was very pale and weak. He opened his eyes though, and when he asked me in a whispery voice who I was, I said I had just come from talking to Luke's wife. That seemed to satisfy him.

"You and Luke must have had a real bad accident in that great machine of yours," I told him.

His watery eyes looked away from me. "Wasn't exactly an accident," he said.

"Can you tell me about it?"

"No," he whispered. "It's my wife and kids, you see. They said they'd look after 'em if I kept quiet."

"Who told you that?"

He tried to shake his head but found it too difficult. His eyes closed and I thought he was leaving me, but then they opened again. I decided to make it fast, so I tried a long shot. "Must have been a big moment for you and Luke when you found the candlesticks."

"It was. Didn't know what to do with 'em at first, but Luke had heard of a place in Finchley—" His voice slid away to silence. He was still breathing though, and at that moment in bustled sister in the crackling white uniform.

"I think he needs some sleep," I said to her. "I'm sure you'll take good care of him."

"I take care of all my patients," she informed me with a stern glare. "Though it's not easy with so many visitors."

My ears pricked up at that. "Has a lot of them, does he?"

"Yes, he does."

"Mostly family, I suppose?"

"His younger brother was here this morning, and then his sister came. Yesterday we had a man from the Transportation Board, and that professor came again."

"A professor?" That seemed a bit unusual. "Probably a doctor," I said. "Some of them call themselves professors."

"Oh, this man wasn't a doctor. I'd know."

"One of Mr. Drew's old teachers," I said, not believing it for one instant. It worked.

She shook her head firmly, rustling all those starchy bits of her uniform. The thought came to me that she was as curious as I was to know why a professor would be visiting a tunnel digger if he wasn't related. I kept going.

"He's been before, this professor, has he?"

"Yes, the day before."

"Seem really worried about Dickie, er, Mr. Drew, did he?"

"Yes, he did. As if—"

She hesitated and I urged her on. "As if what?"

"Well, as if it was his fault."

"How could it have been?"

She gave me a piercing look, as if she thought I was asking too many questions, but evidently my guess had been right and she was as curious as me. She said, "I don't know, but it seemed like it."

"Maybe it was that friend of his," I said. "Youngish man, limped a little . . ."

She may have seen through my trick, but if she did, she didn't let on. "No, an older man, strong and quite large, with a deep voice and a bushy beard," she said.

"Not the friend I was thinking of," I said and was about to leave when she said, "After the professor left, I happened to see Ronald, who is on our front office—you probably saw him."

"Ramrod looking bloke, probably a former military man?"

"Yes, that's Ronald. He was with the army in India. He

mentioned to me that the professor got into a cab when he left, and Ronald overheard where he told the cabby to take him."

You mean you asked him, you nosy old biddy, I thought, but I just looked blank.

"Where was it?"

"He told the cabby to take him back to the British Museum, Reading Room entrance."

"Back? Back to the British Museum?"

"Yes."

"Hmm," I said, and as she waited for me to say what that meant, I said a polite "Thank you, sister," and left.

CHAPTER 9

Like I said, cabbies are a real mixture of human beings. All the way from miners, who wanted to come up from underground and work in the open air, to gardeners, who were sick and tired of the open air. Besides Smiling Sid, who had worked for a lawyer, and Leo, who had been in the Council's offices, we also had a former schoolteacher. And then there was Paddy Reilly, who had been writing pamphlets demanding home rule for Ireland. (There were some who thought he was still writing them.)

These were men with above-average intelligence, and if we had some of those, well, we had to have some of the others too. Outstanding among those others was Benny Harper. Benny the Brain, we called him. We nicknamed him that because when the Lord handed out wits, Benny was the last in line, and when St. Peter lectured on how to use them, Benny wasn't even there. Probably went to the wrong place. How did he manage to be a cabby? we often asked. None of us knew, but somehow Benny managed it. He got his fares to where they wanted to go, and if an occasional sharp-eyed person asked him why he wasn't taking a shorter route, Benny would grunt, "Police got that blocked off."

It was as if the Lord knew he'd short-changed Benny in the mind department, because he made up for it by giving Benny a frame like Hercules, the strength of six men, and the hide of a rhinoceros.

Which is why I asked Benny to go with me to the new underground station they were working on at London Bridge. I didn't know what to expect, but after Jeremy's tales of ghosts and monsters, I wasn't taking any chances. I'd provide the brains and Benny the brawn.

Poor chap, he didn't know I was taking him into possible danger. Two men had died already to my knowledge, and the total might be more. Benny knew me, liked me and trusted me. I felt a bit rotten about risking his life as well as my own, but I was entitled to protect myself was the way I felt. Anyway, I added, I'd be careful . . . of course, I could go alone. Should I do that? My answer to myself was a loud *"No!"* So Benny and I set off just before nightfall with Perseus pulling us along as proud as if he was off to the Lord Mayor's Show.

It was pitch black before we had been out ten minutes—not that late, but a lot of dirty gray clouds filling the sky and a gusty wind that threatened rain soon. Perseus clip-clopped past St. Thomas' Hospital with its big new north wing addition. There was a lot of cross traffic, probably heading for Astley's Amphitheatre, where George Sanger's Circus was packing in the crowds. We went on past Waterloo station, which I used to tell fares who were new to London that it had been built only as a temporary station but had grown bigger and bigger until it was now the biggest and most magnificent in all England. We went by the Royal Victoria Hall that some newspapers called, "The Old Vic," but most people don't want to call it that, so they're talking about calling it the New Victoria Palace.

Across Blackfriars Road, an omnibus roared at us, clanging its bell for me to get out of its way. As I swerved, I came close to an old bloke struggling to get his umbrella up, and he shook it at me as if it was my fault that it was starting to rain. Past the Bear Gardens, we turned toward London Bridge. With the station closed, the area was quiet.

I reined Perseus in, and his hoofs clicked softly on the cobblestones that were now turning black with rain. I stopped at a lamp standard and tied Perseus' reins round it. I unfastened one of the lamps from my cab and turned it low. I took a sack from the back seat.

"Are we there?" Benny asked in a tiny voice. He didn't know where "there" was, and he was too timid to ask. Good thing a temper didn't go with that mighty frame, I thought.

"Yes, we're there," I said. "We're just going to take a look inside."

He looked at the dark front of the station with the iron gates across it. I hadn't told him where we were going or why. I hadn't told him anything, and before he could ask, I beckoned him to follow me. The gates had a big padlock on them.

"Right, Benny," I said. "Let's go in and have a peek." I opened the sack and took out a rope ladder.

See, my old dad rubbed shoulders with some queer types in his business. A few of them were burglars. Sometimes, my dad told me, they went "inside," or maybe they retired to the country and a quiet life. My dad would get their tools, but my mam didn't like that and got rid of them as fast as he brought them in. A rope ladder was all that was left because, as my dad said, "It could have a lot of uses."

It had a use right now. I slung the hooks on to the tops of the gates and went up. I sat on the top, pulled the ladder up and dropped it down the other side. Benny handed me the lamp, then he did the same. He might be big, but he was agile as a monkey. I put the ladder back in the sack, and we went into the darkness.

Some wide steps led down to a big area like a half circle with ticket booths all around it. Posters were already on the walls, advertising Clacton, Eastbourne and Brighton. A bright sun was shining in all of them, and the beaches were full. Lillie

Langtry was telling how wonderful Pears Soap was in another poster, and *Nestle's Milk Makes Babies Grow* said another. Wooden racks and shelves stood empty, waiting to be filled with newspapers and magazines and penny dreadfuls. On the other side, a huge black mouth gaped, leading downward.

"What are we looking for, Ned?" Benny's voice was almost a whisper. Even so, it echoed two or three times before fading away.

"I don't know, Benny," I said, and he nodded, satisfied. "But let's look down here," I added, and led the way toward the dark stairway.

"Can you turn up the light a bit?" he asked.

I wasn't sure how far away it could be seen but I did so, just a little.

I went down slowly, Benny close behind me. We could see nothing but a few steps at a time. They seemed to go on and on forever, but at last they ended. We found ourselves on a platform, flickering shadows in every direction. It was cold and eerie, and I could hear Benny's breathing.

We stood for a minute. I turned up the light a bit more, and the dull orange glow showed we were in what looked like any railway station, except there was no sky, just a low, arched ceiling. The brick walls were new, and steel girders bridged the roof. When I turned the lamp the other way, two sets of rails glittered like strips of mirror. Neatly packed cinders filled in between them and the wooden sleepers were shiny and new.

I moved the lamp again. At one end, the tunnel entrance was blocked with a coach.

At the other end, evidently where the line was going to go under the Thames, a great pile of rocks was stacked, blocking the mouth of the tunnel completely.

Benny's face was pale in the weak light. He looked at me anxiously. I waved the lamp, but could see nothing else. I was about to tell Benny we might as well go when I saw his eyes widen, glistening with fear.

He put a hand to his ear. I listened but could hear nothing. Then I heard it. It sounded like voices, but then it didn't. Sometimes you hear water gurgling over rocks and you think it seems to be whispering to you. That's how this sounded now. As I strained to hear better, the sound faded. We both waited. It seemed like ages but it probably wasn't very long.

It started again, like voices but not like voices. It faded, then it grew louder. As it faded again, I asked Benny, "What does it sound like to you?"

"People talking," he said, but he added, "but then it changes and it doesn't."

I knew what he meant and I agreed. We both strained, listening to the silence. Benny started to wheeze and I waved to him to stop.

"Sorry, Ned," he muttered apologetically. His eyes were big. Fear of the unknown, I told myself. We kept on listening then I heard Benny's sudden catch of breath. A sound came, a new and different sound. It was very soft at first, then it got steadily louder. It was a sort of shushing sound and seemed to be coming closer. It reminded me of something. What was it?

It was a train. It was the chuff-chuff-chuff, like that coming from a steam engine—and it was coming closer.

The trains on the underground were the same as the ones going all over the country on the surface. The Metropolitan Railway people were talking of electric trains, but they didn't have any yet. Right now, they all had steam engines. That was what this sounded like—a steam engine, and coming towards us.

But how could it be? The line hadn't been finished yet, and that great pile of rocks blocking the tunnel at one end and the coach at the other both said a train couldn't come through here. I tried not to look at Benny. He might see the fear in my face, and I had no doubt I looked as frightened as he was.

A ghost train? The idea was ridiculous, and yet . . .

The sound kept getting louder. Then, just when it seemed it must be on us, it began getting softer; then it faded to silence again. I could hear Benny swallow. I swallowed too.

I tried to hear into the silence, but all that did was make aware of my own heartbeat.

A new sound broke the silence. It was the crunch of feet on cinders. I swung the lamp so as to light up the track from the platform to the wall of rocks. There was movement there, but it was too dark to pick out what caused it.

The crunching got louder. The sound was measured, like footsteps but not quite like them.

I raised the lamp higher. Out of the gloom, a shape was forming, walking towards us.

Benny squeaked. I almost dropped the lamp as the shape came into sight.

Walking jerkily along the track towards us, and coming out of the piled rock wall, was a gigantic frog, bigger than a man.

CHAPTER 10

My first fare the next morning was a long one. I picked up two men on Chelsea Bridge Road and took them to Harley Street. Perseus and me—we could do that run with our eyes closed. I didn't, of course, but my mind certainly wasn't on the journey. It was on the strange events of the night before.

When that monstrous frog came along the railway track, Benny had stood petrified, his eyes popping out of his head. He tried to say something but couldn't. I might have been the same way. Benny was the first to move, though—and did he move! For such a big chap, he was off and along the platform like greased lightning. He was already getting out of range of the lamp I was holding. I tried to shout to him to wait, but my mouth was too dry. I raced after him, and together we scarpered up those steps as if the devil himself was after us.

When we got near the top, I had the horrible feeling that we might be trapped, but there was no one else in sight. We were over the gate in double-quick time, and we had Perseus cantering away and across St. Thomas Street before you could say Jack Robinson.

What was it we'd seen? A frog bigger than a man? Ridiculous! Just as ridiculous was that whatever it was had come right out of the wall of rock blocking the tunnel entrance.

And what about all the other stuff? The train that we heard as loud as could be—except that trains hadn't started running yet. Then the mysterious voices—or were they voices? If they weren't voices, what were they?

In my mind, I ran through everything that Jeremy had told me. Voices, monsters, a ghost train; all the very same things that Benny and I had seen and heard. Not that Benny and I had talked about them on the way back. Poor Benny was shaking the whole way and too scared still to talk. I didn't say anything because I thought talking might make him worse, and I couldn't think of anything I could say that would make him feel better.

Was there anyone I could talk to about the evening? Millie would laugh her head off, and so would Cecilia. The other cabbies would think I was going soft in the head and not the right sort of bloke to represent them while we were trying to start a union. Jacko? No, he'd try to run me in for breaking into city property.

I had a busy morning, and all the time, I was watching for the right opportunity . . .

Finally, it came. I got a fare, a posh bloke who wanted to go to the Mansion House. Must have been a big lunch day there, what with dark-skinned blokes, some Chinese, all going inside.

That put me in the right neighborhood, and I trotted Perseus over to Cannon Street Police Station.

Sergeant Barton was again on duty at the desk. I didn't think he'd remember me, but he did. He made it easy for me too. "Come to see your mate Summers, have you?" he asked.

"Right," I said.

He nodded. "Detective Jackson said it was all right, did he?"

I gave him a big grin. "Detective Jackson and me, we—well, let's just say he's a nice bloke—for a copper, that is."

The desk sergeant looked through the papers in front of him. "Can't find the form . . . Said it was all right, though, did he?"

"He certainly did." I was referring to the previous time I had visited Herbert, but I didn't see any need to go into details like that.

"Must be here somewhere . . ." He was having a hard time finding the authorizing form—and no wonder, I thought, as I stood with an innocent expression on my face.

Not being able to find the form, he did the right thing—for a bloke in his position. He held up a sheet of paper that was probably some ruling on the cleaning of toilets and said, "Hmm, yes, all right. Constable, would you take this gentleman to see Herbert Summers in twenty-two twenty-one?"

The walk through the corridors and doors was just as depressing this time as it had been before, and the smells and noises were no better. Since we didn't have Detective Jackson slowing down the process, however, it took only a few minutes before I was sitting there as Herbert was brought in.

He looked bewildered and blinked at me a few times. Then he began to bring himself around. "Real good of you to come, Ned," he said.

"How are they treating you, Herbert?"

"Not too bad. Don't like it in here though."

"Herbert, listen—" I wanted to get it out fast, just in case my unauthorized visit came to the attention of someone besides the desk sergeant. If it did, they might be undecided whether to throw me out or keep me in there. "Herbert, there's been another murder—"

Herbert frowned. His face was pale, but that could be from just being in there, when he was used to being outside all day. "A murder?"

"Another murder. You remember that bloke found dead in your cab?"

"I had nothing to do with it, Ned! I turned around and there he was. I never laid a hand on him, it was—"

"I know you didn't, Herbert. And six thousand pairs of eyes

and ears belonging to cabbies all over London are helping you. Remember?"

His face began to clear. "Yeah, six thousand—all helping me—"

"Right. Well, another bloke has been murdered, see? And in exactly the same way and probably with the same knife."

"It wasn't me, Ned, I swear it, I—"

It was uphill work, but I kept at it. Even a few days in this place would rot a man's mind. "I know you didn't, Herbert. We all know it. Anyway, you couldn't have, could you? You were in here. How could you have done it?"

He was nodding now, his eyes brightening. "That's right, Ned. I couldn't have, could I?" He looked at me anxiously, "Are they going to let me out, Ned?"

"Yes, they are. You've got to hold on for a few more days though—"

"But why? If they know that this other bloke—"

"It's the police way, Herbert. You know how they are—have to do everything by the book. It all takes five times as long as it should, but we'll have you out of here, never worry."

What was most likely the first hint of a smile came over his face since he had been in here.

"You came to tell me, Ned!" He reached out and grabbed my arm.

" 'Course I did. I'm your mate, aren't I? It's not just me, Herbert. It's all your pals, the cabbies."

"When, Ned? When will—"

I didn't want to have to tell him lies. Perhaps I had told him enough already, though I thought of my words as exaggerations rather than lies. I rose to go. "Soon as we can get you out of here, Herbert, we will. Hang on to that."

He still had the hint of a smile on his face as I left, telling myself that I'd better be sure of what I was saying. Somehow, the smells of the place seemed worse as I walked out.

It was an average busy day afterward. A run to Paddington Station, then two women who wanted to spend money at Gooch's Emporium; next was a couple who were going to St. Martin's Church in Trafalgar Square to arrange for a big wedding for their daughter. A family of four I picked up outside the Zoological Gardens wanted to go to Victoria Station, a nice long haul. And then a lawyer coming out of the Saracen Head Hotel in Snow Hill and who looked like he had lots of clients' money to spend, said he had an urgent meeting in a law office on Chancery Lane. He offered me an extra two bob if I could get him there in thirty minutes, and I did it with a minute to spare.

About seven o'clock, I decided to call it a day. Back in Pimlico, I put Perseus in his stable next door, opened a fresh bale of hay for him and filled his water trough. I gave him a rubdown—he loves those—and a pat on the head goodnight.

In my upstairs apartment, the pantry had a piece of ham that wasn't too old, so I had that with a big slice of Cheddar cheese and some pickles. A pint bottle of ginger beer was there too—home made by Mrs. Brown down the street. It was nearly half full, even had a bit of fizz left in it, so I drank that. I washed my hands and face and set off for the Gaiety Music Hall.

Millie had got a complimentary ticket for me. She said that was what they called them when they were free. The place was nearly full when I got there, and it filled up to bursting in a few minutes. Even the boxes were full, and they charged a shilling for them. I was in the gallery, on the third row and near the middle where I had a good view of the stage. We were all squeezed in on the long narrow benches, but nobody minded.

I knew that the Gaiety usually did different turns—comedians, singers, acrobats, magicians, like the show we had seen at the Collins Theatre on Islington Green. But this show at the Gaiety was different; it was like a story but where they sing and dance now and then. Millie was in the chorus here and had been sure management would give her a part to play once they saw how good she was. But she had decided they weren't going to do that after all, which was why she was going to take the other job. I had seen her in this show when it had first opened, and now she wanted me to see it again before she left it.

The show was called *April Morning,* and the story was about this duke who likes to disguise himself as a monk and go among his people. His younger brother is jealous of him and also is fonder of the duchess than he should be, so he gets word to her that the duke is seeing a certain woman in the town. The cast members sing a few romantic songs. Then the younger brother tells the duke that the gypsies who live near the estate are angry at him and are threatening to burn down the castle. The duke goes in his disguise to the gypsy camp and watches them dance. Millie was one of the gypsy dancers, and I thought she was good but sort of lost among a dozen or more girls. I could see why she liked the chance of bigger parts at the Collins.

The story got trickier and I got sort of lost, but the singing was good and I clapped real loud whenever the chorus came on, but they didn't do that often enough. I supposed Millie was right, after all, to make a move if she wanted to progress in her career. From my point of view, I wasn't that sure I wanted to see her become a star. Still, whenever I raised that point with her, she said I was being selfish.

At the end of the show, the audience cheered, and the cast members all came on-stage and took bows. I exited with the crowd, but I went to the back entrance and waited inside like Millie'd told me. Some of the other girls came out, then Millie came.

"What did you think?" she asked right away.

She looked different in regular clothes, a light yellow dress with a sort of shawl and blue shoes. "You were good," I told her. "Perhaps you're right though in trying for a show that gives you more to do."

"That's what I'm telling her," said another voice, and I looked round.

The speaker was an older woman. I mean, she must have been about forty, but very well preserved. She had on a lot of make-up, and her blond hair had come out of a hairdresser's shop, probably an expensive one. Her smart brown outfit of jacket and skirt must have cost a packet too. She had rings on her fingers that I guessed were real diamonds and a pearl necklace with several loops. Her voice was posh but without show. She looked like a real society dame, and I wondered what she was doing here.

"You must be the Ned that Millie has told me about," she said with a little smile.

"That's right," I said.

"I'm Dorothy Radcliffe."

Millie might have told her about me, but she hadn't mentioned her name that I remembered, and I must have looked it.

"I run a few theatres in town," the woman said to me.

I didn't know any theatres were run by women and was just about to say so, but Millie said, "She's the only woman impresario in London." So I just nodded.

Dorothy Radcliffe turned to me. "I'm trying to persuade Millie to join our troupe. I think she is capable of much better roles than she's getting. I know she is giving the Collins in Islington Green a try. I'm wishing her good luck, but whether she succeeds there or not, her career stands a much better chance of growing if she comes with us. What do you think?"

Naturally, I was a bit flattered. A woman in her position asking me what I thought! "Millie's got a lot of talent. It'd be a shame not to make use of it," I said.

She turned to Millie. "There, you see? I told you he'd be reasonable."

Millie looked at me a bit doubtful, as if she hadn't expected this. I must admit that I was surprised myself. Still, I had said it.

"Come around in the next day or two and ask for me," Dorothy said with an inviting smile. I could see she must be good at running a theatre, even if it was an unusual job for a woman. "Just one thing . . ." she took Millie's arm. "You don't mind if I have a word with Millie, do you, Ned?"

" 'Course not," I said, and the two walked down the corridor. People were still coming and going. One bloke in particular I had noticed standing behind Dorothy Radcliffe but some way off, came forward. He was big. Could have been a wrestler once, with wide shoulders and a beat-up face. He blinked continuously. "I thought I recognized you! Ned Parker, right?"

"Yes," I said. "Do I know you?"

"You don't remember me?" His voice was nasal, as if he had been bashed on the nose, maybe more than once. He blinked several times. "They call me Blinker."

"Oh, yes," I said but I was racking my brain to recall where I had seen him.

"You got a minute? Somebody I want you to meet."

He didn't give me a chance to argue. He took me by the arm in a firm, tight grip and steered me down the corridor. We made a quick right turn down another passage and a door opened. Blinker pushed me inside then followed. The door closed.

It was a dressing room, and racks of clothes were all over. Costume clothes, all kind of bright costumes. The lamp was turned down low, but it was enough to see a man sprawled on a settee. He was wearing a clown costume and a painted mask concealed his face.

"Ah, Ned Parker, come on in. It's time we had a chat," he said. A small black thing over the mouthpiece of the mask gave his voice a metallic sort of sound. Blinker pushed me into a chair facing him.

"They call me Mr. John," he said, and I caught my breath. I had heard of him, he was the boss of one of London's biggest criminal gangs. The rumor was that no one knew who he really was, and I could see why.

"What do you want with me?" I asked. I wasn't exactly afraid, but I was certainly nervous.

"I knew your father well, and to keep this talk of ours short, I thought it was time you started working for us too."

So here was another one. Perhaps he didn't know how my father had worked with various criminals in London, found out what they up to, and then informed the police.

I decided to play my hand very carefully.

"My father didn't tell me much about his work," I said.

There was a pause. "Well, that doesn't really matter," he said at length. "Things are different now anyway. I think that you and I could reach an understanding. You could be a help to us, and I could make you richer than you've ever dreamed of being as cabby."

I let another pause pass. "What would you want me to do?"

"You were at the Finchley Auction House. You visited Dickie Drew in Saint Agnes Hospital, you're a pal of Detective Jackson . . ."

He must have spotted the expression on my face. "Oh, yes, Ned, we know a lot about you. Now, tell me just what is it you're looking for?"

I felt cold in my stomach. Mr. John knew altogether too much about me. I was going to have to watch my words with this man.

"I don't know what I'm looking for. That's why I'm looking."

I leaned forward and put on my best truth-telling look. "See, a mate of mine is in jail—"

"Herbert Summers." The voice grated the name.

"Yes, right, Herbert. Well, we all—us cabbies, I mean—know Herbert couldn't ever kill anybody, so we're trying to help him, see?"

The clown mask moved from side to side. "No, there's nothing you can do to help him. You're just putting yourself at risk. Stay out of it, Ned. Take my advice."

"They're saying he murdered that bloke in his cab."

"You don't believe he did?"

"None of us do."

"If he's innocent, they'll return that verdict at the Old Bailey," the metallic voice said.

"I believe in British justice too," I said. "Still, it looks bad for poor old Herbert."

"It's none of your business. Stay out of it. Let the police do their job. If someone else did it, they'll find him."

Well, that's what I thought too. Still, mistakes will happen. Sometimes there's a—what was it they called it? A miscarriage of justice, was it? I didn't want to argue the point with Mr. John, though. It would be an argument I couldn't win. I gave a bit of a shrug, hoping it said that I thought he might be right.

I suppose it did. "I'm glad we see things eye to eye, Ned," Mr. John said. "When we talk again, we can get down to brass tacks and get you started making some money, eh?" He didn't wait for an answer, but when he went on there was a threat in that rasping voice that I didn't like at all. "But watch your step, Ned. Some say that nose of yours will get you into trouble one day. I wouldn't want them to be right. Know what I mean?"

It was a threat all right, but I didn't see any reason not to question him anyway. "I think so, Mr. John, but there seems to be a lot of things going on. How do I know which ones might get me into trouble and which might be information that would help you?"

There was a low chuckle that was like an iron bar scraped along a railing. "I hope you will be able to work out which is which, Ned, I really do. Because if you don't—well, neither of us wants to think about that."

He didn't wait for an answer to that, either. This time though, he waved a hand and Blinker took me out. We went a different way this time, and I didn't know where I was with all those dressing rooms and storage rooms. At last we came out into the front lobby where Millie was still talking to Dorothy Radcliffe.

Millie smiled at me. "We were just wondering where you'd got to."

Dorothy Radcliffe gave me a strange look. "Are you all right, Ned? You look pale. Did you get lost in there with all those good-looking girls?"

"I'm all right," I said. "Been an exciting evening."

Her look changed to a long and lingering one, more personal. "I hope we can enjoy more of those—perhaps even more exciting," she said, and that strong perfume of hers seemed to waft around her words.

CHAPTER 11

Next morning dawned with a blue sky and a sun shining as merrily as if it did that every day. Only a breeze like a baby's breath stirred the air, and people were smiling and asking each other how long this weather was going to last.

It was still lasting when I got my first fare. At the corner of Chester Road, a couple about my age and their two children wanted to go to St. James' Park to see a parade.

The only thing was, they didn't know where in the park the parade was going to be. Well, neither did, I but I assured them I could take care of that. Along Birdcage Walk was a cabstand, and I stopped there, as I knew at least one of the cabbies e there would know about the parade. George Brownlow, twenty years a cabby, knew, and I thanked him and headed for Horse Guards Parade. Sure enough, some stands were up and the route was marked out with banners. The family was delighted, and I told them it was all part of a cabby's job and enjoy the day.

A bloke in a bowler hat waved his prolly as I was driving away. "Are you going Nottingham Court Road way?" he wanted to know. It was a funny question to ask a hansom cab driver—we usually go anywhere a fare wants to go—but I was glad he did. It gave me the chance to say "No," and drive off—not a thing I do at all.

Fact was, I wanted to go east today. Only a few minutes' sauntering slowly brought me to a corner where a man with big muttonchop whiskers waved me down and climbed in. "Great Ormond Street Hospital," he called out. Perfect, I said to myself, and flicked my whip to tell Perseus to urge himself into a trot. That's the hospital the famous writer, Charles Dickens, took such an interest in. He raised a lot of money for it and told about it in a couple of his books, so Millie told me.

Great Ormond Street is a big, bright red brick building that you can see from far off. When my fare had alighted and paid me, it was only a few minutes to where I wanted to go: the British Museum.

The words of the nursing sister at St. Agnes Hospital had given me a lot to think about. Why would a professor be visiting Dickie Drew, a construction worker on a tunnel under the Thames? And a professor from the British Museum, at that? There was a lot behind the deaths of Luke Marston and the dying Dickie Drew. How could I get at it?

Their families had evidently been threatened, and I was not likely to get much out of them.

This professor, though, was a different story. I should be able to learn something from him. I didn't have much to go on. I was looking for a professor with a beard, and in telling the cabby to take him "back" to the British Museum, it sounded like he was there often, so he might be known there. I thought about talking to cabbies, but that was a long shot. Out of six thousand of them in London, I would be more than just lucky if I stumbled on chaps who had driven him. No, the museum was my best bet for a start.

As I walked to the main entrance, I realized I hadn't really noticed the building before. I had passed it lots of times, but never paid attention to it. A huge, eight-sided dome towered high into the air and was the centerpiece. From there, the building stretched out both ways, with great square-shaped structures with a curved top at each end. Brick chimneys popped up here and there like long fingers.

I had put my best clothes on, and the two commissionaires at the double doors didn't give me a second glance. An enormous hall had a marble floor. From the hall, doors and cloakrooms and offices went in every direction. Official looking chaps stood around. I picked one who looked like he'd been there a while.

"The Reading Room?" I asked in a lofty sort of voice. He told me the way and I followed it till I came to a door with a desk blocking it. A big sign over the door told me I was at the right place. A chap about my age with only one leg was at the desk, evidently an ex-Army man. I gave him a friendly grin. "I hope you can help me," I said. "Do you know if the professor is here today?"

"He's here every day," he said, official-like. "What was it you wanted?"

"Just want to ask him a couple of quick questions."

He had a thin face, looked like he'd suffered. I noticed then the medal on his chest. So he was ex-army and probably had other injuries beside the leg. He seemed willing to be helpful, but at the same time, well aware of his job. "The professor doesn't like to be disturbed," he told me. "He's doing very important work."

"That's all right," I said. "I'll only keep him a minute. When he knows what it's about, he'll want to talk to me."

The chap eyed me for a moment then nodded. "All right. You need a reader's card to get in though."

Well, it isn't that I'm not a reader. My mum made sure I was by sending me to that Catholic school, where she said you get a better education, and woe betide me when I sneaked a day off school to go raid the apple orchard. I'm a good reader, but what with having my own cab, I don't have that much time for it. Millie's the reader. She reads for both of us and keeps me informed. He noticed my hesitation. "It's easy to get one. I've got the forms here. I can help you fill them out."

So we did. While we were doing it, he told me how this Italian fellow, Antonio Panizzi, had come to London to escape from Italy where they wanted to shoot him. Seems he was a bit of a revolutionary, but he'd been a real smart bloke in the library business and knew how to reorganize this one. Not only that, but he'd redesigned the building so that it looked like it did now, and it was available to anyone. "You can now take out as many books as you want and keep them as long as you need them," he told me.

"Blimey!" I said, and he gave me a sharp look that said he wondered why a bloke like me would want to ask questions of the professor but he didn't say so.

Holding my reader's card proudly in my hand, I stepped inside and the chap pointed across the room. "See that second row? The professor always sits in that second seat there."

That place was an eye-opener and no mistake. The gigantic dome that I had seen from outside made up the roof. The inside was painted sky blue, and it had a spray of supporting ribs that were painted gold. "The biggest dome in the world after the Pantheon in Rome" the chap had told me. Tall double windows ran around circular wall. From shelves beneath them, stuffed birds looked down on us with sort of disdain. In the center of the floor, desks and shelves were arranged in circles, one inside the other. Outside them, lines of desks went out like spokes in a wheel. I don't know how many people were in there, but there was too many for me to count.

What staggered me more than anything, though, was the quiet. A place that enormous ought to be noisy, a babble of voices like Covent Garden Market or the Corn Exchange.

All you could hear in the Reading Room were occasional soft, twittery sounds. They were probably low voices, but in that massive building, they were lost like a handful of peas in a colander. As I approached, I saw that the professor did have a flowing dark beard. Books were stacked in front of him, and he had lots of papers and two or three pencils. He didn't look up when I stopped beside him, so I cleared my throat. He did then. He looked up and stared at me, but said nothing. The expression on his face said he didn't take kindly to being interrupted.

"Sorry to bother you, Professor," I said, cheerful as I could. "Just a couple of quick questions and you can get back to your work. I know it's important." He glowered as if he was going to throw me out, so I went on fast. "It's about Luke Marston and Dickie Drew. One's dead and the other's dying. They said you were at the station. You might know something to help me find out who killed them."

His eyes bulged and he spluttered, "What nonsense are you talking? I do not know these men! Please let me go on with my work." He had a strong foreign accent. He moved his papers, pulled a book nearer and picked up a pencil.

"I'm sorry, Professor," I said, "but I have to know. You were at London Bridge Station, weren't you?"

"Certainly not! And I have never heard of these men." He was still angry.

"They say you were there," I insisted.

"I do not know them!" His voice was rising. A few faces turned in our direction, and a voice called, "Shush!"

I didn't want to get the place in an uproar, but I can be a very persistent bloke. I was being one now. I lowered my voice and said, "Look, Professor, this may be a subject you don't want to talk about, but I have to know—"

He was getting really shirty now. He kept his voice low too, but it was a hiss as he said, "My name is Karl Marx and I am writing a manifesto to free the workers. I know nothing of the persons you say, nor do I know anything about this station. Now leave or I will have to have you thrown out."

"I have a reader's card," I said, showing it, "and I—"

"I do not care if you have a letter from Queen Victoria herself. Go away and leave me alone!" He turned back to the book he had pulled open and froze in an attitude that said he wouldn't say another word to me.

I went back to the chap at the desk. When he had finished taking care of an elderly man who wanted to know where to find books on fish, I said, "This Professor Marx. You know him?"

"He's been coming here for years, almost every day," he told me.

"What's a manifesto?"

He hesitated. "I think it's a document that sort of says what you want to do."

"He said 'free the workers.' What did he mean by that?" The reason I asked was that it sounded a bit like one of our aims in setting up a trade union for cabbies.

"Oh, he thinks workers are ill-treated, over-worked, under-paid."

"So do I, for that matter," I said, "and a lot of others. Maybe you too."

"You sounded like you were having an argument with him," the chap said.

"He says he knows nothing about what I asked him."

"What did you ask him?"

"I don't think I can tell you that," I said. No need to get him mixed up in this.

"Maybe you've got the wrong professor."

"Blimey!" I said. "You mean you've got more of 'em?"

He smiled a thin smile. "Of course we do. Scholars and learned men come here from all over the country. We have doctors and professors of all kinds. Professor Karl Marx is one of the most prominent so when anyone says 'the professor,' I suppose we think of him first, especially as he's become such a regular visitor."

"They don't all have beards, do they?"

"No, not all. Look, you sure you don't have a name for the man you want?"

"No."

"What's your professor's field? Chemistry, geology, philosophy, literature—"

"I don't know." I was beginning to feel I was at a dead end. "I think he comes here regularly though."

"Hmm." He rubbed his chin. I had to admit the chap was trying to be helpful. "A regular, a professor and he has a beard." He looked out over the sea of desks and books and faces. "See that desk over there?" He pointed to one on the outside circle.

I followed his finger. "Yes, that man has a beard."

"He's a professor. His name's Tryon. Been coming every day for a few weeks."

"Thanks, you've been a big help," I told him.

He laid a hand on my arm as I started away. "Please, no trouble if he's the wrong man."

"I promise," I said.

I approached cautiously. "Excuse me. Professor Tryon?"

He was not as big and broad as Professor Marx. His face looked worried, but that might be natural. His beard showed a few gray hairs close up. He was looking at maps, bright-colored maps that were spread out all over the desk. Lots of blue ocean were on them, and two had a lot of arrows going every way.

He nodded. I breathed a sigh of relief. The right man at last. "It's about the London Bridge Underground Station," I said.

His eyes showed fear. He glanced from side to side to see if anyone was with me.

I felt a thrill of success. This was the right professor. He leaned over his maps, as if trying to cover them with his arms so I couldn't see them. I decided to attack with all guns blazing.

"Luke Marston is dead and Dickie Drew is dying. Herbert Summers is in jail for a crime he didn't commit. I want to see that nobody else gets killed. What can you tell me about all this, Professor? It seems you're in it up to your armpits."

"No, no," he gabbled. "I had nothing to do with all that." He was trying to scoop all his maps together.

"The candlesticks," I said as loud as I dared, and he looked even more terrified.

"I can explain those," he said quickly. "Here, let me show you this book—"

He abandoned the maps, half scrunched up, and rose to his feet quickly. "It's over here." He darted to the nearest rack of bookshelves and disappeared from sight.

It took me a few seconds, then I rushed after him. I couldn't see him down this row and hurried to the next. He wasn't there either. I tried several more rows, then went back to the desk where I had found him.

The professor and the maps were gone.

CHAPTER 12

I made an early start the next morning and had the usual flurry of people being late for trains and wanting to get to the station to catch the 7:15 or whatever. As a result, I was over at Hangman's Corner about half past nine. It being Friday, more cabbies were there than usual. The smell from Preacher's fire was different today.

"Whatcher got there, Preacher?" I asked. "Some rhinoceros meat? The zoo missing an animal, are they?"

"Lamb," said Preacher, licking his lips. "Lovely leg o' lamb."

"Fell off the back of a wagon, did it?"

"Not quite like that," Preacher said. "I was passing the back of Reynolds, the butcher in Cripplegate and—well you know how it is, Ned. Needs a bit longer cooking though. Won't be ready yet."

Bombardier came over, sniffing. "Lamb, you say, Preacher? Got some nice mint sauce to go with it? Lamb's no good without mint sauce."

"This lamb's too good for that. It don't need nothing."

Bombardier had a newspaper in his hand. He waved it at me. "Seen the paper today, Ned?"

"No, I haven't, not yet."

" 'ere, look at this." He pointed to a small column and we read it together.

The sub-headline read, *Hansom Cab Murder,* and beneath it was *Man Arraigned.*

We went on reading. *In the case of the man found dead in a hansom cab at Putney Bridge on April 2nd, a man has been arraigned. He will appear at the Central Criminal Court at the Old Bailey on May 15th, charged with willful murder.* There was, more but it was a mumbo-jumbo of legal words, and neither of us was interested.

"Poor old Herbert," said Bombardier. "He couldn't have done it."

" 'Course he couldn't," I said. "He didn't, and we're going to prove it."

"How will we do that?" asked Bombardier.

"We're going to find out who did do it."

He was just putting the paper down when another small headline caught my eye.

"Half a mo'," I said. "Let me see that."

It was a news item, and it said, *The China Squadron of Her Majesty's Navy returns to its home base of Portsmouth within the next forty-eight hours. The squadron consists of six frigates, three cruisers, one battle cruiser and four supply vessels. This current tour of duty has taken it to Singapore, Shanghai, Rangoon, Calcutta, Bangkok and Hong Kong and has lasted two hundred days.*

Well, that was a bit of good news anyway. The China Squadron was home, and Cecilia would be over the moon about Jack coming home. I'd have to go and see her, tell her; maybe she hadn't seen the paper either.

Tommy Thompson joined us, attracted no doubt by the smell of the cooking lamb.

"Been Oxford Street way this morning, Ned?" he asked.

"Haven't had the pleasure of a fare in that direction yet today," I said.

"Try not to. Fenian Riots again, blocking all the streets."

The Fenian Brotherhood was an organization that said it was dedicated to the creation of an independent Irish state by force.

They believed that all peaceful methods had failed, and they were staging riots to make their point. Many of them had turned violent and a lot of people had been killed. We tried to avoid going into areas where we knew they were happening. It wasn't just self-protection. The police asked us to stay out those areas and keep down the traffic congestion.

I managed to get a couple of fares in the Knightsbridge district—day shoppers in from Surrey, and then a bloke with a case bigger than himself wanted to go to the Albert Hall.

"My bass fiddle," he explained, out of breath.

"No wonder you don't want to carry it there yourself," I told him as we struggled to fit it into the cab.

When we got there, I helped him out with his instrument, and he gave me a nice tip. I looked up and down Kensington Road, saw no prospects and told Perseus to take it slow.

He did a funereal-type clip-clop past Alexandra Gate towards the Horse Guards Barracks, then an unusual thing happened. A cab pulled out of Ennismore Road just ahead of me and a man got out. The cab drove off and as I got closer, the man waved to me.

"I want to go to Guy Fawkes's Cellar," he said.

He wore dark gray trousers and a jacket about the same color. He had on a dark blue shirt. He might have been Australian or Canadian. I'm never sure about the difference.

"I think it's closed, guv," I told him.

"No," he said, very firm. "It's open."

"It closed a couple of months ago and hasn't opened again yet." We have to keep up with all the sights in London and know when they're open.

"It's open now," he said, "and I want to go there." He climbed in before I could say another word.

Well, I thought, it's your money to go there, open or not, so don't blame me. So off we went, me wondering if the other cabby had told the same story.

We didn't see anything of the Fenian Riots. They must have been staying well north of the river. I crossed it at Lambeth Bridge and we went up Millbank and on to Abingdon Street, past the Victoria Tower Gardens. We could see the Parliament buildings ahead and nearer, on the left, the top of Westminster Abbey. I turned into the Old Palace Yard and reined Perseus to a stop in front of a grim, gray-fronted stone building, one of a line that stretched towards Westminster Hall.

"This is it," I said. "Guy Fawkes's cellar."

It used to be a popular place to visit. The notion that Guy Fawkes had of blowing up the Houses of Parliament was one that came to us all now and again, especially when the blokes in Parliament did something really stupid. Of course, not everybody went as far as Guy Fawkes did in 1630. He and his four mates rolled barrels of gunpowder right past where we were standing, into the house, then down into the cellar where they dug into the cellars below the Houses of Parliament. One of Guy Fawkes' mates blew the gaff on him so the fuse never got lit, but still, he had the right idea—or so some of my mates insisted.

Meanwhile, my fare was looking at the front of the house. No signs were up, so you couldn't tell if work was going on there or not. "You said it was closed," my fare said. "I'll bet you sixpence it's open."

That was too much money for me to gamble, and I didn't care much either way, but he wanted me to prove the point, so I went up to the door and turned the big iron handle. It creaked and the door opened. It was then that the bloke gave me a huge push in the back and sent me flying inside. The door slammed.

The first thing I saw was the flagstones near my face and the next was a sign propped sideways against the wall that said, CLOSED UNTIL FURTHER NOTICE.

I scrambled to my feet and bumped into my fare. He pushed me through the doorway and along a short passage. The next room held a burning oil lamp, and two men stood there.

One of them caught my attention immediately. He wore something like an army officer's uniform, but it had ordinary buttons instead of brass. He was tall and lean, with a long aristocratic sort of face, but with a look of cruelty in it. His hair was slicked back with unguent, but the feature that struck me the most was the monocle. You see them now and again certainly, but they're not as common as they used to be.

This one had a metal rim, and the bloke wore it as if he'd worn it for years. It gave him a sort of superior look and as he studied me through it now, I felt like something under a microscope.

"Ned Parker," he said, and I didn't like the way he said it— just my name, nothing else. The other bloke was a bruiser, big and beefy, nose broken a couple of times, a cheek that had been mangled and never grown back together again properly and a big ugly cauliflower ear. There was no sign of the bloke who had brought me here.

"I'm a busy man," the bloke with the monocle said. He had an upper-class accent, Oxford or Cambridge or one of those, and I could imagine him making the poor devils on the parade ground at Aldershot shiver. "So let's get to the point. What did you and Mr. John talk about?"

I knew I was on shaky ground. I also knew it would be better to stick as close as I could to the truth. If he knew that much about me, how much more did he know?

"Mr. John wanted to know why I had been seeing some people, going to some places. He seemed to know a lot about me."

"You had met Mr. John before?"

At least he didn't know that much. "No, never," I said.

"He knew your father though."

"He said he did, yes."

"So did I," said the monocle. "They call me the colonel."

I had heard the name. I didn't know a lot about him, but I knew he and Mr. John controlled most of London's crime between them. I had heard it said that the police were easy on them, as they preferred the two gangs to kill each other off, thus leaving less for the police to worry about. Well, I didn't want to get caught between the two of them. Cabbies hear things, and nothing I had heard about either one of them was good.

"Your father must have mentioned me."

"I think he did, but I was a youngster then."

"You say Mr. John referred to your father?"

"He thought I knew about what my father did."

"You knew he had a cab."

"Oh, yes, I knew that. He took me for rides in it."

"And when he died, you inherited it."

"Yes, that's right."

"But you did know what your father did. Besides drive a cab."

I didn't like him coming back to that. His gaze was on me like a searchlight through that monocle, as if he were looking right inside me.

"Well, Mr. John said that my father worked for him."

"Did Mr. John ask you about Southwark Bridge Station?"

"No, but he asked me why I had been to the Finchley Auction Rooms."

"And why were you there?"

I was thinking lightning fast now. The ice was getting thinner under my feet by the minute, and I had to be quick or I'd fall through. "One of my cabby mates, Herbert Summers, is in jail. He's being charged with the murder of one of his fares. See, Sergeant Jackson, he's a detective, and he—"

"I know who Jackson is," said the colonel coldly. "Go on."

"Well, Jacko thinks that Herbert did in this bloke in his cab and that the bloke stole something from the auction rooms, some church valuables—"

It was spur-of-the-moment stuff, and I was trying to throw in bits that the colonel probably knew about along with one or two more bits that he didn't. Strong rivalry went on between the two gangs. Sometimes one gang had the upper hand, and sometimes it was the other. Right now, Mr. John seemed to have the inside track and I was getting the impression that the colonel was trying hard to catch up.

"So you want to get your hands on these . . . these church valuables, do you?"

"No, no," I said hastily. "I want to help Herbert. I don't think he would murder a fare like that. I don't want to see him hanged."

The colonel got what they call a sneer on his face. "You want to help another cabby? You're not after the jewels? You expect me to believe that?"

"It's true! You can ask any cabby and he'll tell you that I've been trying to get all of them to help."

The colonel turned to the bruiser beside him. "Desmond?"

The bruiser half shrugged, half nodded.

The monocle turned back in my direction. "I'll tell you what I want you to do, Ned Parker. The next time Mr. John asks you questions—any at all—I want you to answer them."

Did that mean I was off the hook? For the time being, anyway? "You do?" I said as if I didn't quite understand him.

"Yes, and then I want you to tell me exactly what he said and what you told him."

I shuffled my feet and looked uncomfortable. "I could get into trouble that way. Mr. John told me to tell him anything I find out. If I tell you as well and he finds out—"

The colonel did not look sympathetic. "They say you're a smart lad. You'd better be smart enough to work that out. Otherwise, there may be another body being pulled out of the Thames." He let that threat sink in, then he added, "I'd like to plant a man inside Mr. John's organization. Maybe I will one of these days. Between him and you, I'd be really well informed."

I kept on looking unhappy, as I knew that was what he wanted. "Your father was good at selling information," the colonel went on, an icy smile on his face. "One day, it proved to be his downfall. Don't you get caught in that position, Ned."

I nodded.

"Inevitably," said the colonel smoothly, "in helping your friend to avoid being hanged, you might lay your hands on these church jewels—or something like them. Ever consider that?"

It was time to ease my way around the truth. "Well, I suppose it would be nice . . ."

"I thought so." The colonel smiled and the bruiser even cracked a grin.

"If Mr. John does ask me any more questions—"

"Oh, he will, Ned, he will. This is a very important matter to him."

"How shall I tell you?" I asked. "Here?"

"No, don't be absurd. We'll be out of here for good in ten minutes. No, don't worry, I'll find you when I want you." He turned away and the bruiser came and grabbed my arm and marched me to the door. As we went out, the fare who had brought me there was standing outside on guard.

"All clear," he said. Desmond, the bruiser, picked up the sign and hung it back up at the side of the door. I walked off fast, trying to make sense of what I had heard.

Whatever this business was with the candlesticks, Mr. John, and the colonel, it was, as the colonel had said, important. The two most dangerous gangs in London were battling over it, and men had been killed already because they had been in the way.

There were a few things they didn't seem to know. Neither had mentioned the professor, though what he had to do with anything was beyond me. Nor had either of them mentioned Paul Worth or the Bishop of Vauxhall. Still, I reminded myself, I drew a blank on them too.

Mr. John knew about me talking to Dickie Drew, and he must have had men talking to him and threatening his wife. The colonel hadn't mentioned either Luke Marston or Dickie Drew though, and he hadn't asked me why I had been to St. Agnes Hospital.

Was I getting in between these gangs? Whether I liked it or not, I seemed to be already. Should I get out of the way altogether? Forget all this? Just be a cabby and let the gangs fight it out? Stick to flicking my whip over Perseus and keep my nose clean?

I pushed those thoughts away. Sounded nice, but I knew I couldn't do it. I was just naturally nosy—like my old dad. My sister Cecilia, my girl friend Millie, all my cab driving friends, Detective Jackson, everybody I knew said that I just couldn't keep my nose out of things.

Then there was poor old Herbert, suffering there in Cannon Street police station, and now going to be tried at the Old Bailey for murder. If I didn't help him, who would? That stuff about British justice was all very well, but once in a while, an innocent man did get hanged for a crime he didn't commit.

As I untied Perseus's reins, he turned his head and gave me a blink of an eye and a gentle whinny. One hoof tapped on the cobblestones. Perseus was saying, "Do what you think is right, Ned."

I gave him a rub on the neck and a quick slap. "I will, old chap," I told him. "I will."

CHAPTER 13

At the top end of Hangman's Corner, the old bandstand is still there. We kept hearing talk about building a new one as an annex to the park due to this one falling down, but nothing had happened yet. It was handy for us though, and we were making use of it now for our meeting.

It was the end of the day for a lot of us and as many as could had gathered there. Blokes stood, sat, or leaned wherever they found a space, and Smiling Sid started us off. He introduced the three of us committee members—as if the others didn't all know us—but he called that "procedure." Then he got down to brass tacks.

"We've all agreed that as cab drivers, we should have a union," he said. "The longshoremen have got one now and it's working well. Others'll be springing up all over the country. It's time we had one. Now, as you all know, we three are going to meet the city council board next week and put our case. The purpose of this meeting is to make sure that we cover all the points that you want us to, so let's start. Who's first?"

Diddy Cartwright waved his hand first. "You told us about that bloke John Fielden who was going round the country talking. You said the dockworkers wanted what you called a minimum wage guarantee. Well, that's what we want too."

Murmurs of approval came from all corners. We should have known that would be the first point to come up—money. Ten minutes later, we were still arguing about it when Sid started waving his arms and finally shouting for quiet. "All right, it's the most important item to all of us. We need to decide if the money should be for each hour or for each day. We'll also have to decide on the amount. We can't settle on all these things here. All we want to do today is get all our points laid out. Now, who's next?"

Tommy Thompson was next. "The dock workers said they were being forced to work excessive long hours. That means too many. We ought to ask for that."

Leo Dempster stepped forward. "If we settled on pay by the hour, a lot of blokes will want a lot of hours. Other cabbies don't want to work more than a certain number of hours a day. How many is excessive?"

After ten minutes of discussion on that issue, Smiling Sid was shouting for quiet again, saying hours would be considered too, and that we had to get on with the meeting. When we did, Bombardier piped up. "Jimmy Laidlaw told us about that swell, Roger Sherrington, who fired all his cabbies who wouldn't work longer hours. Couldn't we ask for something that says a cabby can't be fired without good reason?"

"What's a good reason?" piped up Arthur Young, an older bloke with a lot of years cabbying. That brought on plenty more argument, and it could have gone for hours. The discussion was getting heated.

I gave Sid a signal, and he managed to bring back some order. "Ned's got something to say."

"The railroads are arguing over these same things we are," I said. "Blokes there are trying to get a union going. One big problem they've got is that they employ engineers and mechanics, skilled workers. They also employ laborers, like tracklayers and coal shovelers. They've got a real problem because they don't all get paid the same wages. I just want to point out that we have a big advantage. We're all cabbies. We all do the same job. Let's make it easy on ourselves and get the best deals we can. One way is for us to stick together—make our union strong."

"We're not all exactly the same, Ned," called out Arthur Evans, a cabby for thirty years. "Some of us have been driving a cab a long time. Some others only a short while. Now I'm not saying the new men may not turn out to be as good as us older blokes, but we've got one or two drivers who wouldn't even know where the Coal Pit is."

Laughs came at that. The Coal Pit is a pub in Villiers Street on the Embankment. It caters to a lot of lower types, but swells like to go there too. "Slumming," they call it.

Arthur's comment referred to a young cabby who had a fare wanting to go there and had to find another cabby to ask.

Leo Dempster jumped in. "That's a good point, Arthur. It also brings up a good argument we can use for our cause. We should have a standard for cabbies to meet, prove how well they know London before they take a cab out."

"You mean a test?" shouted Diddy. "Like we was still in school?"

A few objections followed, but as most cabbies have been driving for some time, they—or probably I should say we—had the most voices. "We can use that point," Leo went on, "to prove to the masters how good we are at what we do. Could make us worth more money." Adding the part about money had to prove popular, and it did.

We went on like that. Most cabbies are Londoners, and we've got a reputation for talking a lot. We don't miss a chance to air our opinions, and this was the best chance we'd had to do it in some time. Finally, we broke up. Sid told everybody that we'd present all our points and see what the city board said. Then we'd have another meeting to decide what to do next.

Smiling Sid seemed to be smiling more than usual as we

watched the cabbies leave. To Leo and me he said, "I was getting worried they'd ask the big question."

"What big question?" I asked.

"How much it's going to cost them."

"You mean we'll all have to *pay?*"

"Union dues," said Sid.

"Sid's right," Leo said. "They'll have to know sooner or later, but it's better it doesn't come up till we get a bit deeper into what we're all going to get out of it."

"See," Sid explained, "there's a lot of expenses to running a union. The first thing we need is a fund. If a bloke is off sick or fired or his horse dies, anything like that, then the union has to put its hand in its pocket and pay him. That's part of our strength. Then we may have a pay a lawyer."

Leo was nodding. "Right now, we're too dependent on the masters. When we have a fund behind us, we will be able to bargain on an equal basis."

"Blimey!" I said. "That's not going to be popular."

"Dues'll be low to start," Sid said. "We may have to increase them later."

"How much will they be?" I asked.

Leo answered. He had evidently given a bit of thought to this. "We don't know yet, but somewhere near five pence a day." He glanced at Sid.

"Should be about right," Sid said.

"When do we spring it on the blokes?" I asked.

"Just after they've been paid," Leo said with a grin. "When they're still feeling flush."

"We'll know better after next week's meeting," Sid said. "We'll know a lot of things then we don't know now."

"Speaking of next week's meeting," Leo said, "we'd all three better go together. Whose cab, and where shall we meet?"

★ ★ ★ ★ ★

Next day being Saturday, Perseus and me were out early, ferry-ing folks anywhere they wanted to go. Late in the morning, a couple wanted to go to Great Russell Street and visit the mother-in-law. I dropped them in front of a nice house with a line of big trees in front of it. Then I trotted Perseus the few minutes it took to get to the British Museum and left him in the cab rank. He was getting friendly with the next horse when I left him.

The chap I had talked to before in the Reading Room gave me a sharp look when he recognized me. "I don't want you making a disturbance again like you did before," he told me.

"I won't," I promised. "I have a reading card now."

"I know you do," he said bitterly. "I gave it to you."

"So now I'll be very careful about disturbances."

"I hope so," he said. "I wouldn't want to have to get you thrown out."

"Won't be necessary," I said confidently. "I'm sure the professor will agree. Is he here?"

"I haven't seen Professor Tryon since that unfortunate episode," he said, a bit more hoity-toity than before.

"Got into trouble with your boss, did you?"

"Mr. Rossington did have words with me, yes," he admitted. "Anyway, like I said, the professor isn't here."

"Doesn't matter. Look, just help me this one little bit. Tell me where he got all those maps he had on the desk."

He hesitated.

"That's all," I said. "Then I'll go."

He thought about it and decided it was a fair exchange. "Down there." He pointed. "Section D-twelve."

I thanked him and went down the aisle. Past the rows of books, several big shelves sat in stacks of six or eight. I found D, then I found shelf twelve and pulled it open. Some of the maps were a bit crumpled, so they were evidently the ones the professor had on his desk before. I took one out and smoothed it. It was in bright colors and showed the Atlantic Ocean—it said so in fancy letters. Land showed on the left and the right sides, but the ocean itself was what seemed to be important. It took up almost the whole map.

A lot of arrows were shown pointing across the water, and this map was marked *Trade Winds.* I looked at the others. All of them were of the Atlantic Ocean. This professor really liked oceans, particularly the Atlantic. These maps were similar but not the same. Another was marked *Commerce Routes—English,* the next one said *Commerce Routes—Spanish,* and the third said *Commerce Routes—French.* All of them had little arrows.

Between two of the maps, a small sheet of lined paper had been caught. In fancy handwriting I saw some words in a foreign language. I could have taken it, but the professor might come back for it and I didn't want to upset his work—whatever it was he was doing. So I got a piece of paper and a pencil from a nearby desk and copied the words. They were, *Nuestra Senora de Valencia.*

I had no idea what they meant, but I put the piece of paper in my pocket, replaced the other one between the maps and put them all back. I gave the bloke at the desk a wave and a nod. He looked suspicious at first, then relieved to see me leaving.

At that time of day, the Bayswater Road was a good place to pick up fares who wanted to go to the big stores. I usually got return fares as well. This meant a number of short trips but plenty of them. The traffic was always heavy with omnibuses, donkey carts, delivery wagons going through, carriages and pairs going into Hyde Park and pedestrians dodging across the road all the time.

After a couple of fares amid all this confusion, I was passing Marble Arch when I was hailed. A funny-looking old geezer with a high wing-collared suit and a wide top hat waved his umbrella. I thought he had come out of one of the big houses on Park Lane. When I pulled alongside him, he said in a squeaky voice, "Do you go to Camden Town?"

That was a long, good-paying ride. "I certainly do," I said. "Jump in."

"No, no, I don't want to go there," he said testily.

"You just want to know if I go there," I guessed.

"Of course not," he snapped. "I want you to take this envelope there."

In his scrawny hand he held a brown envelope, the kind lawyers use. He turned it over and I saw a red seal. "Oh, right enough, guv." I reached for the envelope, but he pulled it away.

"Just a minute! I want you to take it to Peat and Harwell at the corner of Georgiana Street. Do you know where that is?"

"Yes, I do, guv. It's near the Grand Union Canal."

"No, no," he snapped, "it's not near it. It's two streets away at least!"

"Know just where it is, guv," I told him. The fare is always right.

I did know where it was. Peat and Harwell were bookies. They had a so-so reputation, and I had been there a couple of times. "Bookie runs," as we called them, were not legal, strictly speaking. Still, every cabby made them, as the person placing the bet paid well, usually two to three times the fare for the same run. A few cabbies I knew had regular runs—clients who bet regularly and who, for one reason or another, didn't want to be seen going into or out of a bookmaker's. A lot of gamblers had their regular local bookie, but some bookie runs were like this one, where the place was a long way away.

He seemed satisfied and held out the envelope, but as I reached for it, he pulled it away again. "How do I know I can trust you?" He eyed me suspiciously.

Aha, I thought, there's a lot of money in here. Placing a big bet, are you?

"Name's Ned Parker, guv. Been a cabby for ten years, own my own cab. Ask any cabby. He'll know me."

"You cabbies have licenses, don't you? Where's yours?"

I showed it, and he read it several times over. I could see his lips moving. He held it in his hand, not wanting to give it back, as if he was disappointed at not being able to find something wrong with it.

"How much is this going to cost?" He sounded like he would argue no matter what I said.

"A thicker."

"*What?*" I had expected it. "A *pound?*" he shouted. "A pound to take an envelope to Camden Town? Preposterous. I'll give you ten shillings."

Ten gen wasn't bad really, but the bloke had started the auction and I kept it up until we agreed on fifteen gen. "I'm going to write down your name and license number," he told me and he did, in a little notebook. "That envelope had better be delivered, or I'll see you in Newgate Jail!" He handed over the money as if he begrudged every penny.

I run into folk like that once in a while; not too many, fortunately. I left him standing there watching me, probably making sure I was going in the right direction.

It was humdrum after that. The best fare I had was a woman taking her daughter to try out at the ballet school on Wimbledon Common. That's a good long ride, and the underground railway doesn't go out that far. They say it will one day, but right now it doesn't. I wonder if they accepted the girl. The usual number of people visiting relatives in hospital filled up much of the afternoon.

I was passing the Flower Market at Nine Elms and picked up a fare, a middle-aged woman who wanted to go to Brixton

Prison and pick up her husband. I was consoling her, telling her he'd get a job, go straight, she didn't have to worry, before she was able to cut in and tell me he was a warder and they were going on a week's holiday. She sounded a bit insulted. Still, I didn't know, did I?

After she collected him, I took them to Brixton Railway Station, wished them a nice holiday and set off for Clapham, this probably being as close as I'd get today.

Cecilia was glad to see me, after she had told me off for not letting her know I was coming so she could have baked a pie for me. "Yes, I saw the paper. Mrs. Jameson down the street showed it to me. Isn't it wonderful the squadron's back?" Her face clouded. "Still, I can't understand why Jack hasn't sent me word by now."

It was my day for consolations. Better get this one right. "It's a bit soon," I said. "I mean, they've got to get all those ships into Portsmouth Harbor, then they've got to pay off all the crew, tell 'em when to get back aboard for the next trip and things like that. Must take a few days."

"But when they come from the East," Cecilia said, "they have to stop at a coaling station—usually Villefranche in the South of France or else the one near Lisbon. Jack always lets me know from there. I should have heard by now."

She looked worried. I reached down into my consolation jar again. "Must be a lot of reports and whatnot to fill out. You know how the navy is, put it all on paper and copy it out four times. Besides, wasn't there word of bad weather in the Atlantic? Slowed them down, most likely." I hadn't seen any weather reports lately, but there often was bad weather there. Might have had some the last few days; who knows?

Young James came running in at that moment. Good timing, just what Cecilia needed to cheer her up. He ran up to me, and I grabbed him and swept him up into the air.

"Blimey," I said, "I'm not doing this any more. You're getting too heavy, young man!"

"No, I'm not. Do it again, Uncle Ned."

I did it a couple more times and when I brought him down to earth, he asked me eagerly, "Can I say hello to Pegasus?"

"Who's Pegasus?"

"Your horse."

"No, my horse is called Perseus. You should know. You named him."

James shook his blond curls. "No, I said Pegasus. The horse with wings, the one in my school book, remember."

"Thought you said Perseus."

James looked at me seriously. "You're pulling my leg, Uncle Ned."

"No, I'm not," I said, and I wasn't. "Let's go out and see him anyway," I said quick-like.

"Just a minute," James said. He ran off to his room. I looked at Cecilia, but she just smiled. He was back in a minute with a big loop of cloth that he had stuck feathers on to. "It's what they call a feathered necklace. I made it in school. They do it in France."

"It's . . . er, it's nice. Want to put it on him?"

He put the thing around Perseus' neck and Perseus behaved very well. After sniffing at it once, he just pretended it wasn't there. James and Perseus had a great time together. The horse liked boys, and the boy liked horses. James looked proud as Punch when I sat him up on Perseus' back. Cecilia had a different worry now. "Hold on tight," she urged James.

"Perseus isn't moving," I said. "James is all right."

"He looks awful high up there."

One of James' pals went by at that moment and the two waved to each other. "It'll be all over the school Monday," said Cecilia.

I had to lift James down so he could run into the house and get Perseus a bun to eat. The horse doesn't like bread, and I never feed him any, but I didn't want to spoil James' day. Perseus felt the same way. He gallantly munched down the bun, getting rid of it in two bites.

"What kind of a school does he go to?" I asked Cecilia. "They certainly teach them funny things there. The school I went to, the nuns never had us making things out of feathers."

"Didn't you learn anything practical in school?"

"No, the nuns at Saint Anselm's were very strict—kept our noses in the books."

Our sister Fanny and her husband Louis had been by to see Cecilia, and we talked about them for some time. Cecilia said their farm was doing well and they were thinking of buying the land next to them and having goats on it. I was waiting for Cecilia to come out with it and get it over. She did. "I hope you're not still on about that business with those candlesticks that were stolen."

"It's just that that cabby friend of mine is being blamed," I said. "If I hear any bit of news about them, naturally I tell the law."

"Like father did," she said.

"It's the duty of all of us to help the police if we can," I said in my goody-goody voice.

"Some just want to help more than others," said Cecilia in that vinegary way she can use when she wants.

I watched James bringing his jigsaw puzzle over to me, half-finished. "Not much happening on that really," I said. "I haven't talked to the police for some time."

That seemed to satisfy her. We talked about Jack again, and she seemed a bit easier in her mind about him. "Tell you what," I told her. "I'll make some inquiries."

She brightened. "Can you, Ned? That would set my mind at

ease. Not that I worry about him," she added.

"Of course you don't," I said, keeping a straight face.

I helped James with his puzzle, although I had to push two or three of the bits real hard to get them to fit. They seemed like different shapes from the holes. He looked up from the corner where we were having trouble with the rest of an ostrich. "What are we going to do about Pegasus?" he asked.

"Perseus," I said.

"No. I told you Pegasus."

"I must have got it wrong."

"You can change it." His little face showed determination.

"I'll talk to him about it."

James thought about that for a minute. "Will he understand?"

"He's a very intelligent horse," I said. "I'll go along with whatever he thinks."

"Can we do it now?"

"It might take a day or two. Changing your name can take time. How'd you like it if we suddenly changed your name to Algernon?"

James hooted with laughter and when I left, both he and his mother were in good spirits. Who would I talk to about Jack? I didn't know, and although I hadn't wanted to admit it to Cecilia, Jack should have been in touch with her by now. But I'd find a knowledgeable person somewhere. London is a wonderful city where you can find out about everything that happens in the British Empire.

It was a nagging question though. Where was Jack?

CHAPTER 14

Spotty Sunday, some cabbies called it. Sunday always had spots where a lot of cab activity could be expected and others where they were as dead as dishwater. I cruised around, not doing much, then headed up into Kensington. Sometimes I could catch people coming to or going from church. I got a fare leaving Brompton Oratory and after a long spell of nothing, I turned Perseus towards Kensington Gardens.

I flicked the whip. "Fancy a name change to Pegasus?" I asked him. He made no reply. "Doesn't come with wings," I warned him. "It's just a name. So I got it wrong. You're still Perseus to me."

At that, he twitched his ears, and he could hardly say fairer than that. "Right then," I said, "Perseus it's going to stay, whether young James likes it or not." He twitched again, and as far as I was concerned, that settled the matter.

Kensington Gardens has three cabstands. The nearest was by Round Pond. It was in one those ditchwater patches this morning. A few pedestrians heading for the pond, a few strollers out after church and stretching their legs, some nursemaids pushing perambulators, and one bored-looking police constable were about it, except for the birds, and there was a lot of those. I hitched up Perseus at the end of the row and walked down to a shiny cab where I said to the driver, "Business is slow, I see."

Eric Newland was a cabby of nearly ten years' experience. Before that, he had been in gentleman's service, first as a bootblack, then working his way up to a kitchen assistant, then a footman. He had been thinking about becoming a butler, but had changed his mind and decided to put the bit of money he had saved into buying a cab.

He was a wiry bloke, not quite skinny, and with black hair and a mustache that he liked to grow, telling us that one of the reasons he had decided against butlering was that butlers had to be clean-shaven. He always looked neat and clean. He was not real pally with any other cabby, but he was always pleasant and polite. He climbed down and shook my hand.

"Hello, Ned. Good meeting on Friday, I thought. Be interesting to hear how next Wednesday goes."

"Interesting for all of us," I said. "Listen, Eric, I wanted to ask you something. When you were in service, you traveled all over, didn't you?"

"Yes," he said. "I toured Europe with Lord Granley and then again later with the Duke of Suffolk. Then with the Earl of Northumberland, I went all over Turkey, Greece, the Levant and—"

"Perfect," I said. "I knew you were just the man. Picked up bits of the different languages, I'm sure?"

"Well, yes, I did. I've forgotten some of them but—"

"No matter," I said, taking out of my pocket the piece of paper with the words on it that I had copied in the British Museum. I handed the paper to him. "What language is this?"

"Spanish," he said, just glancing at it.

"I knew you'd know. Can you tell what it says?"

"Yes, *Nuestra Senora de Valencia* means Our Lady of Valencia. Valencia's a town in Spain. A lot of pilgrims go to the church there, so that's what the church is called."

I was a bit disappointed at his first words, but my mind was racing. A church! St. Mary-in-the-Fields and All Hallows—they were churches too. They were the churches where the silver candlesticks were stolen. Was there a connection with this one in Valencia?

"What else you can tell me about it?" I asked.

He rubbed his chin. "Well, I dunno really. It's famous, particularly in Spain. Like I said, big crowds go there. Pilgrims mostly."

"Is Valencia famous for anything else?"

"Oranges," Eric said right away. "Valencia oranges are among the best. Real juicy and sweet. Known all over." He sensed my disappointment. "Sorry I can't help more, Ned, but I'm not sure what you're looking for. Is it important?"

"That's all right, Eric. Oh, has Valencia been in the news lately?"

"Not that I know. I still read the *Times* regular. Got into the habit when I was with His Grace the Duke. He was one of the directors, you know. If Valencia had been in the news recently, I would have seen it in there."

"Thanks, Eric. If I think of any more questions, I'll come to you. Still doing the Bayswater-Notting Hill run, are you?"

"That's right. I stop in at Hangman's Corner when I'm in that neighborhood. Otherwise, you can find me here at one of the stands in Kensington Gardens."

I thanked him again and watched him walk off. So as far as Eric knew, nobody had stolen any candlesticks from Our Lady of Valencia's church. Still, churches, silver candlesticks, oranges, pilgrims? What did they have in common? Then there were underground stations, giant frogs, ghost trains, murdered men—and the two most feared gangs of villains in London. Not to mention Swiveler Grimes who was "keeping an eye on me."

Blimey—what an Irish stew this was!

The rest of the day was spotty too, and when I got back home that evening, I was as tired as if I'd had a really hard day. To my surprise, an envelope addressed to me was just inside the door. I picked it up. It had a really nice smell to it, like a fancy perfume. Funny, but I thought I had smelled it before. I opened the envelope and read the letter inside.

Dear Ned, Millie is having a try-out for one of our new shows. It will be at the New Vaudeville Theatre on the Strand at 8.30 on Tuesday evening. I would love to have you come along and applaud her. I hope you can stay for a drink or two afterwards.

Fondest regards

Dorothy Radcliffe

Now here was something! I hadn't expected this. I still wasn't sure I wanted to see Millie have a career on the stage. On the other hand, I didn't want to hold her back if that was what she really wanted to do. Perhaps I didn't need to worry, I thought, Millie would do as she liked, never mind what I said. If I went tomorrow and clapped for her, I'd be encouraging her. If I stayed away, she might be angry with me.

It did sound like a great opportunity for her, no mistake about that. The old Vaudeville Theatre on the Strand had been very popular. It had only been pulled down because it got so old. The New Vaudeville was a spanking new building, and the Strand was the real heart of theatreland. When the theatre opened, it would be a big night for the town. Millie had told me that some girls struggled for years to get out of the chorus. Some took a long time to reach the top, others never reached it at all, and here was Millie, being handed fame on a plate! Oh, she had some way to go, but she had looks, could sing, could dance, had loads of determination and—in my opinion—had that little extra that got a girl noticed.

Never be afraid to make decisions, Ned, was one of my old dad's bits of advice.

I always tried to follow this particular bit, but sometimes it wasn't easy. I told myself I had till Tuesday night to decide, but

126

deep down, I knew I'd go. The words at the end of Dorothy's letter—*Fondest Regards* were more personal than I'd have expected. The few letters I got usually ended with *Yours Truly*, but then, people in show business were like that, I had heard. Besides, she was older than me—not by much, it was true, but she was older. All my girl friends had been younger than I. I had heard the other cabbies make remarks about "older women" and the things they knew. When they made the remarks, they usually winked and tapped the sides of their noses.

Still, Dorothy had given me that long and lingering look as I had left. And that sentence at the end about me staying for a drink or two later, I wondered . . . Go on, Ned, you romantic fool, I told myself, make more out of it than is there.

On Monday, the sun surprised London by coming up bright and early, so I made an early start. Just after six, I had Perseus stepping sprightly towards town. The bone-grubbers and the rag-gatherers were out already on the streets, and the dung collectors were busy with their shovels before traffic ruined their livelihood. The cigar and cigarette-end blokes were not such early starter, but there was even one or two of those.

All of these blokes get out early, some as early as two in the morning in the summertime. There's not many rag-gatherers in my district of Pimlico. You see, most of those gathered around Petticoat Lane and Ragfair, as they say Jews throw out the most clothes.

I passed Enoch Bright's scrap metal wagon and he gave me a wave. How he makes a living from those old bits of copper, brass, pewter, tin and old iron, I don't know. Most dealers do well if they make six pence a day, though I know from Enoch that he often finds a good piece that has been thrown out from a posh house because it's broken. There can be quite a few pence in that one piece. If he can't fix it, Enoch knows blokes who can.

The farther I got into London, the better the chances of a fare. A lot of blokes there work long days, starting early and finishing late, so I headed for the railway stations. In my mind, I was mulling over a thought that kept nagging me. Silver candlesticks, was what I couldn't get clear. Church valuables, I had called them when I was being worked over by the colonel, and he had referred to them the same way. Mr. John hadn't mentioned them. Churches seemed to keep cropping up. Then too, the Bishop of Vauxhall was mixed up in the theft somehow— not to mention the poor bloke who had been done in and had worn clergyman's clothes.

How could I get more information without sticking my neck into a noose? If Mr. John or the colonel was holding the noose, neither one of them would hesitate to pull it tight. So as churches and silver candlesticks were rolling through my brain, I realized I was driving past one of the cabstands at Green Park. Five cabs usually plied this stand, and I knew all of the drivers.

I reined Perseus in tight and he gave me a reproving look. I don't normally do it that sudden. "Sorry," I told him, and he nodded to tell me he understood.

Three cabs were there; the others evidently had fares already. One of the three cabbies was Bob Rouse, with a lot of years behind him—the man I wanted to see. "Blimey, it's Nosy Ned himself!" he called out. "What's the matter, mate, lost again?"

"Be a waste of time asking you if I was," I said, and we both got out and had a friendly handshake. The next few minutes were taken up with questions like, "How's old so-and-so?" "Where's what's-his name?" From there, it was easy to slip into asking the question I had stopped for.

"Remember Stan? Stanley Havers? Used to work this parish?" I asked.

Bob Rouse was a grizzled old Scot who still spoke with a touch of the brogue. " 'Course I remember him. We was mates, me and old Stan."

"Gave up cabbying about a year ago," I said.

"That's right. Got a good job in the City, Stan did."

"See anything of him?"

"Ran into him in a boozer a few weeks ago. Looked well, he did. Said the job was going fine, he'd had several promotions, was making more money—"

"Where is he working?" This was the item that I couldn't remember. I may know a great many of the six thousand cabbies in London, but I can't be expected to remember everything about the ones I do know. What I did know was that Stanley Havers was a man I should talk to, even though I wasn't sure why.

"He's at the Silver Vaults."

Bullseye!

I kept the conversation going with Bob. Like most other cabbies, he wanted to talk about our committee's visit to the city council on Wednesday. It was a really important matter to most drivers, and it was good to see that so many took the matter seriously and wanted to have a trade union of their own that would give them a safe feeling they'd never had before. When I left Bob, I had a glow from knowing I was playing a valuable part in all this, and another glow from the hope that the man I was going to see would to able to add one more bit to the puzzle.

Between London Wall and Cheapside runs the narrow street where the Silver Vaults are located. Not everybody knows about them. Talk at one time was about making them into a museum, but it was decided that the place was too active for that. So it continues to buy, sell and trade goods made of silver. It has an auction room and workshops where workers make and repair silver articles.

I had to leave Perseus on Gresham Street where there was a hitching bollard close to a water trough. The sun was still out and it was warm, so he would need a drink now and then. The building was old and gray stone fronted, with a simple sign outside. Only the London Wall across the street, built by the Romans, looked older. The desk had a military-looking bloke at it. He gave me a piercing look.

This investigation was teaching me a lot about people and how to get them on your side. I gave him a similar look back and said, "Edward Parker to see Mr. Stanley Havers."

"Is he expecting you?"

That almost stopped me, but not quite. "No, but he'll see me. Just give him my name."

It worked. "Just a minute." He disappeared.

Less than a minute later, Stanley walked in. "Do I know you, Mr. Parker? I'm sorry but I'm busy at the moment and I—" He stopped in mid-stride. "Ned! For heaven's sake!"

He came up, clapped me on the back and grabbed my hand. "Edward Parker! How long have you been Edward? I was about to say I was too busy—but for you! Come on in. It's been a long time. Oh, only a year I know but—anyway, come on in!"

The man at the desk was watching all this with a puzzled look. Stanley must be higher up here than I thought. Still, that was all the better. He took me back into his office, which was next door.

He didn't look any different. He was still a youngish middle-aged fellow, in his late forties, alert and with a bony face and neatly parted fair hair. His gray suit was posher than any of the cabby clothes I had seen him wearing. He invited me to sit down, and I faced him across his desk that had papers, folders and books all over it.

"I ran into Bob Rouse," I told him. "He said you were doing well." I waved a hand at the office, the desk and him. "Looks like he didn't tell me the half of it."

He grinned amiably. "I've been lucky since I've been here, Ned."

"It's not luck, Stan," I told him. "I bet you deserve it. Tell me, what exactly do you do here?"

"A slice of luck did come my way, Ned. I can't deny it. See, what happened was this. My uncle is a pal of one of the directors of the Vaults. They got to talking in a pub one night—you know the way they do—and this director was complaining that they were firing one of their guards who'd been seen in a boozer telling all sorts of things about this place."

"Things that might help blokes who'd want to break in and steal some of your stuff?"

"Right. So the director was complaining about it being hard to find reliable people for guards. I had been at my uncle's—it was his birthday—and I'd told him I wanted to get a better job than cabbying—" he broke off. "No offense, Ned, but I had another youngster on the way and—"

"None taken, Stan," I told him. "We've all got to look out for ourselves."

"That's the way I felt. Anyway, long story short, I got the job. A month later, a guard on day duty left and I replaced him. The bit of luck I mentioned came then. A bloke came with a delivery. I knew he had a police record as a real trasseno—" he paused again.

"I've heard the word," I told him. "A real bad character."

"Right. Well, I didn't say anything, but then the same bloke came again. I passed the word and a copper nabbed him, took him in for questioning and they found out a raid was being planned."

"Making you a hero! Well done, Stan!"

He chuckled. "It got me a promotion, and now I'm second in charge of the protection squad. My boss is an ex-detective, real nice chap. So here I am."

"With a fancy office, a good job and a nice screw!"

"The office and the job are fine, and yes, the wages are good."

"More than you made cabbying, I'll bet?"

He nodded and grinned again. "Have to admit you're right. Now then, Ned, what brings you here?"

"Well, I was passing—I'd talked to Bob Rouse—and I—"

"It's something to do with those silver candlesticks, isn't it?"

CHAPTER 15

I gave him an admiring look. "This place has got the right bloke in the job with you, Stanley, my boy! 'Course, I was going to tell you." Well, it was true. I was, but I had wanted to ease into it. Now I told him the whole story.

I wouldn't have told it to many blokes, but I knew Stanley to be reliable, honest and absolutely straightforward. His job at the Silver Vaults demonstrated that I wasn't the only one who thought so. He listened closely as I told him of the murder in Herbert Summers' cab, the theft of the two candlesticks, the deaths of Paul Worth, Luke Marston and Dickie Drew. Concerning Swiveler Grimes, Mr. John and the colonel, all I said was that they had warned me to watch my step and that they were involved in a way I didn't understand. I described briefly the visit by Benny and me to the London Bridge Underground Station.

I kept it all short, and when I had finished, Stan leaned back in his chair. "You've got yourself into a right mess this time, Ned," he told me.

"Tell me something I don't know."

"You always did like to poke your nose into matters that didn't concern you," said Stan, shaking his head. He never had been one to mince his words.

"The matter that concerns me most is poor old Herbert there in the Cannon Street clink," I objected.

"I respect you for that," Stan said, "and I'll do what I can to help. You've got yourself some powerful enemies though, Ned. Mr. John and the colonel—now there's two of the worst criminals in Britain."

"So folks say," I agreed.

"You see, the reason I guessed why you came to see me—I got your message through one of the other cabbies about helping out old Herbert. Now here, we watch out for any action involving silver. We heard about the candlesticks and made a note to watch out for them showing up. I could see how Grimes might have got involved. As for Mr. John and the colonel—well, they get into any affair that smells of money. The rest of it is weird. An underground railway station, a giant frog, and those three men you say were killed? Those don't make sense."

"How about the professor at the British Museum Reading Room?"

"Him too. That's also weird."

"You probably get a lot of weird stuff, Stan," I said. "A lot of it doesn't make sense—until suddenly it does."

"True." He nodded. "True." He leaned forward to look at me across his desk. "You talked to the police, of course?"

"I've talked to Detective Sergeant Jackson."

"I don't know him," Stan said, "but I've heard his name. What does he say about all this?"

"When you say 'all—' " I began, and Stan grinned.

"These threats from Mr. John and the colonel made you a bit—shall we say, choosy?—about what you have told the Sergeant. Am I right?"

"On the nose."

"So what can I do to help?"

"I wish I knew," I confessed. "But you blokes here at the Silver Vaults know all about silver. Silver seems to be one of the main points in all this, so I thought I'd come and learn everything you know."

"It's taken me a year," said Stanley, rising to his feet, "and I'm still learning. I'll be glad to take you on a tour, though. Tell you all I can." He waved to the door. "This way."

We went down a wood-paneled corridor and into a big room like a museum. Glass cases lined the walls, while stands had big silver cups, bowls, vases and urns perched on top of them. Everything was silver in the cases, too: jugs, drinking cups, tureens, salt cellars, mustard pots, sugar bowls, sauce boats, snuff boxes, wine coolers, coffee pots, plates, knives and forks, trays, no end of them. Lamps on the walls made the objects shine and shimmer. Stan told me what they all were and kept up a steady stream of information about where they were from and how old they were. "Must keep you busy polishing all these, Stan," I said.

He laughed. "We have a crew that does nothing else."

We went into another room. "All church reliquaries in here," Stan said. "You'll see a lot of candlesticks."

I did. I also saw crosses, monstrances that I recognized from my visits to church with the nuns, Bible holders, chalices and a few I couldn't decide what they were. Stan pointed to them one by one. "Those are handles for coffins, those are christening cups, these are baptism bowls."

We walked to the next room along a wide corridor that had what looked like paintings on the wall. "Take a look at these, Ned," Stan said. Each one of them had fifteen or twenty colored pictures on it. "They're called 'Hallmarks,' " Stan explained. "They tell you that a particular piece of silver has been guaranteed."

"That's a pretty one," I said. "Looks like an eagle."

"It is," said Stan. "It's popular as a hallmark. The ring of feathers around it is unusual, though. This one is from Switzerland."

"Here's another head, a lion this time."

135

"Another popular one. This is German."

The next had a large five-pointed star and several letters under it. "Peru, in South America," Stan said. "They have big silver mines."

"A lot of crowns too."

"Then this one is Belgian. Helmets are another item used a lot."

"I suppose a real knowledgeable cove can spot a hallmark right away and tell you where it's from?"

"Oh, yes. We have a few chaps like that here at the Silver Vaults. One look at a hallmark and they can tell you what country it's from, which assay office guaranteed it, give you an approximate date when it was made and tell you the quality of silver it's made of."

"How long have they been using these?" I asked.

"Hallmarks started as far back as a thousand years ago. Most of them were developed during the past four hundred years, though."

Yet another room held statues, all sizes. Some were of people, some heads, some animals, men on horseback, snakes, fish . . . all silver. Again, Stan explained them all to me. "No wonder you need protection, Stan," I told him.

On the walls were tapestries with thin silver wires woven into them. "These are mostly from Belgium," Stan said. "They are very good at that kind of work."

Down a flight of wooden stairs we went to into a cellar, a dark place, but lit by flickering furnace fires. "This is our foundry," Stan said. The air was thick and smoky, stiflingly hot. Figures moved like black ghosts, covered in leather clothes. "Keeps them from being burned by molten metal," Stan said. "Liquid silver is over a thousand degrees."

A man carrying a ladle full of red-hot metal came past us. He stopped before a sand mold and poured the metal carefully into it. Another man went by, carrying an ingot on each shoulder. He stopped before a furnace, opened a door and tossed the ingots into the dull red gleaming inside.

"Is this how the candlesticks might have been made?" I asked Stan.

"Almost certainly."

It was hard to breathe and I was sweating all over. Stan grinned at me.

"Fancy a job in a silver foundry, Ned? Don't have to worry about those cold days sitting there in a cab, cold wind coming off the Thames, shivering and—"

"No thanks, Stan. Which is the way out of here?"

Back in his office, it was nice and cool. I sprawled in the chair, breathing the air that smelled so good. Stan was rummaging in his desk until, at last, he found what he was looking for. He handed me a notebook and opened it to a page, then pushed the book across the desk to me. "The missing candlesticks look like that?" he said.

It was a sketch, but very realistic. They were real fancy pieces of work, those candlesticks, elaborate and weaving here and there. A figure of a man was drawn beside them for comparison. "They're bigger than I thought," I said. They were probably about four feet high.

"They stood on an altar," Stan explained. "With candles in them, the flames'd be about the top of a man's head."

"How'd you get these pictures?" I asked.

"The clergy at the two churches gave us descriptions and we had an artist draw this. It's not exact, but it's close to what the actual ones look like."

I studied them again. "Lot of work in making them," I said. "Must be."

"Others we know of are more valuable. Others again are bigger and still others are older. But these are quite valuable."

"Are they old?"

"We don't know, but we think about two hundred years."

"Blimey, that's old," I said.

Stan laughed. "It's old if you're a young cabby in London. It's not that old for a candlestick. Lots are several hundreds of years old." Stan laughed again at my expression. "Some items of valuable silver were made by the ancient Greeks and Romans, two thousand years ago."

"Are they more valuable when they're older?"

"In general, yes."

We chatted a while longer, then finally I said, "Well, Stan, I think I know all I can hold for the moment—about silver, that is. I'll be off and let you get back to work."

"Listen, Ned," he said earnestly. "If I can do anything more to help, I will. I don't want to see Jack Ketch get his hands on poor old Herbert."

"You've still got the jargon," I told him. "Comes from your cabbying years."

He grinned, knowing I meant his reference to Jack Ketch, underworld slang for the public hangman. "Not only that," he went on, "but you might run into a word here or there that might lead you to the candlesticks. Don't forget that we've got some of the smartest people in the country here when it comes to silver. Not only that, but our security department is pretty good too."

"I'll remember," I promised.

"One last thing. Be careful! Those two villains you're rubbing shoulders with—they're dangerous, very dangerous. As soon cut your throat and drop you into the Thames as look at you."

"I'll remember that too," I said, but my voice was a bit raspy.

My throat had gone real dry as his words of warning rang through my head.

As I was not too far away, I went to the British Museum and back to library. In the lending department, they just wanted to see my card, and then I got all the help I wanted. Books on trade unions, books on economics, books by Karl Marx. I had to sort them out and pick out the ones I really felt would be the most valuable. With a stack of them under my arm, I went out, feeling like a proper scholar.

I got a few more fares, nothing great, but enough to feed Perseus and me. As I headed home after what I decided would be my last fare of the day, I found myself going across Ludgate Circus, so I stopped and picked up a meat pie from Mrs. Lovatt's stand. Makes one of the best meat pies in London, she does, and I didn't feel like cooking, nor did a cold dish sound appetizing.

Next day . . . well, you couldn't expect two days of sunshine in a row in London, could you? A miserable drizzle was coming down, but at least it wasn't that cold. It was an ordinary sort of day, cabwise, and I knocked off a bit early so as to have plenty of time to get cleaned up and ready to go to Millie's try-out. I was really looking forward to it. I was going to give Millie all the support I could do. That's what I'd decided. At the back of my mind was that tantalizing picture of Dorothy Radcliffe . . . she really was a very good-looking woman. She had a way of using her eyes that said she was interested only in you.

So the evening saw me and Perseus heading for the West End, me in my best clothes and him after a rubdown and a sack of oats. For a treat, I poured half a bottle of ginger beer into his water. The fumes tickle his nose and make him sneeze, but he loves the taste. We went along Greycoat Street where they were trying to start a new evening market. Must have been about fifty stalls, many with one or two of the new gas lamps, but a lot still with the old lights. The first stall held a bloke showing fat yellow haddock with a couple of candles stuck in bundles of firewood. A boy was shouting, "Eight a penny! Stunning pears!" Next to him was a stand with a stove baking chestnuts. They smelled good too.

The pavement and the road were thick with people. Housewives with shawls, small boys creeping about. Some were up to no good. I know. I used to be one of 'em.

"Bonnets! Only four pence," a man was shouting, Next to him a woman was waving big dark bunches in the air. "Lovely grapes. Only tuppence a pound." A fishy smell drifted my way. We were passing a stand selling whelks and mussels. Somewhere nearby, a flute warbled. A butcher had colored paper streamers all round his stand that fluttered in the wind, the strong white light from a nearby gas lamp making the stand look as if it was covered in flames. Anything you wanted to buy was here: shoes, clothes, food, dishes, vegetables, pots and pans, furniture, toys, anything to make a penny. Some folks were here just for a stroll around, enjoying an evening's free entertainment.

I'd passed the New Vaudeville Theatre while they were rebuilding it, but I hadn't paid it a lot of attention. I saw now how big it was, with a broad front with the name in great red letters on a white background. The boards were lined up outside—nothing on them yet—looking eager for a first night. The wide steps going up to the pay box looked enormous, and the glass doors were shiny and new. They were also locked.

I rattled one and a face appeared. The door opened and I said to a mustached man, "My name is Parker. Mrs. Radcliffe is expecting me."

He looked me up and down, then opened the door wide enough for me to get in. "She's in there, up on the stage." He motioned across the lobby to big swinging doors with gold-colored handles. I went on into the auditorium.

It was dark, but the stage in the distance was bright with lights. Voices echoed and a piano tinkled a few notes, then stopped. Row after row of empty seats looked unnatural. I tried to imagine how they'd look when they were filled. My eyes were growing used to the dark, and as I walked up the aisle, I could see the circle above me and two galleries above it. The place seemed bigger than any theatre I had ever been in, and the walk up the aisle seemed endless. I could smell fresh paint at first, but as I went farther, the air held whiffs of cigarette smoke. My feet sank into a carpet so thick nobody could hear me coming, and I realized it must be too dark for anyone on the stage to see me.

Voices still came. One was arguing, and the piano started up again. I could see the stage more clearly now. A man smoking a cigarette was at the piano, and another man in shirtsleeves was waving his arms and talking in a thick voice and an accent. A woman's voice silenced both of them. It was Dorothy Radcliffe's, and I could see her near the piano. She was wearing a silvery-white dress that fitted her closely, every inch. I supposed it was all right on the stage, but you didn't see many dresses like that in public. I admit I had to keep looking at it though.

She was talking to a young girl who was even more stage dressed than Dorothy was. She had on a short very tight, red and white tunic that showed all her legs, and it was lower on her breasts than it should be. She had a lot of make-up on her face, and her hair was fluffed with a red ribbon in it. Her high heels caused her behind to wiggle as she walked and she turned and—it was Millie!

I couldn't believe it. I had stopped at the top of the aisle at the front row. Dorothy saw me and called out, "Hello, Ned! Glad you could come. Have a seat. We're just trying out this number. Won't be too long."

141

I collapsed into an aisle seat on the front row. I was looking up at the stage and Millie's dress—if you could call it that—showed even more of her legs from here. As for her breasts, well, they looked ready to pop out at any time.

"Run it through again, Otto," Dorothy called out and the piano tinkled. Millie began her dance. She twirled, her chin high and her arms out. She kicked and stopped, posing with her hands on her hips, smiling. I'd never seen her like this. Not in any of her shows before.

"Knees higher!" called out Dorothy a few steps later, "Shoulders back!" I hoped the tunic had strong seams, and I wondered how Millie kept her balance in those high heels. "Looser from the waist!" called Dorothy, and Millie swayed and I could see her eyes shining.

They finished the number. Millie stood panting. Dorothy was shaking her head and talking to the shirtsleeved man. "Try it faster, Otto. This isn't a turtle dance." He played some notes, but Dorothy shook her head impatiently. "Faster!" she ordered. She seemed satisfied this time. "All right, Millie, try it at this tempo."

When Millie had gone through the routine again, she was glistening with sweat.

Dorothy shook her head. "Better, but not quite right yet. That kicking—you have to make it higher. Keep your head up all the time—you have a lovely profile, but you must hold your chin up. Otto, give her the lead again . . ."

It looked good to me this time, but at the end of it Dorothy was still shaking her head. "This time, Otto, increase the tempo more for the last two or three minutes. Build up to a real climax."

Millie looked worn out, leaning against a prop at the side of the stage. I went up the steps and said to Dorothy, "Can't she have a rest? Look how tired she is."

Dorothy came over to me, took my arm and firmly pulled me away. We walked to the far side of the stage, and she turned to me and looked into my face. I could smell that perfume of hers again and her eyes were beautiful but stern. "Ned, I know you're concerned for Millie, but you have to realize something. She's been in show business enough that she shows talent—definite talent. But she has a long way to go to reach where she's heading, and that's the top. This theatre is going to be one of the finest in London. We're going to put on only the best shows in Britain, and that means the boys and girls in it have to be the best too. We'll have some stars, of course, but we also intend to develop some stars of our own. I can see Millie as one of them, but it's going to take work, hard work. Now, can you go back to your seat in the front row and let her go on climbing to the top of her profession?"

I wanted to say I wasn't sure that I did, but I glanced over at Millie and saw her glowering at me. "All right," I said and went back down the steps to my seat.

It must have been the best part of an hour before Dorothy called out to the piano player, "That'll do, Otto." To the shirt-sleeved man, she said, "Marco, get Louise and Tess up here and go through that Egyptian dance number with them. It needs a lot of rehearsing. I'm off to the Doll's House with Ned and Millie. Have my coach brought around to the front, will you?"

Millie looked ready to collapse, but she limped over to me. "It's very nice of Dorothy to invite us to the Doll's House, isn't it? I've never been there. Have you?"

She knew perfectly well I hadn't. It's one of the swankiest places in London, sort of a club, but women go there as well as men. A lot of them go for the casino, where they say small fortunes change hands. It has a cabaret like the French have, with singers and dancers, but it has a reputation. Well, I suppose that's like the French too. If the Doll's House weren't so posh, the police would shut it down for what are called "lewd" performances, but when the likes of the Prince of Wales and other members of the Royal Family go there, . . . Well, then, it can stay open and be as lewd as it likes.

It wasn't the time to say any of that, but then there was no need to, as Millie knew it all well enough. So I just looked bored and said, "Don't believe I have," just like a toff would.

CHAPTER 16

Shepherd's Market is in Mayfair and just south of Piccadilly. You can tell from the name what it used to be. At least you think you can, but you'd be wrong if you picture sheep being bought and sold.

That's what I like to tell visitors, anyway, because Edward Shepherd was the name of the architect more than two hundred years ago. The Three Jolly Butchers was one of the first buildings there, a real famous pub, and they used to hold the annual May Fair around it. From that start, shops sprang up, and today it's a sort of village right in the heart of the city.

It's getting quite a reputation too. Shepherd's Market has several bawdy houses that cater to the upper classes, gambling houses, and there's a big room where they have illegal boxing matches—bare knuckle and fight to a finish. A lot of blood gets spilt in those places, and I've taken quite a few senseless and battered blokes home from it. Visitors to London often asked to be taken there—just to see it, no getting out of the cab. Perseus and me give them a good run-through but—almost needless to say—I hadn't been in the most famous place in Shepherd's Market until today.

Doll's House is that place. Everybody knows it, but not many get in there.

I felt quite pleased that I was being invited now, and Millie had dropped a remark or two on the way that showed she was impressed too. She had recovered herself after sitting in the coach, and was getting back to her usual chirpy personality. Dorothy sat, sort of regal with a slight smile, as she looked from one to the other of us. I wondered what she was thinking.

Doll's House was not much from the front. Windows that were too high up to see into and covered on the inside by huge velvet curtains. A long row of shiny iron railings on both sides from the entrance; a gigantic oak door that would take a dozen men to break down. The door opened as we went up the steps to it and swung wide. A bloke who looked like he could have been a butler at Buckingham Palace let us in. He bowed to Dorothy. "Good evening, Mrs. Radcliffe. Good to see you this evening."

"Thank you, George." She gave him her ermine wrap and he took it very carefully, then reached out a hand for Millie's shawl and disappeared with both of them. The lobby we were in was lit with dim orange lamps and had a thick carpet that looked Chinese.

The wood paneled walls held paintings that looked old and valuable, as well as a couple of old tapestries.

"Let me show you through Doll's House first," Dorothy said.

The first room was like a men's club, though there were a lot of women too. Everybody was dressed to the nines, and posh accents bounced off all the walls. It was a clubby atmosphere too, some folks sitting, some standing, most chatting, drinking and smoking. Millie gave me a sharp nudge, and I found I was staring at the girls serving the drinks. They were all dressed like French maids with skimpy little black and white costumes and black stockings.

"You'll see more activity in here," Dorothy said, leading the way. The next room was bigger, fuller and much noisier. Roulette wheels were spinning, and various card games were going on. I looked at the stacks of money on the green baize tables and met Millie's astonished gaze. A small group of army officers in uniform were getting loud at one table, and an argument was breaking out at another, but they quieted down.

Dorothy led us to another door that she opened just partway so we could peek in.

We breathed steam and hot air that gushed out. Inside was a pool with several heads bobbing about. Some looked like men and some like women, but with just heads, it's hard to tell. "It's heated," Dorothy said. "We won't go in. We don't bother with bathing costumes, you see."

She closed the door and we followed her to another. "This is our cabaret room," Dorothy said. "It hasn't started yet." The room was set up like a small theatre, but with tables and chairs instead of rows of seats. "It's a copy of the Moulin Rouge in Paris," she told us.

She led us back to the first room, the clubby one. More people were there now and it was much livelier. Dorothy waved to one of the waitress girls who came over with a tray and filled glasses on it. "Have a glass of champagne," Dorothy said, handing us one each.

I heard Millie stifle a cough as the bubbles got up her nose. I had the same urge, but held it back. I'd tasted champagne before, naturally, but not more than twice, though there was no need for anyone to know that. "Here's someone you need to meet," said Dorothy, motioning a tall man to join us.

"This is Ivor Dunstan," Dorothy said. "He's going to be in one of our next shows."

She introduced Millie and me. "This is the young lady who'll be working with you, Ivor."

He was a good-looking bloke, I had to admit. Big, broad-shouldered and with a sort of swaggering manner that said he knew he was important and popular. He spent longer over kissing Millie's hand than I would have liked, and he kept on looking at her afterwards. She seemed to be enjoying the attention, so I was polite. He ignored me until Dorothy said, "Ned has his own transportation company." That made him at least notice that I was there. He gave me a nod.

"Millie had a real work-out this evening, Ivor" said Dorothy. "She's going to be great. Needs more work, but she has the ability to get to the top."

"Hope you didn't work her too hard," he said, still not taking his eyes off her. "She needs to be able to enjoy the rest of the evening."

"What do you do in the show, Mr. Dunstan?" I asked.

"I sing, I dance, I act," he said loftily. "Didn't you see me in *Midnight Rapture*?"

"I think I missed that one," I said. "Probably one of my busy periods."

"It ran seven months," he said.

Dorothy came in swiftly with, "Our next show will run longer. It's going to be a real hit." She squeezed Millie's hand. "And so will you, my dear."

Millie's eyes sparkled. She had got over her tiredness and was loving all this. Ivor Dunstan took her hand away from Dorothy. "Come with me while I have a little flutter at the blackjack table. I can see you'll bring me luck."

"All right," Millie said brightly, avoiding my eye. The two of them walked off.

"Let me get you another glass of champagne," Dorothy said, waving to a waitress.

I looked at my glass in surprise. I had drunk it without even noticing. Probably the excitement of meeting a famous star of the London stage.

"Ivor's been with my troupe for a long time," Dorothy told me. "He's one of the finest tenors in London and has a wonderful sense of timing. He can play light comedy roles. He even dances and the women love him."

"I'm sure they do," I said. The empty glass in my hand was replaced with a full one.

Dorothy led me around and introduced me to more people. One was a member of Parliament and another had a big department store in Hampstead. A burst of laughter broke out across the room and everybody looked. A burly man with a beard had a gorgeous redheaded woman on his arm, and people were all around them.

"Who is that woman?" I asked curiously.

Dorothy frowned at me. "Oh, come now, Ned, you don't have to ask me that. You see her face on half the buses in London."

I looked again. "It can't be . . . it surely isn't Lillie Langtry!"

Dorothy shrugged. "The two of them come in here a lot. You recognize him, of course."

I was almost speechless. Me—in the same room! "It's the Prince of Wales!"

Dorothy nodded. "Want to meet them? Maybe you will later."

Blimey! I thought. Me, meeting the Prince of Wales! Wouldn't my old mum have fallen off her chair if I had told her that!

"Most of the important people in London come to the Doll's House," Dorothy said matter-of-factly. "I see the Duke of Buckingham coming in. He's probably heading straight for the gambling tables—yes, he is. The Under-Secretary for Foreign Affairs is usually here by this time unless he's attending a late-night session in the House." I turned my gaze back to the group around the Prince. I had seen someone who looked familiar. But I couldn't have. I didn't have a lot of friends in circles like these. And then I saw her. I caught my breath.

I tried to sound casual as I said to Dorothy, "It's Lillie Langtry on the Prince's right, but who is that woman on his left?"

Dorothy moved slightly so that she could see clearly. "Oh,

that's Margaret Tinsdale." She gave me a questioning look. "You know her?"

I laughed. "No, never met her. She looks familiar though. Maybe I've seen her picture in the papers."

"Probably. She's prominent in society circles and does a lot of charity work."

I hadn't seen her picture in the papers. I'd seen her in person with a bishop's arm around her. She was the woman the bishop had visited at Mildenhall Mansions in Belgravia the day this had all started.

"She's the sister of the Bishop of Vauxhall," said Dorothy.

Sister! Well, the old boy wasn't the gallivanter I thought he was. Shows how you can jump to wrong conclusions.

"I'd rather she didn't come to the Dolls House," Dorothy was saying. "Among the charity she does is saving fallen women, and I think she has her eye on some of my girls here."

"Ah," I said, and thought it best to leave it at that.

"Still," Dorothy went on, taking my hand, "That's enough shop talk. Let's find a quiet table."

It wasn't so much of a table, but a small booth by the wall. We squeezed in, facing each other, knees touching. "They would have a problem serving a banquet in here," I joked.

Dorothy smiled. Her teeth were very white and she had a lot of red lipstick on. Her face was not many inches away from mine. "They wouldn't try," she said. "This is for drinks and intimate conversations only." She pointed. "Those are for real intimacy."

She was pointing to heavy silk curtains that could be pulled across the entrance to the booth. A waitress walked by and Dorothy called to her. "Jenny, our glasses are empty."

Mine wasn't quite, but I was enjoying the champagne. Two more fizzing glasses appeared quickly.

A tall, whiskered man walked by and bowed to Dorothy.

"Hello, Frederick," she called out. "Nice to see you again." She watched him go past then said to me, "Frederick Olmsted, an American, a very nice man. He's designing a large park in New York and is in London spending his time studying Kew Gardens. He intends to copy it."

I was looking around the room. "I wonder where Millie is," I said.

Dorothy shrugged. "Ivor is probably showing her how to lose money. He's good at that—among other things."

"He probably makes a lot of it in your shows."

"He likes to keep busy but then he *has* to keep busy. But yes, we pay him well. We pay everybody well in our shows. We want the best, and we're ready to pay for it."

"It must be an exciting business," I said and meant it.

She raised her glass and I raised mine. She clinked the two together. "I find life exciting," she said. Her eyes seemed bigger, and I noticed for the first time that they were green. As we drank, her other hand was on mine. It was warm and velvety. She moved slightly and her knees pressed tighter against mine.

"Is your life exciting?" she asked.

It was warm in the room. A dozen or two buzzing conversations charged the air. Maybe it was the champagne, but nothing seemed to matter other than what was happening in this booth. "It is at this minute," I said and squeezed her hand back.

"You know, Ned," she said softly, "I know almost nothing about you. Tell me everything."

"That would take all night."

"I'm not going anywhere," she said.

"I'll keep it short," I promised. I did . . . well, as short as I could. I told her how my mum was strong in favor of sending me to a Catholic school when I was five. I told how I had done well in school and about my dad and his cab business. I said he had been an advisor to the police and how important they had found his information. I went on to tell how a gang had beaten him up and how he had died afterwards. My mum died right after, and I had taken over my dad's cab business. Now I was on the committee to start a cabbies union.

"A self-made man," she said admiringly. "Ned, are you as hungry as I am?"

I hadn't thought about it but now she mentioned it . . . "I am a bit."

She called to one of the waitresses and spoke a few words to her in a voice too low for me to hear. I did hear, though, as she added, "—and fill our glasses."

I was about to protest when I realized all that talking had made me thirsty. The girl returned with a bottle and when our glasses were full, Dorothy pointed out more guests whose names I knew from the papers. "I see the Prince of Wales is still having a good time," I said as loud laughter burst out from the small crowd around him.

"He usually does," said Dorothy. "Still, we may not be seeing so much of him in the future. I hear he's going to open his own club. He was a member of White's but he insisted on smoking in the morning room where it is not allowed. He told the managing board of members to change the rules and they refused."

"Even for the Prince?" I was amazed.

"Even for the prince. So he's opening his own club and will call it the Marlborough. It's on Pall Mall."

"I thought princes could do as they liked," I said.

Dorothy looked at him, waving his arms, waggling his beard and telling another story. "He thought so too—and found he was wrong."

The same waitress came past and said a couple of words to Dorothy. She stood.

"Let's get a bite to eat," she said, taking my hand and leading me across the room.

A wide wooden staircase with a plush carpet and a carved banister did a curling sweep upward, and we followed it. On the next floor, we went into one of the first rooms. It was small, with paintings on the walls. The first one I saw had blokes with horns on their heads chasing through the woods after young women who looked like they didn't have any clothes on.

In the center of the room was a table with a snowy white tablecloth. We sat in armchairs, and only then did I notice that the table was loaded with food. "Let me help you, Ned," said Dorothy, and she started heaping a plate.

My eyes must have bulged as I watched my plate being filled. I could see oysters, sardines, pickled tunny fish, salmon, smoked eel, eggs in jelly, radishes, spring onions . . . Dorothy paused with a fork into some small fish that I hadn't seen before. "Anchovies?" she asked. "I know everybody doesn't like them."

I'd never seen one before but I wasn't going to admit it. "Yes," I said, "I like them."

We tucked in. A silver bowl had a fresh bottle of champagne in it and Dorothy looked doubtfully at the label. "Oh, yes," she told me, "that's the one, the Royal Charter from Epernay. You'll like this."

I did, too. It had a dry taste after the other. How could a drink be dry, I wondered?

"Really good, isn't it?" said Dorothy. "We have a case of it on the *Lady of Gloucester.* You'll have to come on a cruise with us some time and help us drink more of it."

"What's that?" I asked, "a boat?"

"Yes," she said and I wondered who the "we" meant, but didn't ask. Anyway, my mouth was parched. I had to have a long drink of the champagne after tasting those funny little fish that Dorothy said were anchovies. They were very salty and sort of pickled at the same time. I cast a glance or two at bowls of food that she hadn't served and I wondered why. I found out when we emptied our plates and she put them aside, took some clean ones and began piling food from those bowls on to them. She told me what they were, one by one.

"Chicken darioles." They were little barrel-shaped pastries filled with chicken in a thick white sauce. "Beef galantine in aspic, zephires of duck, saddle of hare . . ." This had a dark brown sauce. I didn't know people ate saddles, but by this time I was ready for anything. She gave me slices of roast partridge and then big pieces of goose that she said came from Toulouse and were in another kind of sauce. My plate was full by then. Dorothy handed it to me together with an empty plate. "For your vegetables," she explained.

I have a good appetite, but Dorothy kept pace with me. It was all so tasty. As I was eating, I found a thought creeping in to my mind. Why me? She was a well-to-do, striking-looking woman who could probably pick and choose from dozens of men in London. Why was I getting this special treatment?

Perhaps she was reading my mind, for in between mouthfuls of goose, she said, "Not still worried about Millie, are you, Ned? Ivor will be taking good care of her. It's important they get to know each other because they will be working together."

"Millie can take care of herself," I said. Perhaps it was the champagne that she was still pouring that made me believe it. The same champagne might have been the reason, too, that I stopped wondering *why me?* Dorothy would want me to give all the support I could to her new star and not stand in the way of her climb to the top.

We had finished eating. Bowls of fruit were on the table as well as tureens of syllabub and frangipane with cherries, but I shook my head. Dorothy rose and came round the table. "You're wise to say no," she said, taking my hand. "There are sweeter ways to end a meal than with food."

As I got to my feet, the room seemed to move. I stood still

and the room did too.

Maybe that champagne was having its effect on me after all. My feet moved, and I followed Dorothy as she opened a door and took me into an adjoining room.

It was a bedroom, or, more likely, what they called a *boudoir.* Two of the walls were bright red and the other two were covered with a full-size mirror. Another mirror covered the ceiling. The bed had a lacy cover that had been turned down. I felt another wave of haziness sweep over me, but that was swallowed up by Dorothy's arms round my neck and the pressure of her body against mine. Her hands slid down as she began unfastening buttons and pulling, pulling . . .

CHAPTER 17

Hammers were banging away on the inside of my head. I put my hands over my ears, but those hammers were just as loud. My eyes tried to open but got stuck partway. My stomach churned, but my head hurt worse. I lay there for a few minutes, then my eyes opened a bit more.

I was in my own bed at home. How did I get here? I had vague memories of Perseus trotting through the quiet, darkened streets. Good thing he knows his way back home. Like a bloomin' carrier pigeon, he is. I tried to get out of bed, but the room rolled sideways and I couldn't. I lay still until the world righted itself.

It took some time. I must have dozed on and off, but when I finally came to, I felt just well enough to sit up. It was a mistake, and I had to lie down again. Next time, I got to a sitting position and even on to my feet, but only by holding on to the bedpost. The next half hour was a sad story of dizziness, groaning, a heaving stomach and a headache worse than any I had ever known.

I managed to stagger over to the stove and put the kettle on. A hot cup of strong tea helped, and my head and my eyes belonged to me again. What day was it? Why was it important? This was Wednesday; what meaning did that have? It came flooding back: the meeting with the city council committee. The clock showed five past ten—and we were meeting with the council at eleven-thirty! I flung on clothes and raced out of the door.

What about Millie? I had told Dorothy that Millie could take care of herself. I hoped I was right, but I had to find out. I ran all the way to Millie's house. Luckily it wasn't too far. Her mother opened the door. She didn't look pleased to see me. I was still trying to decide what to say when she snapped, "What time of night was that to bring a girl home? I thought you were against all this stage nonsense anyway."

"I am," I said. "I'd just as soon she forgot all about it."

"Doesn't look like it. Bringing her home at four thirty in the morning indeed!" Her mother was going on. "I heard you, the two of you, giggling and who knows what else out here. Well, there'd better be no more of it or her father will be talking to you, and he can be a very violent man when he gets mad."

She slammed the door in my face.

I was relieved. At least Millie had got home all right. As for the "giggling and who knows what else," I'd have to take that up with Millie, but right now I had an important meeting to attend.

Leo and Sid were waiting for me at Sid's place in Battersea. I had run all the way and was out of breath when I arrived. The running helped my hangover a bit, but not much.

"Blimey," Sid said, "look what the cat dragged in!"

"I'd rather not hear any comments," I said stiffly, and Leo gave me a pitying look.

"I bet you wouldn't. Are you sure you're up to this?" he asked.

"No," I said, "but let's go."

The city council buildings on the Embankment look across the river at the Houses of Parliament. Leo had been with the county council that also had their offices here, so he knew how to find his way. It was just as well, as the place was like a rabbit warren inside, with dozens of little offices, miles of narrow corridors, and people coming and going, up and down staircases, with papers in their hands.

We reached the hearing room with five minutes to spare. They kept us waiting anyway, but at last, we trouped into the hearing room. Nearly half of the room was at a higher level than the other, and a long table sat on the higher level with five chairs for the magistrates. We sat on chairs out in the middle of the room, spaced enough apart so that we couldn't whisper to teach other. The place had an atmosphere like a courtroom. Judging by the couple I had seen, however, this room was smaller.

Sid sat in the middle, Leo on his left, me on his right. The bloke who brought us in wore a blue and white sash with some kind of medal pinned to it. "The magistrates will be here in a few minutes," he told us with a friendly nod. It must have been fifteen minutes, then the door opened and the magistrates walked in and took seats at the table. They wore sashes too. I supposed only judges wore full robes.

We had expected to be outnumbered when we saw the chairs at the raised table end, but there were only three magistrates. Nice of them to have an equal number to us, I thought.

One of them, a bloke sitting in the middle, was top dog, evidently. He was a prosperous looking character with a red sort of face that usually means plenty of good food and drink. Them in glass houses shouldn't throw stones, I told myself. On his right was a cove with short muttonchop whiskers, not quite gray yet, a beaky nose and sharp eyes. The third fellow was small and shriveled, narrow shouldered and with a pinched face.

Red Face in the middle started us off. It was, he informed us, a meeting of the Hearing Committee of Her Majesty's Home Office. The petitioners (I soon learned that was us) had presented their request for the forming of a trades union branch, members to be composed of hansom cab drivers within the limits of the Metropolitan City of London. The findings of this hearing would be forwarded to the Under Secretary of Transportation who would then present it, along with his recommendations, to the Right Honorable Home Secretary.

He had a strong voice, not really loud, but the kind you hear from people who use their voices a lot. I managed to stay awake during the next bit too, when he gave the titles of the three blokes up there. My stomach was starting to play up, and I hoped that Red Face's strong voice would be louder than my stomach that was protesting all over again about its treatment last night. My eyes felt drowsy too, and my eyelids were sticky.

Sid was then invited to present his petition. He did so very well, saying that six thousand cab drivers provided the transport for the entire City of London. He was aware of the very competent bus system, but they only had seven hundred buses, and the big area they had to cover meant that people usually had distances to go to bus stops. There, said Sid, they would have to wait up to twenty minutes, sometimes longer, and in the rain and snow. It was true, Sid admitted, that the new underground railway system was providing transport for many, but routes were few and so were trains. It was very expensive to dig underground tunnels—

Pinched Face chipped in here, talking right over Sid. It was unnecessary, he said, for the petitioner, Mr. Morris, to talk costs of underground railway tunnels to this hearing committee. He himself had spent several recent years on financial committees debating the costs of such work, and all three of them knew far more about this than all the cabbies in London.

Mr. Prosperous Red Face seconded these comments, adding that it needed to be pointed out that while the current bus service consisted of only seven hundred buses, another one thousand two hundred were now being built. As some of these were larger and others were double-deckers, when these were completed before the end of the year, more than four times as many seats would be in use.

The three of us tried not to look at each other. Perhaps we should have known this, but we didn't. It was bad news, whether we had already known it or not. Leo spoke up, asking to make a statement. He has a nice speaking voice—cultivated, they call it. Perhaps he could make a point for the cabbies' team.

The main point, Leo said, was not so much how many people different transport methods could move. Six thousand cabbies deserved to have their working conditions improved and to be protected against exploitation. Leo went on to compare cabbies' wages with those of the dockworkers—who already had a union—and those of the railway workers, who expected to have their petition accepted in the near future. He made references to "certain masters," who wanted their cabbies to work a fourteen-hour day and fired any who would not. He didn't mention Roger Sherrington by name, but it was likely one or more of the three magistrates knew who Leo meant.

Beaky Nose asked about our affiliations, and it turned out he meant with other unions. Sid explained that we had none, but he got in the good point that we kept abreast of the dockworkers and the railway unions, and it was possible that all would one day be united in a "transport workers" union. Beaky didn't like this. He said anything like that was too far in the future, and anyway, it was irrelevant. That meant it didn't matter.

Pinched Face asked who our legal representative was. Leo answered that one. Smooth, he was. I would have answered that we didn't have one yet, but Leo put it to him that we were considering several possible firms and would decide very soon. Truth was, we had asked two or three, and all had turned us down.

The magistrates battered away at us. Some questions were reasonable, but some were not. It had taken the dockworkers years to get a union, and as there was fewer of us, we were likely to take longer. But we knew that, and like Sid had said to us, "The sooner we start, the sooner we get a union." Sid and Leo had both pointed out in our meetings that it would be an uphill battle, and it now looked like it would be uphill Mount Bloody Everest rather than Highgate Hill.

The questions kept coming, and Sid and Leo did wonders in fielding them. My part in all this was small, and I hoped I wasn't letting them down. I did get in one or two answers here and there. Then Red Face asked, "What is your opinion of the *Worker's Manifesto*?"

Leo and Sid looked at each other, each silently urging the other to answer. I was still feeling as if I could be knocked-over with a good-sized feather, but I had been reading books and doing my homework. And besides, it was time I began pulling my weight here.

"It's an important document in the development of a strong work force in this country," I piped up.

Beaky pushed in, sounding as if he was ready for an argument.

"By strong, you mean strong enough to challenge management."

I took a few seconds over that one. "It shouldn't be seen as a challenge," I said. "Conflict between labor and management is not helpful." I hoped I was quoting Professor Karl Marx correctly.

"Isn't the *Workers Manifesto* an endorsement of Socialism?"

I had to watch my step here. It sounded as if he was leading me into a trap.

"Political power comes from economic power," I said, trying not to sound as if I was quoting from Karl Marx—which I was.

"Doesn't the *Workers Manifesto* say that all men are equal?" said Red Face with a sneer if ever I saw one.

He was leading me into a trap, all right, but good old Karl had an escape route for me.

"The economy of the whole world has always been the creative work of a small number of superior thinkers," I said. "If we didn't have their brilliance, nothing else would come into being. After that, it takes millions of workers to turn their ideas into practice. The thinkers and the workers may not be equal in brains, but they are equal in the eye of God."

That last bit wasn't from Karl Marx. He didn't think much of God. I added it, knowing that even Prosperous Red Face couldn't argue against God.

Red Face and Pinched Face exchanged sour looks. Beaky looked down his nose.

I had won the point though, and the questions that followed were tame. Finally, Red Face rapped the table with a little hammer. "This hearing is adjourned. The committee desiring to obtain trades union representation for London cab-drivers will retire while the magistrates confer."

The bloke with the blue sash came in and took us into a waiting room. When he left, Leo gave me an admiring look. "Blimey, Ned, where did you get all that stuff?"

Sid was smiling as always, but more so than usual. "Proper stopped that bloke in his tracks, you did."

"I've been doing a bit of reading," I said. Actually, that little exchange had made me feel better. My stomach was settling and my head was no longer a battleground.

"What do you think, Sid?" Leo asked. "How did it go?"

Sid sighed. "Could have been better."

"Still, we made all our points." Leo was always optimistic. We chatted for about another ten minutes, then the blue-sashed bloke came in. "They're ready for you."

The magistrates were still in their seats. We took ours. Red Face looked at the papers in front of him.

"In the matter of the request for the formation of a trades union for London Metropolitan cab-drivers—this hearing has decided . . ." He paused, and we were all holding our breath. "The request is denied."

It was a glum group in Sid's cab as we rolled along the Embankment. Sid had the little connecting door open so we could talk. Leo was the first to ask, "Sid, can we appeal?"

"No," Sid said. "No appeals. But we can apply again."

"How soon?"

"There's nothing in the rules, but if we apply too soon, they might let it sit there for ages."

We had to slow to allow a column of blokes with banners to cross the road.

"Who are they?" Sid asked us.

"Clerical workers, unemployed," said Leo.

"They need a union," Sid said.

"Not as much us," I said.

"Just as much as us," said Sid firmly. "They're already discussing it."

It was quiet for a while. We all had our own thoughts.

"Just where did you get all that stuff?" Leo asked me.

"Books. A lot of 'em written by Professor Karl Marx."

"He's that German bloke," said Sid. "Lives in London now. Getting famous."

"And you've read 'em?" Leo said to me.

"Certainly," I said, "and I've talked with Professor Marx too, of course."

Both looked at me in amazement.

"Where'd you do all this?" Sid asked.

"The British Museum Reading Room," I said, looking casually out of the window.

"You?" said Leo.

"I have a reader's card," I explained.

CHAPTER 18

I'm usually feeling peckish by that time of day, but after last night, I had no appetite. So when Sid dropped me off, I hitched up Perseus and we set off in search of a penny or two. I was feeling as miserable as Sid and Leo over the denial of our application, but I knew there'd be another day. They knew that too, but they were taking the decision more to heart.

I'd only gone a couple of streets when a bloke stepped out in front of me and held up a hand. He was well dressed, although when I got closer, I could see he had a nose that had been broken a couple of times. He was polite enough though, and asked me if I knew where the Smithfield Meat Market was. It was the kind of question I get a lot. Sometimes I say, "Why not ask me if I know where Buckingham Palace is?" but I wasn't in the mood for banter, so I just said I did and off we went.

I guessed that he had some business there; he was probably a merchant of some kind. But when I asked him if he was a visitor to London, he only said he spent a lot of time here. He was quiet the rest of the way. When we got near the market, I drove through Leicester Square, which they are trying to rebuild. Some of the construction slowed us down, but it was better than taking the Long Acre approach as that's where the trade wagons unload.

I got as near as I could. "This all right, guv?" I asked.

He climbed out and reached in his pocket. Instead of the purse I expected, he brought out a small pistol and pointed it at me, holding it close to his side. "I want you to come with me," he said, and his voice was a lot less polite than it had been before.

"I've got to hitch up Perseus," I said. "My horse," I explained. He nodded, and I took a little heart from that. Fact is, I wasn't as nervous as I might have been. Perhaps I still had enough alcohol in me. I made Perseus secure and the man moved the gun slightly. "Walk," he ordered, and I walked, him keeping a step behind me.

He must have done this kind of thing before, because he was good at it. I couldn't make a dash into one of the crowds of laborers, butchers, buyers, sellers, or wagon drivers as he was too close. On the other hand, he was not close enough that I could wrestle the pistol out of his hand even if I had wanted to try that—which I didn't. Either way, he seemed too professional for me to want to do anything other than what I was told.

"Keep going straight ahead," he said, and we did. We passed wagons being unloaded, a man with a long bar on his shoulder with a dozen rabbits hanging on it, another bar carried by two blokes that had partridges, and another with plovers, streaks of bright colors showing through their shiny feathers.

We went on into the market. We had to wait for a line of blokes staggering under the weight of hogs' carcasses inside. I watched for a chance to dodge between them, but my bloke was no mug. He'd thought of that too and poked the pistol barrel into my back ribs. When the hogs had gone, he barked, "Get going," and I did.

Merchandise was still coming into the market, even though it was late in the morning. I had brought people here a number of times, but I had never been inside—no reason to be. The only reason I was inside now was a pistol in my back. Still, every time I'd been here I had noticed that, though most stuff came in early in the morning, the market went on all day, stuff coming in and stuff going out. It came in from the farms and went out to the butchers.

What I saw in the next building almost made me sick on the spot. Cows were hanging with a hook through their necks. Farther down, blokes with knives were ripping at the carcasses. One would slash through the skin, the next would make quick strokes across, and by the time the carcasses had got all the way down the line, the separate pieces of meat were there for the butcher shops. Well, that was bad enough, but all were dripping blood and the floor was half an inch thick with it. Blokes with hoses were trying to wash it down holes inset in the floor, and other blokes with long brooms kept sweeping it down the holes. The stench was awful.

"Turn right," said the voice behind me. I did, in between two of the carcasses. Ahead was a wooden door to a small office. "In there," I was ordered.

The colonel sat on the corner of a desk. He had a sort of military uniform on made of a white denim material. It had no insignia or military buttons though. Its pure whiteness was dazzling after the masses of thick red blood I had just seen. Standing nearby was the bruiser with the mangled cheek and the cauliflower ear, the same man he had had with him in Guy Fawkes' cellar. The man who had brought me remained behind me. Besides the desk, all that was in the room was a heap of boxes.

The colonel put his monocle in. He did it the way most blokes with monocles do it, as if they were screwing it in. It magnified his eye in a nasty sort of way. He studied me through it. "I thought talking to you here might have some symbolism, Ned. You know what I mean by that?"

I did, but thought it was better to play stupid. I shook my head and looked frightened. It wasn't difficult; I already had a head start.

"The symbolism I'm referring to is the blood. A lot of it out in the market, isn't there?"

I nodded.

"Yes, cows have a lot of blood. Humans don't have as much. Now, if that were your body hanging out there with a hook through your neck, you wouldn't bleed enough to need a man to push the blood down the drain. Do you understand me, Ned?"

"I—I think so."

"Good. Now, the reason for this little chat is that I'm disappointed in you, Ned. The last time we talked, you didn't tell me everything."

That didn't seem to call for an answer so I didn't give one.

When he went on, his voice was sharp as a whiplash. "You didn't tell me what was going on in the new underground railway station at London Bridge, did you?"

"I—no, I didn't." My voice wanted to be shaky, and I let it.

The colonel shook his head sadly. "Not wise of you, Ned. Not wise at all. Do I have to have Desmond take you outside and rub your face into one of those bleeding carcasses out there? Would you understand my point then?"

"You—you don't have to do that," I said weakly.

"Because the next step after that would be to have your carcass hanging there alongside the cows. Of course, you needn't be dead—well, not at first anyway."

I was getting his point; there was no doubt about that. But while he had been talking, I had been racking my brain, and I got the germ of an idea. I let him keep talking to give myself time to work it out.

"I couldn't tell you anything if I was dead," I said.

"True," the colonel said in a honeyed voice. Then it turned to acid. "But I'm sure you could tell me a lot in those painful hours before you died."

"What do you want to know?"

His tone hardened. "I want to know what's going on in that underground station. I want to know why Mr. John has his people guarding it so carefully. What's in there that he has so many men keeping it secret?"

So that was why the colonel needed my information. Mr. John evidently had a lot more men than the colonel, and they were doing a proper job of keeping quiet what they were doing. I thought I had my story ready for him now.

"It's true I didn't tell you about this before," I said. "The reason I didn't is . . ."

I faltered and he slapped a hand on the desk he was sitting on. "Go on!"

"I knew you wouldn't believe me."

There was quiet for a few seconds, then a soft chuckle came from the man behind me. The other bruiser, Desmond, took his cue and he chuckled too. The colonel shook his head slowly. "Like I said, I'm disappointed in you, Ned. You didn't think I'd believe you?"

"No, I didn't."

"And why, may I ask?"

"It's too . . . too weird."

Another chuckle came from behind me.

"So tell me, Ned," the colonel went on, in a voice like he was humoring me, "What was so weird that you couldn't tell me?"

I said nothing, then I said hesitantly, "You'll just laugh."

"Better I laugh than do what else I might do to you if you don't tell me," the colonel said.

I waited as long as I dared. Then I said, "The station isn't open yet, but you can hear trains moving, and you can hear train whistles down there. Strange voices sound like murmuring, coming closer, then going away but you never see a person. Worst of all . . ."

"Don't stop now, Ned," the Colonel said, bringing out each word.

"Giant frogs."

"Giant frogs?" he repeated.

"Yes, big as a man."

The Colonel eyed me. "You've seen one of these yourself?"

"Yes. Yes, I have."

That clearly surprised him.

"What did you do when you saw it?" he asked.

"I ran like hell," I said.

"Were you sober?"

" 'Course I was."

The colonel looked past me, in the direction of the man behind, the one who had brought me in.

"What is it, Vern?"

"Can I have a word, boss?"

The colonel frowned, nodded. Vern came from behind me and went to the colonel. He talked into his ear, but all I could hear was a whispering sound. He finished and went back to stand behind me again.

The colonel was examining me, still frowning. After a minute or two, he said, "Vern tells me that all you're doing is repeating local rumors. He lives near Elephant and Castle and picks up all the local gossip. People who live near the underground station talk about ghosts they have seen. They say they have heard strange noises, heard ghost trains."

He shifted his position on the corner of the table. "Your story is not good enough, Ned. Repeating local folklore? No, you can't get away with this. I need to teach you more of a lesson."

I was nervous. The state was genuine now. "It's true! I heard the voices. I heard the ghost train! I even saw a giant frog!"

He took out the monocle and rolled it between his forefinger and thumb. The eye where the monocle normally sat studied me without blinking. This went on for so long, I began to sweat.

He screwed the monocle back into place, and the eye gleamed through it, seeming to be without pity. At length, he said, "You're saved, Ned. Saved for the moment anyway. Saved by Vern's cousin. You see, Vern tells me that his cousin, who lives near the station, has heard the ghost train himself. He also has a neighbor who has seen one of these giant frogs. Vern's cousin is a reliable witness." He sighed as if he had wanted to get on with some torture and was being cheated out of it. "I say he is a reliable witness because he is a policeman."

I was tempted to turn and shake Vern's hand but resisted the temptation. The colonel was speaking again. "Another matter though, Ned. You're keeping some bad company, aren't you?"

It was another of those questions you don't answer.

"The Doll's House is what I'm referring to," he said, and that shook me up a bit. The colonel managed a tiny smile, but it wasn't the kind that comes from hearing something funny. "Yes, I know about your visit there. I just mention it so you know that I'm keeping an eye on you."

I nodded. It seemed the best thing to do.

"I should ask you again what you were doing there in the underground station, but I suppose you'll tell me that you were looking for ways to prove your friend Summers innocent of the crime of murder."

I gave him another nod. "Yes, right."

"And did you find what you were looking for?"

"No. Like I said, I ran like hell when I saw that monstrous great frog," I said.

"So Mr. John is raising big frogs, is he?"

"I don't think so," I said. "There must be some other explanation. But," I added hastily, "I've got no idea what it is."

"Ah, well," the colonel said smoothly, "we'll find out. And you'll keep helping us won't you, Ned?"

"I'll tell you what I can."

He waved a hand to Vern, behind me. "You can take him back, Vern." He gave me that wintry smile again. "Keep him out of the way of those fleshing knives out there. They can do a lot of damage."

Chapter 19

I got two fares after I unhitched Perseus. In between the two, I had time to think. The pot was getting hotter and was soon going to be up to boiling point. The colonel was behind Mr. John in this two-horse race, and he was determined to catch up. People could easily be hurt as he did this, and I could be one of them. The only way he could have known that I was at the Doll's House was if someone had seen me there. A lot of soldiers were in the place, and one of those could have been on his payroll. I had squirmed out of being worked over by his bruisers this time, but I might not be so lucky again.

Not only that, but the date of poor old Herbert's trial was getting closer. Jacko had told me that no new evidence had shown up, which meant that he would be found guilty.

It was high time I got moving and got on to something new.

After the second fare, I went on to Millie's house. She was out, her mother told me and added with a spiteful look, "A gentleman came and picked her up. Going for a walk in the park, he said."

A gentleman? Millie didn't know any gentlemen.

"A singer, she said he was." So it was Ivor Dunstan. Millie's mother didn't sound fully approving, but she probably thought anybody was better than me. Ivor wasn't wasting any time though, was he? I thanked her mother very politely and left.

Well, I had done my duty by Millie and made sure she was all right. Now to get on with my investigation.

I had an idea that was worth a try, and I turned Perseus in the direction of the British Museum. Professor Tryon knew more than anyone else. I didn't know how or why, but I was going to find out. I didn't expect him to be any more helpful than he was before, but I'd face that difficulty when I faced the professor. I turned Perseus off Great Russell Street and towards the entrance to the Reading Room at the library.

I was looking for a place to hitch Perseus when a familiar-looking figure came hurrying out of the main door. The build, the beard, the quick motions—yes, it was the professor himself, coming out of the building. Another minute and I would have missed him. I reined in Perseus and watched the professor go to one of the cab ranks. He climbed into the first cab and it moved out.

I let him get well in front, then I followed. I kept the other cab in sight as we went east along High Holborn and along Newgate Street, then through Cheapside and along the Cornhill. Where on earth was he going? He could live out this way, I supposed, but I wouldn't have thought so. The Tower of London loomed up ahead. This was getting to be a long ride. We went along Leadenhall Street, made a sudden turn into Lime Street and stopped. The cab door swung open and the professor got out and went into the building. I moved in closer to see what the building was, although I already thought I knew . . .

It was Lloyd's Shipping Register—Lloyd's of London.

This professor certainly was keeping me guessing. What could he be doing here? Well, I wouldn't find out sitting here. On the other hand, how could I get inside?

Still, I reminded myself, I got into the Reading Room at the British Museum, so I should be able to use my wits enough to get in here. I had brought fares here on occasion, but had never been inside the building. How could I do it?

I rummaged around under the seat in the cab. There was the

cardboard box that Cecilia had given me with the flowered necklace young James wanted me to hang round Perseus' neck. I didn't want to have the poor horse hanging his head in shame with a thing like that round his neck, nor did I want to tell James or Cecilia that, so the box was still there. It was a good size, big enough to look important. With it in my hand, I went into Lloyd's.

The commissionaire looked like an ex-navy man, weather-beaten and bow-legged.

"I have a parcel for Professor Tryon," I told him. "He said he would be here."

"He just came in," the old sailor said. "I'll give it to him." He reached out for the box.

"Personal delivery," I said. "The professor was very firm about that." I looked apologetic. "Don't know why, but he said it was valuable and he couldn't take any chances with it."

"Oh, all right," the man said. "He's gone down to the warden's office." He pointed to the far end of the room. "Know where it is?" I nodded. "You can take it to him," he said.

The place was buzzing with activity. Small cubicles surrounded by wooden railings had one man in them, sometimes two. Messenger boys bustled all over, bringing files or bundles of paper. Half a dozen different tobacco smells hung in the air, some English, others foreign. Paintings on the walls showed passenger ships, mail ships and some that were called "clipper ships." Once in a while, a bell would clang, and all of the blokes in the room would stop and listen while a whiskered bloke with a big voice read out about a ship that was lost or sunk or had arrived in harbor. Most of the information he read out told of a cargo of this or that, weighing so many tons.

Some of them were grain, some machinery, some tea, some lumber, some coal. Never having been in here before, I didn't know where the warden's office was, but somebody would tell me. I was looking for the right bloke when I caught sight of the professor. He was going into a glass-sided office at the far end of the room. I went nearer.

A bloke with a white beard and hair and wearing a sort of blue naval jacket was sitting at a desk. He looked up as the professor came in and nodded as if he knew him. Perhaps the professor came here as often as he went to the British Museum. I moved closer.

Three blokes stood near the office and were having a good old argument about pepper. It didn't seem to me to be a subject worth arguing about, but from what I could hear, a shipment was coming from Madagascar and was very valuable. In fact, one of them had arranged for a Royal Navy ship to escort it through the Straits of Somewhere-or-Other. Blimey! I thought. All this over a pinch of pepper! Then I caught the words, "A six-hundred-ton cargo." That was a lot of sneezes.

I wasn't paying that much attention to the three, but they moved a pace or two to keep out of the way of messengers and other blokes scurrying to and fro, and they were waving their arms as they talked. They made a good cover for me so I went close to the warden's office, but stood so it looked as if I was part of the pepper group.

I could just hear the conversation inside. The warden was saying, "It was some years later when Royal Navy records were made available to Lloyd's that it was realized a great prize was waiting to be revealed. The laws of salvage were reviewed due to the question of location, and it was only then that the reports of sightings from the observation tower at Tilbury and the Coast Guard station at Purfleet came to light."

The professor had his back to me, so I couldn't hear him, but I could tell he was asking a question. The warden listened, then nodded his head and answered. "Certainly the storm drove it farther up river, but the problem is how much farther?"

The professor asked another question that I couldn't hear. The warden said, "Ordinarily we would know that, but as it was not one of ours, I can't tell you."

The pepper boys got a bit more heated at this point, and when one of them said something that ended in "assumption of risk," there came shouts of disagreement from the other two. I couldn't hear what was being said in the glass office, and I almost asked the peppers to quiet down. I edged a bit closer, but the professor was half-turning. I didn't want him to see me, and another bloke joined the pepper argument, so I beat a retreat. I wasn't sure what I had learned, but I guessed they were talking about a ship. What was "the great prize," though? It certainly wasn't two candlesticks.

Near the door, I found I still had the box under my arm. I saw a bloke get up and walk out of one of the open cubicles with a little wooden fence around it. I plunked the box down on his desk and as I left, I wondered what he would think when he opened it and found a feathered necklace.

The commissionaire gave me a glance as I passed him. "Find him all right?" he asked.

I nodded and smiled and exited.

After that much excitement in the last twenty-four hours, I could have done with a spot of shuteye, but it was not to be. We had arranged a meeting of cabbies for the end of the working day. It wasn't an event I was looking forward to, but I knew that Leo and Sid weren't either. It was a long ride back to Hangman's Corner. I took it slow in case a fare wanted to go my way. Nobody did though, and I got back, hitched Perseus near one of the watering troughs, and walked slowly over to the bandstand.

I gossiped with the blokes for a bit, then Leo and Sid arrived. Sid was still smiling like he always did, but he didn't look amused. The rest of the cabbies drifted in and we started the meeting. Sid told it the way it had happened and came to the end. "So when the magistrates came back, they turned down our application for a union."

There was silence. Maybe we had sounded too optimistic and led the blokes to expect forming a trade union was easy. Regardless, some unhappy murmuring began. Leo stood up. "It's only fair to tell you that the first three applications from the dockworkers were turned down. But they didn't give up, and the fourth one was approved."

"You mean that's what we have to do?" a voice called out.

"We're going to keep on trying as long as it takes," Sid said.

Diddy Cartwright raised his hand. He didn't have to do that. In fact, he was the only cabby who did, but he wanted to prove how much he knew about meetings. "Mr. Chairman," he began, which was a bit of a laugh, although nobody did, "Is it perhaps time to reconsider the committee members? Maybe we need another vote. The present members haven't been very success-ful with this application. Is it not time to seek new voices, new ideas, new approaches?"

He sounded like one of those letters to the *Times*. He prob-ably wrote those too. Sid knew how to handle him, though. "If you or any other member, has any ideas, please put them forward. We will give them full consideration."

Diddy just wanted one of us off the committee so he could get on, and I was the easiest one to lose. He had no new ideas. The silence that followed was broken when the question was asked, "Can we appeal?"

Sid explained that we could not, but we could reapply. That caused some discussion as to how long we should wait. I said we would be looking at the dockworkers' second application and see how they changed it from the original, as well as their others, all the way up to the one that worked.

"But they have so many more members than us," said Eric Newland.

"Shouldn't make any difference," Sid said. "We can get six thousand signatures. That's enough for a union."

"Do we know what reason they gave for turning us down?" asked a cabby called

Basil, who had worked as a clerk in a big store, and knew how to use his head.

"They didn't give us one," said Leo. "They don't have to, but I know a bloke in the council offices. Used to work with him. He can find out."

More questions came and were answered. All the blokes were unhappy. Maybe we had got their hopes up too high. Still, we had made a start, and they all realized that. They also knew that we would keep trying until we got our union.

"They're beginning to drift away," Sid said to me out of the corner of his mouth. "Time for us to shut up."

So we did. I'd had a long day, and too much had happened. I went home and fed Perseus his oats and saw he had plenty of water. I gave him an apple—he loves those—and left him. All I had was a potato and leek pie. I ate it cold and had an apple myself. What's good for the horse is good for the master, I told myself. Then I went to bed—my earliest in a long time. But if I didn't, I'd fall asleep on my feet.

CHAPTER 20

A good night's sleep did wonders for me and I woke up feeling ready for anything. I had vague memories of a dream in which I was trapped in a room full of men, all with knives dripping blood like those cow carcasses. I pushed it into the cellar of my mind and had Perseus on the road before six o'clock. He looked a bit surprised. Maybe he thought hangovers lasted longer than that.

At that time, London's day was already started. The water carts were out on the streets, sluicing them down, and the milk carts were rattling their bottles. The wonderful smell of fresh bread came drifting out of Swanson's bakery on St. George's Street where Fred and Hilda, who had been at school with my dad, made the best buns in Pimlico.

The knockers-up were still clattering at the windows of those who didn't have time pieces, and the flower sellers were dragging their carts into position on the corner of Warwick Square and starting to unload their boxes and baskets. It would be one of the most colorful sights in this part of London within the next quarter hour.

Victoria Railway Station was my destination. Today was the day out-of-towners came in for the markets, and it would be a good place and time for fares. Not that it looked much like a real station. The London, Brighton and South Coast Railway had only opened seven or eight years earlier, and several platforms were reserved for it at the new Victoria Station that opened on the same day. The Victoria Station had wooden fronted buildings and looked like one of those towns you see in pictures of the Canadian backwoods. I felt I should be driving a stagecoach instead of a hansom.

It was busy though. The papers said ninety-four trains left the station the day it opened, and the number was a lot higher every day now. I got a fare as soon as I moved into the rank, a choirmaster and his wife, wanting to go to Brompton Oratory for some rehearsals for a big festival coming up. Two more fares followed, and they put me where I wanted to be by about nine-thirty. I still had my duty to do by Cecilia.

I left Perseus in an empty rank at the side of the Admiralty building I walked to the front. A couple of smart-looking sailors were on guard with their rifles and their bayonets. Their black boots were shiny and their buttons must have to be polished every day. Those men might have been wax, they were so still. Inside the big doors, two uniformed sailors sat at desks. I went to the nearer.

"My brother-in-law is in the China Squadron. They've come back from the Far East and the ships docked already, but Jack hasn't come home yet. Can I talk to somebody who knows what happened to him?"

I had been working out that little speech, and it sounded to the point. The papers had been printing columns lately about the need for the armed services to improve their relations with the public. I was going to give them a chance to do just that. A couple of months ago, they might have fobbed me off but now, with the spotlight on them, I was hopeful of some result.

It looked like either my question or the newspaper articles were working. I was taken through a maze of passageways and into an office where a pleasant-looking older bloke sat with big ledgers on his desk and on racks on all the walls. He asked what he could do for me. He said he was Captain Gridley. I told my story again.

"Ah, the China Squadron, yes. It docked on the eighteenth. Which vessel is your brother-in-law on?"

"HMS Venomous."

"Six thousand two hundred tons, fourteen guns, crew of three hundred and twelve, launched in Plymouth 1849—" He gave me an apologetic grin. "Sorry. Not trying to impress you. I like to keep up my mental record of all our fighting ships."

"You did impress me," I said. "The navy must have a lot of ships to remember."

"Yes, we have in service at this moment—" He broke off. "Ah, that's secret, of course."

"Perfectly all right," I said, wanting to match his politeness. "I understand."

"Not that we have any enemies in the world who can match us on the high seas. The French have not rebuilt their navy since Napoleon, the Spanish haven't recovered from losing their Armada yet, and the Dutch and the Portuguese are concentrating on merchant ships rather than naval. Still, our intelligence chaps insist on keeping our strength to ourselves."

"Of course." The stuff in the newspapers had worked. The navy was being friendlier with the people.

"Anyway, back to your question—let me see now." He thumbed through one of the ledgers on his desk, then stood up. "Just a moment." He went and opened the door. "Henson, do you have a moment?" He talked to somebody outside and came back in.

"Your brother-in-law has been in the navy a long time?"

"Yes," I said, and we chatted until there was a knock on the door and a bloke—must have been Henson—brought in a blue folder. I realized that Captain Gridley was being courteous and could have had me just sit and wait. During our chat, he'd told me that he missed being at sea, but he had been invalided out after a collision with another ship. I didn't say a word, but wondered why two ships couldn't avoid each other, the ocean being such a big place.

He went through the blue folder page by page, then stopped. "Ah, here we are," he murmured. There was a silence while he read. He looked up at me. "It's bad news, I'm afraid."

I felt cold. "He isn't dead?"

"No, no, he's quite well," he said. I breathed a sigh of relief.

"So why isn't he at home? As long as he's all right. Well, I mean, that's the most important thing, isn't it?"

"I'm glad you take that attitude," said Captain Gridley. "It is more important, yes. I hope your sister will see it the same way."

"So where is he?" I asked.

"He's in Hong Kong."

"That's in China, isn't it?"

"It is. Hong Kong is one of our biggest naval bases in the Far East and—"

"Why didn't he come back with the squadron?" I asked, puzzled.

He pursed his lips. "Not to mince words but . . . he jumped ship."

"You mean he deserted? Stayed there!" That didn't sound like Jack.

"It's the army that deserts. In the navy, we call it jumping ship. Let me explain. Britain has built up the colony of Hong Kong until it is now one of the biggest trading ports in the world, and it's still getting bigger. Our navy protects it and goods flow in and out at a tremendous rate. Hong Kong has become the commercial gateway to the Oriental world. This has created opportunities for Westerners—particularly British—to set up businesses in Hong Kong and make a lot of money."

"And that's what Jack is doing?"

He looked at the file again. "We have statements here from two of his shipmates. You see, HMS Venomous was laid up in Hong Kong for engine repairs. The crew were given shore leave while the repairs were being carried out, and your brother-in-law ran into a chap who was a friend of a friend. This man had a good job in one of the merchant houses, and he persuaded your brother-in-law to stay and work with him."

"Making a lot of money."

"I'm sure that would be his intention," said Captain Gridley dryly.

"Then as soon as he's made his packet, he'll be coming home."

He hesitated. "We would hope so."

"I would hope so too," I said bitterly. "My sister, his wife, will hope so too. What's she going to do in the meanwhile? How will she live?"

He thought about that. "Having jumped ship, officially we don't know his whereabouts. That means we won't have any way of paying him."

"His pay continues?" I said, a bit surprised.

"Until some action is taken by the Lords of the Admiralty. Luckily for your sister, Her Majesty's paymaster grinds his mills extremely slowly."

"What does that mean exactly?"

"It means it will be several months before any decision is reached." He drummed fingers on the desk. "Is she here in London?"

"She lives in Clapham. Got a little boy."

"All the more reason." He opened the blue folder and looked inside it again. "His record has been excellent until now. Pity that he—still, the temptation is strong, I suppose."

He was thinking hard. "What I may be able to do is to see that his pay goes to his wife. Mind you, I don't know how long we can do this. The most I can do is to stretch out the time until he is officially proclaimed 'absent without leave.' After that, it will be difficult, but at least she will have a few months of income. That's about the most I can do."

"I thank you very much, Captain," I told him sincerely. "You are a true gentleman and a credit to the navy."

He smiled slightly. "Thank you, Mr. Parker, but don't tell the navy about it. What they don't know won't hurt them."

"One of my mottos too."

We shook hands and I was taken away. All those letters that people had written to the newspapers about the armed services needing to treat civilians more civil had worked. I might even write one myself—no names, no pack drill, of course, but they deserved a pat on the back.

The bloke taking me back to the main entrance had a stiff arm. Must have been why he had an Admiralty job. I asked him how he got it, and he was real pleased to tell me all about it. We were pals long before we got to the entrance and I had a sudden thought. "Tell me something. Do you have any blokes who know the history of the navy?"

He grinned. "You gotta be joking. Naval historians! We got dozens of 'em."

"Could I get to talk to one?"

He looked doubtful. "Dunno about that. What for?"

"I have a friend in trouble. His future might be a bit grim unless I can find out certain things. It's to do with the navy— nothing bad," I added quickly.

He rubbed his chin. "I wonder who . . ." He raised a finger in the air. "I know! Lieutenant Waverley. He's being transferred to Scapa Flow. Doesn't like the idea much, but he has to hang around till he can get posted. Made all his arrangements. Bored to death, he is. Be glad to talk to you. Come on. I'll take you to him."

Lieutenant Waverley stood gazing out of the window at St. James' Park. He was in an office with six desks, and when my bloke introduced us and told him what I had said, he looked interested.

"Take him away," called out one of the blokes to me. "He has nothing to do, and he won't let us work."

"Let's go through here," the lieutenant said with a laugh, and took me into an empty office. On the walls were pictures of old warships. We sat at a desk, facing each other. "So what do you want to know?"

He was probably about my dad's age, with short-cropped hair going a little gray. He looked active and with an alert sort of face that hinted he might be interested in a lot of things.

"I don't have much to go on but . . ." I told him about a friend whose future might depend on what I could learn, like I had told the bloke who brought me. That got him on my side right away. He seemed a sympathetic sort of chap and would probably have been a lot more sympathetic if I had told him that Herbert was facing hanging, but I decided not to get into all that.

"A ship with a valuable cargo came up the Thames. It was sighted by the Coastguard Station at Purfleet and seen from the observation tower at Tilbury."

"When was this? What year?"

"I don't know."

"Make a guess?"

"Not really. Not too long ago, I shouldn't think."

He made a clucking sound. "All right, go on."

"A storm drove it up the Thames—"

"Wait a minute, you say 'a ship with a cargo.' This is the Royal Navy. You want to talk to the people at Lloyd's Shipping Register." He was starting to lose interest.

"I just came from there."

"They couldn't help?"

They might have helped if I had been able to overhear any more of the conversation, I thought, but that wasn't the right thing to say to keep this bloke going.

"The reason I came here," I said, "is that Lloyd's only knew about it when navy records were made available to them. Doesn't that mean the navy should know about it?"

His interest came back. "Yes, it does. Hmm, I don't quite understand this. Lloyd's couldn't identify the vessel? They have records of ships back to the ark."

"I remember what they said. They said, 'It wasn't one of ours.' "

He leaned forward eagerly. "Not British! That might explain it." His expression changed. "Still, Lloyd's have records of foreign ships coming into British ports. That must mean . . . what does it mean?" He looked angry with himself for not knowing. I could see his brain was buzzing though. "It must mean it wasn't coming into a British port—but then what was it doing in the Thames?" He eased back in his chair, thinking furiously. "A storm, you say?"

"Yes."

"A bad one?"

I didn't know, but I said, "Yes." It sounded good.

A look came into his eyes. He pointed a finger at me. "Have you ever heard of Professor Tryon?"

I swallowed a gulp. "I . . . er, I met him in the British Museum Library, the Reading Room."

"You've talked to him?"

"A little," I said.

"Did he ever mention *Nuestra Senora de Valencia*?"

I reached into my pocket and took out a piece of paper and laid it on the desk before him.

CHAPTER 21

Lieutenant Waverley looked at the piece of paper that said those same words in my handwriting. He pushed it back at me. "You already know."

"I don't know anything about *Nuestra Senora de Valencia.*"

He cringed a bit at my pronunciation. "Why do you have it written on this paper then?"

"I thought it was a church."

"Oh. Well, it is that too." He smiled at the blank look on my face. "You see, churches all over Spain have that same name. *Nuestra Senora* means Our Lady in English."

"I know that," I said and added quickly, "but it's about all I do know."

"Right. Every town has its own church by that name—towns like Barcelona, Oviedo, Tarragona, Cadiz, Toledo. A few of the more prosperous towns put up money for Spanish galleons to go to the New World and bring back goods. The galleons were named after the town, which was the same as the church."

"Spanish galleons! I remember learning about those in school."

"You would. Every English kid does. The galleons brought treasure back from South America."

"Treasure!"

He didn't seem to mind my interruption and went on. "Exactly. Treasure looted by the Spaniards from churches and cities and great homes, as well as gold and silver from the mines in Peru and Mexico."

"And this ship was one of those?" It was all beginning to fit together now.

"Yes. The trade winds blew them across the Atlantic." I could see that map in the British Museum Reading Room in my mind, all those little arrows on it.

"The galleon, *Nuestra Senora de Valencia,* was a hundred and fifty feet long. She displaced two thousand tons and had a loaded draft of twenty-one feet. She was one of a convoy of ships bringing back to Spain millions and millions of pounds worth of treasure. She became separated from the rest of her convoy and two British frigates, belonging to a fleet of English privateers, sighted her and gave chase. She was no match for them and flew a white flag rather than be sunk. They were bringing her back to England as a prize when there was a great storm." He was filling in the story for me now.

"The three ships were separated," he went on, "and the crew of the Spanish ship seized the chance to escape the frigates. The storm carried them into the mouth of the Thames. They probably didn't know where they were, and it didn't matter, for if they stayed out in the Atlantic storm, they were going to sink. The ship was sighted both at Tilbury and Purfleet—you're right there. It was being blown in, towards London. The storm continued. It was one of the worst of the century. She was blown up river, and no one knows what happened to her after that. She sank somewhere and was never heard of again."

He gave me a keen look. "First the professor, and now you. Why all this interest?"

"If it had treasure on board, wouldn't somebody have found it by now?" I asked.

He laughed. "Lord, no. Do you know how many sunken treasure ships there are? Fifty Spanish galleons alone were sunk, most of them on this side of the Atlantic where the weather is always worse. To my knowledge, only three wrecks have been located, and two of those are too deep to salvage. In the Thames, it's true it's a smaller area, but the tide runs high. Thousands of tons of water race in and out twice a day. Tons and tons of silt get pushed up and down the river. Any ship that sank nearly two hundred years ago could be buried deep by now and no way of knowing its location."

"So the *Nuestra Senora* is there—somewhere—but nobody knows where?"

"Wherever it is, it's under ten feet of silt. That's fine sand. Maybe twenty feet. Maybe someday we'll have the technical ability to locate it but today . . . well, it's sheer chance, and anyway, who is able to comb the bed of the River Thames?"

Maybe nobody, I thought. But a giant machine, digging deep below that riverbed might, by chance, hit . . .

He laughed again. "Don't tell me you're after the lost treasure of the *Nuestra Senora de Valencia!*"

I laughed louder than he had. "Not me. I'm no treasure hunter." He waited for me to explain but as I didn't want to, I spun him a yarn. "No. I thought it was a church, and I'm interested in churches. You might call it a hobby. Last week, I was going round this one in Kent and they had . . ." I don't think he believed a word of it, but he was too polite to call me a liar.

At the end, he said, "I'd like you to keep me informed. I mean, in your . . . er, your study of churches, you might run into some information that relates to this galleon."

Perseus sauntered along as if he had all the time in the world. I was giving him his head so I could think, and I had plenty to think about. I had the whole picture at last, even if some of the earlier parts were missing. I still didn't understand about the two candlesticks and why they had been stolen from the churches. It seemed obvious that Luke Marston and Dickie Drew in their massive digging machine had been working on the tunnel when they had somehow run into the wreck of the *Nuestra Senora de Valencia*. The galleon must have been blown much farther up the Thames than anybody had realized. Another reason for going slow was I was putting off telling Cecilia the bad news, but it had to be done. I turned Perseus in the direction of Clapham.

Cecilia opened the door and immediately said, "Come in, Ned. I see from your face that you have some news."

We sat at the little kitchen table. "First of all and most important, Jack's well."

Her expression relaxed a little. "That's good news anyway, but the way you put it, there's more to come. What is it?"

"Not to put too fine a point on it, but he jumped ship in Hong Kong."

Her eyes widened. "Hong Kong? In China? What do you mean, he jumped ship? You mean he's still there?"

"Yes, that's right . . ." and I told her what I had learned from Captain Gridley at the Admiralty. She looked sad. I could understand it. I said right away, "At least, when he does come back, he'll have a lot of money."

"I'd rather have Jack," she said simply. But she's a practical girl and added, "So what am I going to do? Sell matches on the street corner?"

I told her of Captain Gridley's promise to do what he could to get Jack's pay sent to her, and she brightened. "That'll be something at least. For how long though?"

"Jack'll be back by then," I said. I thought it better not to say that, as a navy deserter, he might have trouble getting a job.

"I'll make us a cup of tea," she said. Tea the same as that brought on those clipper ships in the pictures on the wall at Lloyd's of London, I thought. When she came back and put cups and saucers on the table, she looked like she had shed a few tears, but she was calm, and I remembered she had been the calmest of all of us when my dad had died. I had already been taken by my aunt Ada when my mum died, so I didn't know for sure, but I bet Cecilia had been just as calm then.

"How's Millie?" she asked as she poured the tea.

"Very well," I said. "Got a job at the New Vaudeville Theatre."

"My goodness! Isn't that the big new one on the Strand?"

"Yes, that's the one."

"Millie's really coming up in the world," said Cecilia.

"Yes, she is."

She's a sharp girl, is Cecilia. She caught a tone in my voice. "Something wrong between you two?"

"No, not really," I began.

"Ned!"

"Oh, all right. We're a bit on the outs at the moment, that's all."

"You don't want her doing what she wants to do, is that it?"

"In a way. But no, I don't mind her being on the stage if she really wants to, but she may be climbing too high, too fast."

"Sounds like she's going fast, that's true, if she's at the New Vaudeville. Is there another man?" she asked suddenly.

"Sis, you are nosier than I ever was!"

"So there is another man?"

"Ivor Dunstan, he—"

"Ivor Dunstan? I've heard of him. Wasn't he in *Midnight Rapture*?"

"So he says."

"He had a long run in that. The papers said he was very good. He sings and dances. They say he's a good comedian too."

"Ha ha."

Cecilia giggled. "A bit of competition might be good for you.

Remember Bernard Lovell? Jack was so jealous of him."

"Yes, you liked Bernard, didn't you?"

"Not that much. But I let Jack think I did. It got him to propose to me."

I was astounded. "You did that?"

"Of course. A woman has to do those things. That's what Millie may be doing."

"Maybe I should do the same," I said.

"Not you," Cecilia said. "It's not your nature."

An image of Dorothy floated through my memory. Sisters didn't know as much as they thought they did.

"I made some scones for James," she said. "Do you want one?"

"You make the best—" I was starting to say but she was already fluttering a hand at me. She brought me two scones. I was glad I'd got her off the subject of Jack. I really did think that there was a good chance he'd be back soon, and with a wallet full of money. But Cecilia was a good wife, and I could see she would be worried. Jack was a nice bloke, and he and I got on real well. He had done well in the navy, but I could understand that he might be tempted to make a lot of money if the chance was there. Maybe Hong Kong was the place to make it.

Cecilia brought the pot and poured me another cup of tea. "Not still poking your nose into that business with the silver candlesticks, are you?"

"Herbert is being tried at the Old Bailey for a murder he didn't commit. I'm still trying to find out what I can to help him."

"Isn't that the job of the police?"

"They think their job is done. Now it's up to a judge and jury."

We had a bit of a disagreement about British justice for some time, and then young James came romping in. He flung his arms around me. "Did you change his name to Pegasus?" was his first question.

"I talked to him about it."

"Pegasus was the winged horse, you know."

"Yes, he was."

"Perseus wasn't a horse at all."

"I should have remembered that," I admitted.

"He doesn't mind having his name changed?"

Cecilia was trying not to laugh, and I was trying to be serious. Young James is like a terrier when he gets his teeth into a thing.

"I don't think he's made up his mind," I said.

"I said hello to him outside. He's not wearing his feather collar either."

"He may be keeping it for special occasions. It's not the kind of collar a horse would wear every day, you know."

James thought about that. "No, I suppose it isn't," he agreed.

When I left, Cecilia was still giggling and James was happy, and that was what I had come for, really.

Late afternoon is an in-between time in the cab business. The midday and lunchtime customers are done, and the leavers from work and the people going to railway stations haven't set out yet. I could still get in another three or four hours. But in the meantime, I headed towards Hangman's Corner. Perhaps one of the cabbies had some news for me that might help. I also wanted to talk to Leo and Sid about getting ready for our next application for a union.

A bit of a shower came down, but it didn't amount to anything. We went up Silverthorne Road and on to Queenstown Road. At Queens Circle, I turned on Prince of Wales Drive, then on up into Battersea Park. A few nursemaids were still pushing prams. Some kids were playing cricket, and the usual strollers and fresh-air fiends and those with nothing to do were out. The air was crisp, and as I got near to the entrance to Hangman's Corner, a bloke stepped out from behind a tree and waved me to a stop.

As soon as I had stopped, another bloke came from behind him. One grabbed Perseus' reins and the other came to the cab. He looked like a bruiser. I was seeing enough of 'em these days to spot 'em right away, even if I hadn't before. This one had lost a few teeth and his grin was not pleasant.

"Mr. John thought we should come and see you. He hears that you've been passing words with the colonel."

"That wasn't my idea," I protested. "The colonel—"

I didn't get any farther. A long arm reached out and seized me by the throat. Next I knew, he'd pulled me out of the cab and on to the ground. I hit it with a thump that knocked most of the breath out of me. From where I was lying, he looked enormous. Then the other bloke came up to join him, and he looked even bigger.

"We got to teach you a lesson, Mister Parker," the first one said and a boot belonging to the other bloke crashed into my ribs. The park went swimming away into a dark red haze.

Chapter 22

The haze cleared; perhaps the pain in my ribs helped. I was aware of being flat on my back, looking up into a blue sky with patchy white clouds. The only thing spoiling that view was two ugly faces.

"Don't worry, Ned," said one mocking voice. "We're not going to kill you."

"No," said the other, deeper voice. "You might wish you was dead though!"

They both laughed as if that was funny.

"Listen," I managed to croak, "Mr. John doesn't want you to do this. I'm telling him all I know."

" 'ave you told him about havin' your secret meeting with the colonel?" asked deeper voice.

"No, I haven't. I don't know where to talk to him. He always arranges to talk to me."

"That's just too bad," the other voice said. "It's goin' to cause you a lot of pain."

Another kick came right on the same place, and that side of my body felt as if it was on fire. I tried to squirm away, but a foot on the other side pushed me back. Two hands grabbed me by the shirtfront and jerked me to my feet. A fist hit me in the stomach, not real hard but hard enough to knock the breath right out of me. I struggled for air.

"Come on, Mister Nosy Ned, be a man! Stand up on your own two feet," said a jeering voice. I tried, but found myself

196

falling. The other man put his hands around my neck and lifted me, half choking me in the process. I staggered, but a hand propped me up.

"We was going to 'ave a word with that girl friend of yours," said deeper voice, "but the orders got changed. Now we want to make sure you understand to keep what you know to yourself." He ended with a snarly tone I didn't like. I tried to clear my head so I could see where the next blow was coming from.

I could see a bit. I could see Perseus and my cab—but I must be seeing double. There were two cabs, two horses. I started to crumple, but a rough hand hoisted me back on to my feet. I could still see two cabs, but something was wrong. The second horse wasn't Perseus. What had happened to my eyesight?

The head of the bruiser nearest me suddenly turned and I twisted my neck to see where he was looking. I wasn't seeing double. Another cab had pulled up nearby. One of the bruisers waved a hand at the cab. "G'warn!" he shouted. "Get away!"

I tried to call out but I had no voice, just a whisper.

"What are you doing?" came a new voice, one that sounded familiar.

"Get off if you know what's good for you," snarled deeper voice

I took advantage of those few moments to shake my head again and try to clear it. A figure was stepping down from the cab, a huge, looming figure with a massive body, long arms and a face that I couldn't quite see but I thought—

"Benny!" I called out with all the strength I could muster.

"Ned?" Alarm was in the voice and the figure came nearer.

"Get back in that cab!" shouted deeper voice. "This is none o' your business—"

The threat came too late. Benny the Brain, my valiant companion from our night visit to London Bridge Underground Railway Station, lumbered towards us at a surprising speed for such a big man.

Mr. John's men were accustomed to doing the attacking, not being attacked. Both of them were taken unawares by Benny, who was on them without a second's hesitation. Deeper voice was growling another threat at him when Benny's round arm swing crashed into the side of his head. He staggered, fell to one knee. The other man leapt at Benny and the two struggled for a few seconds, but big as the other man was, Benny was bigger.

He was also a lot stronger. Each man was battling to get his hands on the throat of the other, but Benny was first to tighten his grip. The man's mouth opened and Benny gave him a shake that must have rattled every bone in his body. There was a horrible gurgle, and the man's arms dropped to his sides. The other bruiser had got back on his feet and leapt on Benny's back, trying to get his arms around his throat. I don't do much fighting, but when I was in school, every kid had to do what he could to defend himself. As a result, I never learned to box, but I did pick up a few dirty tricks. One of the most useful was a knowledge of where the kidneys are and how sensitive they can be.

I punched the man hard in the kidneys. The first couple of punches got no result, but then he yelped and dropped off Benny's back. Quick as a flash, he turned to swing a fist at me. Benny reached for him, but not in time to prevent the fist from hitting me. Then the other bloke was on his feet and coming.

"Behind you, Benny!" I shouted.

He twisted just in time to meet the bloke full on. They crashed together, dazing both of them for a second. Benny's size gave him the advantage and he recovered first, jabbing a left fist into the face of the other. The bruiser went down in the dust.

The fist that hit me just missed my face and hit me under the ear. My head rang like a bell, but I had no time to listen to it. I dropped to one knee as if I was falling. Then I threw my arms round the bruiser's knees and pulled him to the ground. He was stronger and more experienced than me, and he aimed a kick that caught me on the thigh, sending stabs of agony through my leg.

I lay paralyzed for a moment and the man jumped at me—only to be grabbed by a pair of long arms that held him, twisted him, and delivered a tremendous blow to the jaw. There was a cracking sound, and as I watched him fall, I saw a still body already on the ground. I had missed whatever Benny had done to that one, but it had ended the battle.

I struggled up, Benny helping me. "Blimey, Ned, you do know some nasty people!"

"Wouldn't call them people," I gasped.

"Can you stand up?"

I tried, fell at first, but got up and stayed up though fiery pains were still pulsing through my leg. Benny was evidently a more seasoned fighter than I was, because his first action after I was on my feet was to look at the two bodies. Both men seemed to be still alive, but breathing heavily and not likely to give us any more trouble for the time being. One had a broken jaw and the other lay still with one hand to his throat. "Had to throttle him," Benny said by way of explanation.

Benny was not even out of breath. He fussed over me as I insisted I was all right.

"You was coming in?" he asked.

I nodded. I had left Perseus pointing in that direction. "Think I'll call it a day instead," I said. "Benny, you're a hero. I'm glad you're my friend."

"You gotta be careful, Ned" he told me in his most serious voice. "I told you that before."

"You did."

"Is this something to do with that station we went to?"

"It is, and it's something that I hope will soon be over."

"I might not always be there to save you, Ned." There was concern in his voice, and my heart warmed to him.

"I hope you won't have to be, Benny, but if I had to have anybody, you'd be the one."

He smiled. It was considered a vacant smile by some, but to me it was one of sheer friendship.

"What are we going to do with these two?" I asked. "We'll likely have the police asking questions if we leave them here."

"I'll take care of 'em," Benny said, taking them by the scruffs of their necks, one in each hand.

"You're not going to drop them in the—" I started to say, alarmed.

"No," said Benny. "Enough nasty things in the river as it is. I'll just drop 'em on the rubbish tip up there by the gate. It's where they belong."

I insisted on thanking him again. He got all embarrassed, but I did it anyway. He tossed the two bodies into his cab as if they were sacks of coal and drove off.

Perseus gave me a look that said, "Have you been fighting again?"

"You sound like my mother," I told him and flicked the whip just over his head.

I used plenty of cold water to rinse my bruises when I got home. The one on my neck just below the ear was tender and made my neck stiff. My ribs ached, but none seemed to be broken. My stomach hurt and my throat hurt, but no bruises had showed up yet on either one.

I ate a slab of bread and a piece of cheese and collapsed into bed. I couldn't get to sleep right away even though my whole body felt exhausted. I was thinking of what one of those bruisers had said. They were going to have words with Millie, but the orders got changed.

So, Mr. John was threatening her as a way of getting me to tell him all I knew and say nothing about him. I wondered why he had changed his mind. Instead, he had sent those two brutes to rough me up to teach me a lesson. Did he still intend to do anything to her? I would have to talk to Dorothy and tell her in a quiet way that Millie might be in danger. She could arrange for somebody to keep an eye on her—beside the one that Ivor Dunstan had on her. He was a good-sized bloke, but no match for Mr. John's nobblers. Still worrying about what else I could do, I fell asleep.

I hadn't even got a fare next morning. In fact I was just rolling along up Bourne Street towards Sloane Square when a familiar figure stepped out and hailed me. It was Detective Sergeant Jackson. I stopped alongside and gave him a cheery good-day.

I wasn't feeling all that wonderful, but my body had sunk into a dull ache all over, the aches in the different parts of me all merging into one. Being achy was better than having broken bones or worse though, and I'd certainly have been in worse shape if Benny hadn't arrived.

Sergeant Jackson rested a hand on my cab and looked up at me. "Been keeping out of mischief, Parker?"

"You know me, sergeant," I said in my chirpiest voice.

He kept on looking at me as if he could see my bruises, but I didn't think they showed. I tried not to look too stiff.

"I know you only too well, Parker. Reason I asked, we got a call to come out to that hangout of yours. Somebody found two bodies on the rubbish tip at the entrance."

"Dead bodies?" I tried to keep my tone normal.

"I think you'd better come with me for a ride," he said and climbed into my cab.

"Here, wait a minute!" I protested. "I've got a living to make, I have."

" 'Always ready to help the police with their inquiries.' " He didn't do a very good job of mocking my voice.

"Well, it's true, I am but—"

"Then keep driving."

I drove. "Right here," he would say, then, "The next left." We went along the Embankment and up Cheyne Walk into Chelsea. Between St. Stephens Hospital and the World's End pub. Jacko said, "Tie up at the next corner."

I did, and we walked a little way and went through a doorway with a blue lamp over it. The sign said, Chelsea Police Station.

Jacko gave a nod and a wave to the policeman at the desk, who was evidently expecting him. Jacko led the way along the corridors, and he only spoke once.

"This is getting to be too much of a habit, Parker."

A nasty shiver ran down my spine, and I forgot my aches and pains. The familiar smells of antiseptic and urine drifted in the narrow, murky corridors, and our footsteps echoed. We went into a room with whitewashed walls. It held boxes and crates and a few sacks, but the scary part was the table in the middle of the floor. It had a sheet over it.

"We don't have a hospital or a morgue in the Chelsea Station yet," Jacko said. "So we have to make do but—"

Like a magician in a show, he whipped the sheet away. The body was fully clothed in a dark suit, waistcoat with a fob, black boots. The beard made him recognizable at once.

It was Professor Tryon.

Jacko's remark about "too much of a habit" should have prepared me for something like this, but it hadn't. Even as I saw the sheet-covered table and Jacko reached for the sheet, I had a bad feeling. But I half expected that the body I saw would be one of the two bruisers who had attacked me, certainly not the professor's.

The professor knew about the *Nuestra Senora de Valencia,* he knew about the seizure by the two navy frigates, and he knew about the storm that had rescued the galleon from the navy and driven it up into the Thames. He knew about the silver candlesticks, and he probably knew what else was on board the treasure ship. He had found out where it sank after talking to Luke Marston and Dickie Drew.

All this was flashing though my mind. I said quickly, "You said you found two bodies on the rubbish tip. Where's the other?"

Jacko flipped the sheet back over the professor's body. "This isn't one of them. This one was pulled out of the Thames right near the station here. Just this morning. That's why he still has clothes on. He's only been examined. They'll do the autopsy this afternoon."

"But the two punishers?"

"Did I say they were punishers?"

"Yes, you said—er—"

I expected him to pounce on me but he didn't.

"Those two aren't dead. They're badly hurt, but they're not dead. They refused to go to a hospital, and we had to let them go. But one of our sharper constables spotted one as a punisher—got a real bad reputation, he has. Moreover, we know who he works for."

He turned his full attention on me. "You know a lot about what's going on. You can probably tell me the connection between the professor and those two ruffians."

"Professor?" I said.

"You know right well who he is."

It was the moment for a fast decision and I made it. "I was so shocked at first, but you're right. I do know who he is. His name's Professor Tryon."

Jacko hadn't expected that. He was expecting my usual denial. "And how do you know who he is?"

"I've seen him at the British Museum. In the Reading Room of the library."

"You? In a library?"

"I have a reader's card," I said haughtily.

"You?"

"Yes, me. Want to see it?"

He opened his mouth, changed his mind, and then said, "What are you doing in the Reading Room at the British Museum?"

"I'm one of the committee of three that's trying to get a union for the cabbies."

"I know that," he snapped.

"Well," I said, "I've been reading a lot of books about economics and stuff like that so as to help our case. The British Museum has the finest collection in the—"

"Never mind that," said Jacko. He was getting annoyed at the way I was wriggling my neck out of the noose that he thought he was pulling tight around it

"I talked to Professor Karl Marx," I said. "He's written a lot of these books, and I've talked to Professor Tryon as well."

I was keeping away from the full truth. I would have liked to ask him to keep an eye on Millie, who was being threatened by the two bruisers he had pulled off the rubbish tip, but that would mean too many explanations. Besides, I wasn't all that sure that the police could protect her if Mr. John was really determined.

Everything I was telling Jacko was the truth—as far as it went. Then there was the colonel. How threatening might he be if driven to it? My last meeting with him in the Smithfield Meat Market indicated that he could be just as dangerous as Mr.

John and maybe even more so. I recalled Stan Havers' words about that pair: "two of the worst criminals in Britain."

It was too risky to tell Jacko much more right now, but the day might be fast approaching when I had to. I wanted to keep him ready if I needed him. How could I do that . . . ?

We were still standing facing each other across the dead body of the professor. Poor bloke, he had got himself into a bad position. It had turned out to be a deadly position.

"Too bad about the professor," I said, shaking my head. "Pulled him out of the Thames, did you?"

"Yes."

"Drowned, was he?"

A week ago, Jacko would have snarled something at me and hustled me out of the building. Now he was floundering. Poor old Jacko. When he had the first body, he probably thought it was just another of London's violent deaths. Nothing special about that; he saw a lot of them. With a second body, and killed the same way, suddenly he had a case. Now with a third body . . .

"He was already dead when he was dropped in the river." Jacko sounded almost civil.

"Stab wounds? Like the others?"

"Yes."

I decided to keep going while I was on a roll. "When you said one of your constables spotted one of those blokes on the rubbish tip as a punisher, and you knew who he worked for . . ."

Jacko gritted his teeth. He needed help—from anybody, even me, I could tell. Perhaps I was the first "anybody" he had come across. He might find others, but right now I was all he had. He knew me. He knew I knew more than I was telling him, but he was no longer able to browbeat me—or even beat me. Not that he had ever done that, but he had threatened it a few times. He was a smart copper. His best chance was to use me and dangle a carrot instead using a stick.

"Go on," he urged.

"Do we both know who that is?"

He wasn't going to make it too easy for me. He got that look of his again, the one that looks as if he's going cross-eyed, but he doesn't.

I helped him. "I can understand that without proper evidence, you don't want to name him, but shall we just say he's boss of one of London's two most dangerous gangs?"

"We could say that."

"You probably know this already, but London's second most dangerous gang—the one with a sort of military connection—"

"I know the one." His look was easing, now that he thought he was in with a chance for some really vital information.

"It's in on this as well."

He nodded. I didn't know if already knew or not.

"But the murders—well, they're the work of that first bunch of villains."

He nodded again. "And where is all this leading us?"

"To a conclusion—and very soon, I think."

"I need more than that," he said, showing his teeth and looking a bit more like his old self.

"I'd give you more, only someone close to me is under threat," I said. I hadn't been going to say that, but putting it this way might do what I wanted.

"Is that the young lady I think it is?"

"That's the one."

He nodded, considering. "We made a midnight raid on the London Bridge Underground Railway Station," Jacko said, watching me carefully.

"Did you? Why did you do that?"

"Information received."

"What sort of information?"

"Accounts of unauthorized persons in a station which is officially closed."

Unauthorized giant frogs too? I wondered, but I said, "Train whistles and noises like that? When the station's closed and there's no trains?"

"That sort of thing," Jacko agreed. "What do you know about them?" he asked suddenly.

"I have a friend lives near there. He said there's been a lot of stories. Natural, I suppose. I mean, a station closed when they're desperate to get it finished so they can open it."

He sort of nodded.

"How did the raid go?"

He looked down at the sheeted body. "Place was deserted. No people, no trains, not even any ghosts."

He looked quickly up at me to see my reaction. I managed not to have one.

"Any signs of anything going on there at all?" I asked.

"No. Should there be?"

I shrugged. "Been a lot of rumors, that's all."

"You believe in rumors?"

"Not always. What are the plans for the station, do you know?"

He got his shrewd look. Perhaps he thought he was still on to something.

"No plans to open it yet. Still quite a bit of work to be done. They've had a few cave-ins, you know."

"Have they?" I asked innocently.

"Let's get out of this place," Jacko said sharply. "I hate the smell in here."

We left the room and walked quickly back to the entrance. There I stopped. "One more thing—"

Jacko eyed me suspiciously.

"Herbert Summers," I said. "You know more than enough to be sure that he couldn't have committed these murders. You've got to—"

"I haven't *got* to do anything. Besides," he added, "I recommended his release already. He should be out day after tomorrow."

Jacko stayed to talk with the constable who had been led to the body, and I went to work. I was humming to myself as I unhitched Perseus. "Hoo—bloomin'-ray! Herbert's getting out!" I told him. He caught the note of joy in my voice and his ears twitched like they always did when he understood.

CHAPTER 23

I read the letter through again for the third time.

My Dear Ned,

You'll be pleased to hear that Millie is making good progress and the show is almost ready to put onstage. Wonderful news! The opening will be announced to the press and the public at a grand celebration to be held at the New Vaudeville Theatre on Saturday night and I shall expect you to be there as my personal guest. Who knows? We might find the opportunity to spend some time together—just the two of us! I'll have a brougham collect you at eight o'clock.

Fondest wishes,
Dorothy

A brougham to collect me! I was coming up in the world. So was Millie, by the sound of it. She was going to be in a big show at a new theatre with top stars. Well, it was what she had always wanted and I was happy for her. The truth was that I had been good and drunk when Dorothy and I'd had our roll in the hay. Otherwise, I would not have been unfaithful to Millie. But did I really owe her anything? If our close friendship had been ended, she was the one who had ended it, not me.

Did Millie know about Dorothy and me, I wondered. I thought not, but if she did would she say anything? Probably not, and even if she did know, I was beginning to understand that her career meant more to her than I did. Besides, I didn't know what she and Ivor were up to; perhaps the same as Dorothy and me.

The thought of seeing Dorothy again sent a delicious little shiver up my spine. Maybe I had been drunk that night, but I could remember enough of it. The thought of a repeat performance was more than I could resist. I was not going to turn down an invitation like that.

A few fares brought some more pennies in to feed Perseus and me. A doctor I picked up on Old Brompton Road told me he wanted to visit a patient in St. John's Wood.

"A pleasure, doctor," I said, "but don't patients usually visit you?"

"Usually," he said, quite pleasant. "But this one is a director of the Cunard White Star Shipping Line and he pays me to visit him."

Then I had two ladies, one of them from Scotland, visiting her friend who lived on Grosvenor Place. Very posh, they were, but very nice and polite. They told me exactly what they wanted, and I took them to Messrs. Lewis and Allenby in a terrace off Conduit Street. " 'Drapers and Milliners' they call themselves," I told the two ladies. "One of their best customers is Her Majesty, Queen Victoria, and nearly all the female members of the Royal Family go there." The ladies were delighted and gave me a nice tip.

After delivering them, I headed off on some business of my own. I directed Perseus in the direction of the Edgeware Road and then over on to the Finchley Road, where I headed for Fountain Street. Near the Red Lion pub, I found a good spot to leave Perseus. From there, I walked to the Finchley Auction House.

I was a bit less nervous this time than I had been when I'd

come here before. Still, Swiveler Grimes was a tricky character, and Walter and his other boys weren't far behind. I sauntered in and called loudly, "Anybody here?" so that I couldn't be mistaken for an intruder. Most auction houses don't have intruders, but then not many auction houses do the same kind of business as Swiveler Grimes does.

Walter Greenfield appeared, just as beefy, just as red-faced as before, and wearing the same tweed suit. "Can I help you—" he was asking when he recognized me. "Oh, it's you. Parker, Ned Parker, right?"

"That's right. Mr. Grimes around?"

"He might be. Let me see."

He disappeared and left me alone in the room with the stacks of chairs, the boxes, the crates and the pieces of furniture, rolls of carpet, sinks, paintings, tapestries. He was back in a couple of minutes. "He'll see you. I'll take you to him."

When we walked into his office, my feet sank into his carpet again. I hoped that when I left, I wouldn't have to do it in a hurry. It would be like running through quicksand. The big pendulum clock was still ticking quietly, and its pendulum swung merrily as if it hadn't a care in the world.

Swiveler Grimes sat at his desk, skinny and unhealthy looking as before. One eye looked as if it was glad to see me, anyway. "Well. Young Mr. Parker, is it? I was just saying to Walter the other day, 'I wonder if young Ned Parker will come back one day.' That's what I said, didn't I, Walter?"

"You did, Mr. G. Your very words."

"And here you are." He switched eyes—or at least, that was the way it looked. I was prepared for it this time though, and it didn't give me the shakes like it had before.

"Yes, I'm back, Mr. Grimes. I've been thinking over what we talked about."

"Yes, Ned, go on. Is it that crib you were thinking about?"

"Er, in a way, yes. You said the last time we talked that you handle all kinds of swag."

"We do, all kinds."

I took a deep breath. I hadn't dared mention them before but here goes, I thought.

"Have you heard about those silver candlesticks?"

Neither eye moved. It probably meant something, and I waited.

"A pair of silver candlesticks did pass through here some time ago," Swiveler said. His words were slow and cautious. "What about it?"

"Did you learn much about them?"

The thin lips twisted. "This is not the kind of business where questions get asked and answered. Is it, Walter?"

"No, indeed, Mr. G. Most of our clients require that confidences be kept."

"Exactly. Well put, Walter."

I pressed on. "I'm not asking any questions, Mr. Grimes. Well, perhaps I am but it's this. Have you had any other, er, goods from the same place as those candlesticks, and would you be interested in more?"

The pendulum clock sounded as if it was ticking louder, perhaps because it was the only sound in the room.

"We are always interested in goods of value, Ned. Won't you come to the point?"

"Yes, all right. It's like this. I might know where a lot more items like the candlesticks, a lot of them more valuable, might be found."

There, I'd said it. I knew it was risky. I waited.

Swiveler cleared his throat, but his voice was just as croaky when he said, "Ned, I said we didn't ask a lot of questions. Still, we often learn a lot about the items that pass through the auction rooms. Do you know the history of the candlesticks?"

"Just bits, here and there. Not much, really."

One eye was on me now and the other was moving off to the side. Was that the same as before? I thought it was the opposite. Perhaps Swiveler did this just to unnerve people. If he did, it worked.

"The candlesticks were brought here by a chap called Marston. He died, didn't he, Walter?"

"He did, Mr. G. Very sad."

"Yes. Well, Sir George Willoughby, the well-known philanthropist, owner of the bus line and a very generous man to charity, bought them from us and gave them, one each, to two churches. They were stolen, unfortunately, and haven't been heard of since."

He waited and I waited. "Do you know where they, Ned?"

He sneaked up on me with that sudden question, but I managed to handle it. "No, I don't know where they are, Mr. Grimes, but I do believe they are part of a great treasure. That's what I've come to ask you about."

"I see." The eyes switched, but I was getting a bit more used to them now. "Do you know where that great treasure is, Ned?"

"No, I don't, not at this moment. I expect to be able to find out soon though."

I had a strong suspicion that I knew where it was: in the tunnel that was being dug for the London Bridge Underground Railway, where Luke Marston and Dickie Drew had dug into the wreck of the *Nuestra Senora de Valencia*. Two silver candlesticks had evidently been washed through in one of the many cave-ins, and Marston and Drew had taken them to Swiveler Grimes and said nothing about them to anyone else.

How Mr. John had found out about the candlesticks, I didn't know. Nor did I know whether Mr. John's digging had unearthed the rest of the treasure, but certainly he had been able to work in peace, thanks to terrifying locals and possible intruders with ghost trains and whistles and whispering voices.

Maybe the treasure wasn't still there, was another possibility. The station was quiet according to Sergeant Jackson, so perhaps the work was done and the treasure gone, but I meant to find out if I could. If the rest of it had been brought out, there was a good possibility it had already been offered to Swiveler Grimes.

"I'll tell you the truth, Ned. I've heard some rumors, but I haven't seen any more valuables from that source since the candlesticks. If you can help me get my hands on it, you could do very handsomely out of it yourself."

So that answered that—if Grimes was telling the truth. I didn't doubt that Grimes and the truth were strangers to each other, but still, it could be true. The gleam of greed in his eye, the one not moving at the moment, said it might well be.

"Are these valuables all from the same source, Ned?"

They were in the sense that he meant the question, but I saw a good chance to mislead him a bit. "Some of the valuables are from churches, yes, but there's also jewels and some gold bars." That's what Lieutenant Waverley had told me anyway.

"Come and see me again, Ned. Don't come alone."

"What do you mean?"

"Have your cab full of valuables." He chuckled and Walter joined in. He probably always did.

Walter showed me out and I was glad to go. I had learned what I wanted to know, and I was happy to get out of the place.

On the corner of the Finchley Road and Baronsmere Road is one of the best fish and chip shops in London. It's a small place, but Reggie and Edna Merritt, who own it, would rather have a line of customers and serve good fish and chips than get a bigger place and worry about making ends meet. At lunchtime, they're not too busy, and I got a nice piece of haddock and some chips—extra ones for Perseus because he loves them. I kept his separate from mine because I like plenty of vinegar, and vinegar makes Perseus shake his head.

Brixton was a longish haul but Perseus took it steady, and he hadn't even worked up a sweat when he pulled up in front of All Hallows Church. It was an old church. This part of Brixton must have been in the country when it was built. A neat fence ran all around it, and the churchyard had some ancient looking tombstones. A few graves had flowers on them, so it was an active little parish.

The front door to the church was unlocked and I went in. It was cool and a smell of incense still hung in the air. Some nice stained glass windows sent colored beams of light across the floor and stacks of hymnbooks were carefully piled on the back seats.

A candle burned smokily, but it seemed to be the only light. When I heard movement, I started to look about me. The noise came from a few rows up, where a bloke in a black cassock got up from where he'd been kneeling. "Good afternoon," he said softly. "Welcome to All Hallows."

He came towards me. He was middle aged with a kind face. "Good afternoon, padre," I said. "My name's Parker. I wonder if I could ask you a couple of questions."

"I'm the vicar," he said. "Neville Mountjoy. How can I help you?"

I decided to take the bull by the horns. "It's about the candlestick that was stolen from your church."

"A sad business. It's dismaying to think that a man, even a thief, would take a candlestick from a church. How did you hear of it?"

"I was talking to Mr. Meecham over at Saint Mary-in-the-Fields," I explained.

"Oh, are you a parishioner there?"

"No, but my sister is."

"I see. Yes, it was really a blow to us. Such a generous gift from Sir George Willoughby, and we had the candlestick only a short time."

"So I understand. Tell me, vicar, have you had any word of it?"

"None whatever, I'm afraid. The police were very diligent, but unfortunately they were not able to retrieve it. I was talking to Canon Chesterton at Saint Mary's the other day and he said the same thing. Neither one of the candlesticks has been seen or heard of since they were stolen."

"Were the two exactly alike?" I asked.

"They were a pair," said the vicar. "Both apparently cast in the same foundry."

"Why do you think they were stolen?" I asked.

He paused. "That's an interesting question. If just one were stolen, it could be for money, for whatever it might fetch. But two—and from different churches—well, that suggests someone wanted the pair. But for what reason?"

"The police couldn't guess why?"

"Not in the visits I had from them, and I gather the fellow who was also making inquiries about them couldn't guess either."

"Who was that?" I asked innocently.

"Oh, the Bishop of Vauxhall was very concerned about the thefts. He had his nephew asking questions here and there. Fellow called Paul Worth."

"Ah, yes."

"You know him?"

"I wouldn't say I know him," I said, "but I have seen him." I didn't add that he was dead and with some nasty stab wounds in him as Dickie Drew.

The vicar seemed willing to keep on chatting. "At least," he said, "looking on the bright side, if they should turn up—by the

Grace of God—we'll be able to identify them and claim their return to us as their rightful owner."

"Really? How?"

"By the hallmark. You know what a hallmark is?"

"Oh, yes, I know a lot about hallmarks. They're like a guarantee. Some are eagles, some are castles, some helmets—all sorts of things. Hallmarks can tell you what country the piece is from, which assay office guaranteed it, and even the date it was made and the amount of pure silver in it."

"You surprise me, Mr. Parker. You are unusually well informed."

I had impressed him. I could see that. It wasn't what I had set out to do. I only wanted to let him know how interested I was in these candlesticks so that I could get everything out of him that he knew.

"What sort of a hallmark do these candlesticks have?" I asked.

"I can show you. Here . . ." He led me to the back of the church. In a little room, he got a piece of paper and a pencil and sketched the hallmark. It looked like a church steeple with some numbers, and under it was a star. It was the same star that Stan Havers had showed me when he had said it was from Peru, in South America, where they had big silver mines. It fitted with what I knew about the *Nuestra Senora de Valencia* coming from South America loaded with treasure, but it didn't explain about the thefts from churches.

We chatted on, but he didn't have any further information that was helpful. As he was walking with me out on to the front stone-flagged pathway, he asked the question I had been expecting.

"Might I inquire what is your interest in the candlesticks, Mr. Parker?"

"I'm helping the police with their inquiries," I said, using the expression that my old dad had been fond of. "Sometimes a member of the public can learn a fact or two that might not come to the attention of the police. Know what I mean?"

He probably didn't, but he nodded his head. "I see." He looked past me to where Perseus was having a good old nibble at the graveyard hedge. "You came by hansom cab," he said, a little surprised.

"I go everywhere by hansom cab," I told him, shaking his hand.

Chapter 24

Those silver candlesticks were getting to be a pain in the neck. Who had stolen them and why? Where were they now? Then there was Mr. John. He knew that I had been at the Finchley Auction House, but he had made no mention of the candlesticks. The colonel hadn't mentioned them either, and when I let out the remark about church jewelry, he didn't pick up on it and ask me about candlesticks. I wasn't sure about Swiveler Grimes. He hadn't mentioned them, but I was sure he had fenced them. When I had faced Professor Tryon with the simple words "the candlesticks," he had started to babble, saying "I can explain those."

I doubted that the police knew anything about them, because if they did Jacko would have been all over me. But surely the blasted candlesticks were the clue that set Mr. John to looking in the London Bridge Underground Railway Station and start digging. How did that happen?

I felt really pleased that Herbert was being released. But it didn't end there. His release wasn't going to stop my poking and prying. I couldn't get out of this now; I was in too deep. Both Mr. John and the colonel had me in their sights, and if I needed any other reminder that I was still in a hot spot, seeing Professor Tryon's body was it. In any case, I couldn't walk away. My natural curiosity wouldn't let me. I was nosy and I admitted it. What's more, I was going to keep on being nosy.

First thing I did next morning was to go to Hangman's

Corner and pass the word about Herbert. Every cabby would tell two or thee other cabbies. Every cabby would stop at cab ranks throughout the city, and before noon, nearly all of the six thousand cab drivers in London would know about it.

"Great news!" said Leo, pumping my hand.

"I'll tell the blokes who are going out to cover the Empire Exhibition," said Smiling Sid, "that'll cover a few hundred cabbies."

I sought out Stoker Francome. He'd been a stoker on a battleship but burned both his hands real bad. He took up cabbying when he got out of the navy. "You live near Herbert Summers," I said after I'd told him the good news. "How about making your first trip this morning over there and tell his wife? Don't suppose the police will do it."

I was chatting to a couple of other cabbies when Leo took me aside. "Remember I said I'd have a word with a friend of mine in the council offices about our application for a union?"

"Yes, I remember."

"Well, I saw him last night. He said the records have our application and a statement about the committee's decision. It said—and I wrote this down—" Leo took out a piece of paper and read, " 'The general level of behavior of cab drivers in London is reprehensible'—that means bad, Ned—'and it is recommended that higher standards be established and maintained before any further consideration of an application for a trade union.' "

"Why, the rotten so-and-so's!" I was furious. "I'd back London cabbies against longshoremen, railway men, anybody. We're better blokes than any of those, and they've got their unions!"

"They added this," Leo said and read again. " 'Cab drivers are, to a notable extent, representatives of London to visitors from outside the city, and a sense of responsibility, honesty and decorum is essential before an important step such as the sanctioning of a union can be granted.' "

"There's a bit more," said Leo, his voice serious. "It's an affidavit from a bloke complaining about a cabby running a bookie business. It gives a date, a time, places and names of a recent bet being placed. It's got your name on it."

"Let me see that." As I said it, I had a sinking in my stomach. As soon as I glanced at the paper, names leapt out at me. Marble Arch, Camden Town, Peat and Harwell, Bookmakers—and the image of a funny-looking old geezer in a high winged collar suit and a wide top hat. I handed the paper back to Leo. After one look at my face, he said, "You were set up, Ned."

I nodded glumly. "He wanted my name and my license number."

"We all make a bookie run now and again," said Leo. "Usually it's just word of mouth when anybody has a cabby deliver a bet, but this is written proof." He put the paper back in his pocket. "If it's any consolation to you, there's more still."

"It isn't," I said, "but what—?"

He avoided my eyes. "Oh, the petition refers to my being let go by the county council offices—for misconduct, they say. And poor old Sid, they haven't left him out. It says, 'Though not proven, Sidney Morris was dismissed by Gerrard, Clyster and Allison, Lawyers, for misappropriation of funds.' "

"Blimey," I said, "they got us all, didn't they?"

"Somebody's got it in for us," said Leo grimly. "I've talked to a bloke I know in the dockers' union. They had the same problem early on. Bad examples, they called 'em. Dockers who drank and got into brawls. They made out that they were typical examples."

"Terrible," I said, sarcastic as I could be. "Getting into a fight in a bar—men who do that are worse than dynamiters. It's hard to fight this kind of stuff, Leo."

"I know. But we have to. I'll talk to some pals still in the law business. They might be able to give me some ideas."

We parted to go to our own cabs.

It was a cold spring day with those gusty winds and stinging sprays of rain—the kind of weather that makes Londoners want to jump into a cab. True, they do now have the choice of the Underground, but a lot of people don't like it down there. Lots of steps going deep into the bowels of the earth, long waits on drafty platforms, breathing smoke from the engine, an uncomfortable ride in slow and jerky carriages, staring out at brick walls in the darkness. Who wants that when they could have a smooth, pleasant journey in the fresh air looking at the storefronts and the buildings and the passers by?

Naturally, we have to charge a bit more because the public's getting fast and personal service, but when the weather's like this and you want to go somewhere, the sight of a hansom trotting by is too much to resist. All of which says why I had a brisk morning.

I was still thinking of that rotten chap at Marble Arch and wished he could have kept his fifteen bob. I was also watching out for evildoers under the command of Mr. John or the colonel, but I didn't think I'd meet any. I'd had enough attention from them already.

So after a worthwhile morning, I stopped for a couple of hot potatoes at One-Armed Arthur's stand on South Park in Fulham. I've known him for years, and so did my old dad. Arthur put an extra dollop of butter and extra sprinkles of black pepper on the potatoes for me. I got one for Perseus, and he wolfed it down so fast it was like a conjuring trick.

I was directing him up towards the King's Road when a woman waved to me.

She had on a dark blue wool dress and a small blue and

white hat. She had an anxious look on her face. "Do you know where Mill Hill School is?"

"Yes, missus, I do."

"It's out of London, isn't it?"

"On the edge, you might say," I told her.

Mill Hill is about the only real "village" left in London. Some others claim to, be but Mill Hill really is. It's best known, I suppose, for Harrow, the posh public school, but Mill Hill School has a good name and it's in a nice spot, surrounded by wide lawns and groves of trees brought from tropical countries.

"My daughter's there, you see, and the headmistress wrote to me and said I should come and talk to her about my daughter's future." She looked up at me on my high perch. She was worried. "I do hope she isn't in trouble."

I hoped so too, especially after she explained.

"Mill Hill had been a school for boys only but now, on a sort of experimental basis, they are taking girls. It's older girls only—sixteen years old, they have to be. They're supposed to be more responsible at that age, you see."

I nodded sympathetically. Sixteen was also an age where boys might be more interesting to them than schoolwork. She had reason to look worried.

"I went to the bus station, but I have to make two changes to get there. That means three different buses. It would take too long. I can get back all right, that doesn't matter, but I want to be there as soon as I can this morning. How much do you charge?"

"Three bob," I said. "That's the best I can do. Three bus fares would cost you nearly two bob."

Her face brightened. "All right." She climbed in. Perseus gave a small whinny in approval of my generous offer, as well he might, for it was half of the normal fare.

We had a nice ride, with the sun popping out now and then

just to show us it was still up there. Mostly, though, it was the same gusty winds and showers. I stayed off the main traffic routes but still made good time.

As we drove into the village of Mill Hill, I pointed out Vincett's to her.

"Ooh, I've heard of that," she said.

Lots of folk say it's the best butchers in England, and customers come from all over London. The sixth generation has it now, and they say it has got better with each generation.

We passed a wide-open green field with a five-barred stile going to it. "That's a short cut the children use," I told my fare. "But don't worry. I'll take you to the main entrance."

"Thank you," she said, not familiar with my humor.

When I dropped her off, she gave me three-shilling pieces and fumbled in her purse for a tip. "No, no," I told her. "That's all right." She smiled thankfully, and I was glad I had done that. She didn't look too well-heeled, and she might have some bad news coming.

For the return journey, I kept to the main traffic roads where there was a better chance of picking up a fare. I always enjoyed going down the Great North Road, particularly when I could tell a fare from out of town that the Romans had built it. Outside Neasden Hospital, I got a husband and wife wanting to go home to Shoreditch after visiting her mother.

As they climbed in, I said, "Hope she'll be well soon."

"I don't," said the husband. "She'll be back home as soon as she is, and she lives with us." I saw the jab in the ribs his wife gave him.

I had been half looking for a fare to the Shoreditch area, and after leaving them, I set out for the London Bridge Underground Railway Station. I tied up Perseus and walked towards the steel gates. It didn't look any different than it did when Benny and me were there, though that was at night. Not many people were about. I stood and took some long looks in all directions. Nobody seemed suspicious, nor were any coppers in sight. I strolled slowly to the corner of Lower Thames Street. The old church of St. Magnus the Martyr was built by Sir Christopher Wren and is two hundred years old, though, as I tell visitors, it looks a lot older.

I remembered driving by and seeing a beggar on the steps one time. Sure enough, he was still there. He didn't look too scabby as I drew closer, and he looked up when I stopped in front of him. His legs were like pipe stems and he was thin as a rail. His eyes were clear despite his age, which must have been eighty or more.

"Spend much time here?" I asked by way of openers.

"All of it. Except I go in to mass every morning." His voice was weak.

"You can see the new Underground Station from here," I said conversationally.

He nodded.

"Is it worth a thrummer to you to answer a few questions?"

"Why?" he wanted to know. That surprised me. An offer of three pence would usually be grabbed before the words were past my teeth.

"My friends say I'm nosy," I said with a smile. I think it was the smile that did it. He held out his hand and I counted three coins into it.

"The police raided it the other day," I said.

"S'right. I watched 'em."

"They didn't find anything."

"No, they didn't. Looked real down in the mouth, they did, when they came out."

"But before that, there was a lot of stuff going on there."

"There was?"

"You know there was if you're always here," I said sternly.

"What did you see?"

He thought it over. "Seen you and that big bloke."

He saw me and Benny! "Anybody else ask you about this?"

"No. Nobody."

"What else did you see?"

"Blokes would come alone, go in there."

"How did they get in?"

"Through the gates. They had a key."

"How long were they in there?"

"Long time, most of 'em. Some didn't come out."

Was he making this up? "How could they not come out?"

"Dunno. Some others, they come out and never went in."

"Now, wait a minute," I said. "I gave you a thrummer. I expect my money's worth!"

"Givin' it you," he said with unexpected firmness. "It's the truth. Some went in, never come out. Some come out who had never gone in."

That was a stunner and no mistake. How could that be? There was only one answer. There had to be another way to get on to the platform. Of course, that made sense. I knew that some stations already built had two different ways to get in and out. That meant there was another entrance somewhere.

"These blokes you saw going in and out, were they carrying anything?"

"Think they was. It was hard to tell. Most times it was night."

I kept up the questions but didn't learn anything new. He was willing to tell me what he had seen, but he wasn't that close and it had mostly been nighttime. The one useful item, though, was that another way in and out was somewhere near, probably on another street. I gave him another thrummer and told him to keep his mouth shut if anyone else asked him questions. If the police asked, he wasn't likely to tell them a dickey bird. I thought about Mr. John and the colonel who, would have more violent ways of getting the truth. I couldn't expect him to keep silent under torture.

"At least don't tell 'em about me and the big bloke," I said, leaving. But he was busy counting and recounting the six copper pennies.

CHAPTER 25

Time went by slower than a hundred-year-old turtle with gout. But go by it did until Saturday night, and I was putting my best suit on again. It was getting more wear now than it ever had since I'd bought it three years ago. I put another splash of bay rum on my hair. It tends to stick up a bit. I ran my razor over a patch on my chin that looked a bit rough and gave my shoes another spit and an extra rub.

I gave Perseus a night off again and he looked happy about that, but perhaps he was more swayed by the carrot and the apple I gave him. I had a half bottle of Mrs. Brown's home-brewed beer left over—it had gone a bit flat—and I poured that into his water bucket. He tasted it, twitched his ears and ignored me in his haste to empty the bucket.

The arrival of a brougham to pick me up caused a bit of a stir in the neighborhood. Curtains twitched apart, folks opened their front doors a few inches to get a better look, and a couple of windows screeched open. Customers in the butcher's down below me turned their heads to goggle. The two bays pulling the brougham could smell Perseus and whinnied to him. He answered back, and I wondered what they were saying. I hoped he was telling them to take good care of me.

The driver looked posh in his uniform and held the door open. In a brougham, you can't talk to the driver as easy as you can in hansom, so we clip-clopped through London with me able to sight see, which was unusual.

The New Vaudeville Theatre had big colored banners all over the front. *Opening Soon!*, *The Finest Show in London*, and *Song, Dance, Laughs* were some of them. Several buskers were at work on the pavement in front—one doing cartwheels, one blowing fire, a juggler keeping four balls in the air, and a bright painted hurdy-gurdy churning out music while a little brown monkey jumped up and down on top of it.

A bloke in a brown and gold commissionaire's uniform asked me who I was, and found my name on his list. He stood aside and let me in.

Inside, the theatre was nearly full of people, on the stage and up and down the aisles, while some were sitting in the seats. An orchestra was playing, though you could hardly hear the music over the babble of voices. A lot of people were in stage costumes. An elegant young man with a rouged face and in a milk-white tunic and salmon-colored trousers fluttered his kerchief at me as he hurried by, and a couple in Pierrot costumes was trying to dance to the orchestra but finding the aisle crowded.

At a bar at the back of the stage three perspiring bartenders poured champagne. Another bar had been set up at the top of each of the aisles. I was about to move in the direction of the nearest when a familiar voice said, "Why, Ned, how handsome you look!"

Dorothy was wearing a gown that took my breath away. It fitted like it had been poured on to her, and looked to be made of gold threads. She wore delicate golden slippers with long toes and very high heels and had a gold bracelet on each wrist. Round her neck, she wore a band of very fine gold wire, woven tight. In her silvery blond hair was a narrow tiara that gleamed gold, and she had a gold earring in each ear.

"You look like you're worth a million pounds," I told her. If all that decoration was real gold, I'd bet my assessment wouldn't be far off.

"It's a duplicate," she said, "you know—a copy of one the Duchess of Devonshire wore. You know who she was?"

"Think I read about her in the papers," I said.

"I'm sure you did. She was the mistress of our late King William the Fourth."

"Oh," said I, at a loss for words for once.

"I always considered her a brazen hussy, but for an occasion like this, I thought this gown was appropriate." She twirled round slowly, holding out her arms. She looked gorgeous. "Do you think it fits me all right?" she asked, lowering her voice in spite of the noise around us.

I had to swallow before replying. She smiled wickedly, seeing where I was looking. "Yes, it does," I said, "especially at the back."

She faced me and took a step closer. "You don't think the front fits?" she whispered.

I looked down at her breasts, perfect mounds, almost touching me.

"It's a perfect fit."

She laughed, a tinkling laugh of satisfaction. "Ned, you always know the right thing to say." She grasped my hand. "Let's get you some champagne."

We pushed through a knot of people, evidently actors and actresses because they were talking loudly about sets and cues. Champagne fizzed and bubbled into glasses, and Dorothy touched her glass to mine. "Here's to us," she whispered, and at that moment, if she'd told me to hold my nose and jump in the Thames, I would have done it.

"You say the show's nearly ready to open?" I said, recovering my speech.

"Yes. It needs a little sharpening up and we need bring in a couple more songs, but it's almost there. Millie's great, by the way," she added, casual-like.

"I'm glad," I said.

"She and Ivor make a good team and—oh, there she is! Have you said hello to her yet?"

"No, I just came in."

She took my hand again and pulled me through to call out, "Millie! Having a good time?"

Millie looked younger than I had ever seen her. Perhaps it was the simple, pale blue muslin dress with dark blue tucks. Her hair was cut a bit shorter. "Hello, Ned," she said and waved a hand at a young man who was evidently with her. "This is Simon."

She didn't need to explain that he was an actor. He had tweezed eyebrows and his lips were too red for nature. He was wearing a yellow shirt with two rows of frills up and down each half of the front. His pants were tight—too tight—and made of a shiny, light brown material. His high buckle shoes had gemstones on the tops. He smelled nice, though. I didn't know that men wore perfume, not even actors. He nodded to me without interest.

"How's the boating number coming along, Simon?" Dorothy asked crisply.

"I think it's ready," he pouted, "but Mr. Morton wants more rehearsals."

"You must have heard of Charles Morton, Ned," said Dorothy. "He opened the Oxford Music Hall that was so successful. He was going to open another one, but we persuaded him to produce this show for us first."

"He's a demon to work for," Simon complained. "He wants too much from us."

I nodded. I had heard the name. Probably everybody in London had.

"He is a bit of a slave driver," Dorothy said sweetly, "but you'll be a better performer after he's had you a while."

"I'll be too worn out to perform," whined Simon.

Millie squeezed his arm. "Not too worn out, I hope," she murmured, and he gave her a weak smile.

On the stage, something caught my eye—it also made me catch my breath. A couple in white robes like Romans wore— togas, I think they call them—moved across the front of the stage and blocked my view. For a moment, I wasn't sure what I had seen.

"What's the matter, Ned?" asked Dorothy. "See someone you know?"

I moved up to get a clearer view and for one second, I saw him again. A man wearing a clown costume and with a painted mask over his face. It was the costume that Mr. John had worn when he had questioned me in the dressing room in the back of the Gaiety Music Hall.

Dorothy was asking me the question again.

"The man in the clown costume!" I said. "Who is he?"

She craned her head to see the stage. More people were coming in and there were more cramming the aisles. "I don't see him," she said. "Where—?"

"I can't see him either now," I said. "Too many people in the way."

"A clown costume, you say?"

"Yes."

"They're a common fancy dress," she said, matter-of-factly. "Must be scores of them in London."

I kept on looking but I couldn't see him, not even when the people there moved.

"Thought it looked like a man I know," I said. "Doesn't matter."

"Let me get you some more champagne." She moved close to take my glass and I was aware again of how extraordinarily attractive she was.

"What is it?" she asked, amused.

"You notice everything, don't you?" I was a little embarrassed at how easily she could read my thoughts.

She smiled as she brushed past me to refill my glass. Millie and Simon had gone and I couldn't see them. Two girls with wings went by. I guess they suppose they were supposed to look like angels, but I didn't know angels wore skirts that short.

A chap with a sad-looking face turned and gave me a nod. "Want to talk to you. I need more light on my face."

"You do?"

"Yes, I do. You're not giving me nearly enough." He had a pint glass of beer in his hand. It was nearly empty, and from the look of him, it wasn't his first.

"I don't think I—"

"Yes, you can." He hiccupped. "Just turn up that knob at the side of the klieg. It's easy." He took a big swallow.

"I'm not—"

"Yes, you are going to!" He waved the now-empty glass at me. "It's not fair. The girls get plenty of light. Just because I'm a comedian, why do you think I don't need light?"

"I'm not with the theatre."

He frowned at me. "Yes, you are. You're the lighting electrician."

"No, I'm not."

He looked closer. "You look just like him."

"I'm not," I said. "I'm a . . . I'm in the transport business."

He hiccupped again. "Not a lighting electrician?"

"No, never have been."

He shook his head. "I need more light. Know where the lighting electrician is?"

"No but if I run into him, I'll tell him you're looking for him."

He nodded, staggered, then moved away, swaying slightly.

A girl appeared in front of me. "Are you in the new show?"

"No, I'm not," I said. She was pretty, with long black hair and wearing a gypsy costume. "Are you?"

"I'm not in the show here, I'm in the other one, over at the Apollo," she said. "Third lead, trying to get to be second."

"I hear this one is going to be a big hit," I said.

"They all are till opening night," she said, sipping a green colored drink.

"Have you been in a lot of them?"

"The last three. Tried out for the Saint James last month, but no luck."

"You don't like it here?" I asked.

She made a face. "It's all right, but they work you real hard. Get no time to myself."

Dorothy came back with a champagne glass in each hand. The girl looked alarmed as Dorothy handed one of the glasses to me. "Ooh, sorry, Mrs. Radcliffe," she said and squeezed into the crowd.

"Ned!" said Dorothy. "Can't leave you alone for minute, can I?"

"She was saying she's the third lead. Hopes to get to be second."

"She never will be. Not enough push and drive," said Dorothy. "If she doesn't pay more attention at rehearsals, she'll be back in the chorus." She nodded towards the stage. "See who's up there?"

It was easy to see who she meant. A big man with long, wavy hair, parted in the middle, full cheeks and uneven teeth was talking, and a small group was pressing close to listen. His shirt was very long in the arm and was turned back over his coat sleeves. The stage was more full than before, but this man stood out.

"It's Oscar Wilde," Dorothy said. "You've heard of him, Ned?"

"Writes plays," I said, having heard Millie talk about him, but I didn't mention that. "He's Irish and has the gift of gab."

Dorothy laughed. "That he does. Oscar talks like others write or paint. Talking is an art with him. He has no equal at it."

"Does he write plays for you?"

She looked thoughtful. "You have a good eye, Ned. No, he doesn't, but I would like to get him to do so. I must make that my challenge. It's time to start moving away from musicals."

I thought about Millie, singing and dancing. "You don't think musicals are going to be popular anymore?"

"Oh, they will. Of course they will. But a lot of people want the witty, clever plays that Oscar writes. Especially when it combines another element, in the way that his play *Salome* does."

"What element is that?" I asked.

She looked into my eyes. "Sex, Ned."

"Ah."

"You haven't read *Salome,* have you?"

"I don't think we had it at the Catholic school I went to."

She chuckled. "I'm quite sure you didn't. I'll have to give you a copy."

"I'll read it."

"I have some other books you might like to read too. I didn't know you were a reader, Ned."

"The nuns at Saint Anselm's School had us reading all kinds of books, and I still like to read when I have time."

"Not *all* kinds surely!"

"No, perhaps not all," I agreed.

Somebody bumped into me from behind and I would have spilled my champagne, but luckily I had drunk most of it. I noticed Dorothy trying to look over people's heads. She must have seen something, for she turned to me suddenly and her whole manner changed.

"It's getting too noisy here, Ned. Let's go somewhere quieter, shall we?"

I was prepared to stay and meet more actors and actresses, maybe even have a word with Mr. Oscar Wilde, but I was under her spell. "All right," I said.

She was looking around again. A big bloke—looked he might have been a prize fighter at one time—pushed his way through the crowd and came up to her. He said a few words into her ear. I looked at the bloke. I thought I had seen him before and decided it was probably at the Doll's House, where he was one of the bouncers.

He began to push his way into the crowd. If that didn't get them out of the way, one look at his build and punched-up face caused them to step smartly aside. A brougham was at the door, two handsome horses and a driver at the ready.

We climbed in, Dorothy rapped on the partition and we set off.

CHAPTER 26

The brougham driver was good. He kept up a steady pace and hardly ever stopped, but knew how to slow ahead of a traffic-clogged area and how to speed up a little when the way was clear. Turning corners, he knew just how fast it was safe to go without tilting. I liked the way he handled two horses. It wasn't an easy thing to keep them in step with each other and keep one from pulling ahead of the other.

Dorothy snuggled close. "I'm feeling amorous tonight, Ned," she whispered, and she began to prove it. I get a lot of couples in my hansom who feel that way late at night, and I always feel like apologizing to them. The cab of a hansom is just not big enough for couples to do what couples want to do. A brougham is a little bigger, but it's the shape, if you know what I mean. It just wasn't designed for that.

We came close, but we were trying to come closer when we both had a breather. Actually, we were gasping for air. Bright lights flickered past the window. I stared at them and Dorothy pulled me back to her. I tried to struggle up. "Where's this bloke taking us? This isn't the way to Shepherd's Market, to the Doll's House!"

"Who said anything about going to the Doll's House?" Her hands were still busy.

"I thought you did."

"No, I didn't say that."

"Then where are we going?"

She sounded annoyed as she snapped, "We're going to a celebration. Now pay attention!"

I was still trying to pay attention, but it was only a few minutes later when the clip-clop slowed, then slowed some more, and we stopped. Dorothy swore, then forgot me as she struggled to get everything back into place. The driver called out and Dorothy snarled, "I know! I know!"

The driver opened the door and held it for us. Dorothy stepped out and I followed. We were in a dark street with no lights visible except in the distance.

"Where's the celebration?" I asked. Dorothy made no answer. The driver went ahead of us to what looked like a storefront that had been boarded up. He seemed to be measuring, then he reached for one of the cracked boards and pressed on it. A whole section swung open on silent hinges, bigger than a big door. Blackness yawned inside, but the driver reached on to the wall behind the door and turned up an oil lamp.

I looked up the street to where lights could be seen. They had a familiar pattern, and I knew they were on London Bridge. That meant that we were now about to go down into what I had looked for and hadn't been able to find.

The other entrance to the London Bridge Underground Railway Station.

Lamps flickered as we went deeper down the steps. I was jittery about what was happening, but any thoughts concerning doing anything else were out of the question.

The driver—he looked more like a bruiser now—hung behind us and blocked any retreat. Reluctantly, I followed Dorothy down the steps. She was tripping merrily away, just like one of her leading ladies on the staircase at the theatre.

It was a long way down, and Dorothy was too far ahead for me to ask any questions. Behind me was the driver/bruiser. I could see the platform now, and then Dorothy was on it. talking to someone, but her voice echoed and I couldn't make out the words.

Over my shoulder, I could see the driver. He was close but staying far enough away that I had no choice but to go on down. I remembered this descent from our previous visit—Benny and me. At one end, the tunnel mouth was blocked with a fall of rock. Two men were pulling at the rocks.

But they weren't. Something was wrong. Their hands were coming away empty. As I watched, they pulled at some ropes, and the rock face looked to be disappearing. What had looked like a big pile of rocks was really a huge tarpaulin with rocks painted on it. The weak lighting when Benny and I had been there before had made it seem all too real.

Some kind of celebration was getting started. A long table had a white tablecloth on it with lots of food and bottles of champagne in buckets of ice. The platform certainly wasn't as crowded as the New Vaudeville Theatre had been, but there were nine or ten men and nearly as many women. All wore costumes, and they looked like the same costumes I had seen at the theatre. I supposed they had come from there.

Dorothy had recovered her good spirits and beckoned to me to join her. "So what is the celebration?" I asked again as I did so. She glanced along the platform. Two men stood, looking into the mouth of the tunnel at that end. "You'll see in just a moment," she told me.

Some of the others were talking. Everybody seemed to be waiting. The air was charged with excitement. Suddenly, all conversation stopped. A light crunching could be heard. It seemed to come out of one of the tunnels, and all heads spun that way. The crunching continued. It sounded like footsteps traveling on gravel. Something appeared out of the tunnel, and there was utter silence.

It was a giant frog. It came into the station, a horrible creature, waddling like a duck, but erect like a man. It came on with slow plodding footsteps, then it climbed, painstakingly slowly, up the iron steps at the end and on to the platform. It came towards us.

It stopped and stood swaying slightly, dripping water. Two of the bruisers ran forward and each took a grip at the sides of the head. Two huge bulbous eyes stared forward. Then the two men gave a wrench, and the head came off.

Except it was a helmet. It was a diving helmet, and the two huge eyes were big lenses. Clips were unfastened and catches released. The upper half of the diving suit fell away, leaving pools of water. Then the great clumsy boots were pulled off, and then the pants. "Judas Priest!" said the diver. "What a relief!"

Another man had gone forward. "Is it all out?" he asked.

"All we can get," said the diver, breathing as deeply as if the musty air in the tunnel were summer wine.

Everyone froze. A whispering had started. It was quiet at first, then got louder. It seemed to come from everywhere and fill the station. It faded rapidly as a gust of air rushed out of the tunnel and dust swirled along the tracks between the platforms. The sound of a train whistle split the air, not too loud at first, but getting louder until it seemed like it would pierce our eardrums. A roll of thunder burst from the tunnel, and the whistle died away.

Out of the tunnel came a train, a black and orange monster with wheels six feet in diameter and flashing pistons. Steam spurted from under it, and some of the women on the platform screamed and shrank back.

The train was not moving fast, but its size was frightening. The massive pistons slowed, and the wheels screeched on the shiny new rails as they fought to get a grip. It was a breathtaking sight though, and nearly all else was forgotten as the train slowly rolled to a standstill. A bit of a cheer went up.

Dorothy turned to the steps. Others were coming down them and on to the platform. We had not heard them due to the excitement. One of the approaching figures captured my attention though.

I thought I had seen him on the stage at the theatre, but then he had disappeared. Now here he was—in the same clown suit. It was Mr. John.

Behind the train was a small wagon. Two men in overalls jumped down from the locomotive and went back to the wagon. They pulled away a cover, and a gasp went up—and no wonder. The view was dazzling: gold and silver cups and bowls, baskets of jewels, belts, and tiaras glittering with stones, sparkling diamonds, blood red rubies.

Everyone moved closer to get a better look. The sight was magnificent, like the sun. "Aren't they beautiful!" said a woman's voice. It was a familiar voice, and it belonged to one of the group that had come in with Mr. John. It was Millie.

I was not the only one to recognize the voice. "Millie!" said Dorothy in astonishment. "What are you doing here?"

We both saw why she was there in the next moment. Standing beside her was Ivor Dunstan.

"Why did you bring her, you fool?" cried Dorothy furiously.

Ivor looked at her as if he didn't understand. He swayed unsteadily, and Dorothy spat her words at him, "You're drunk, you stupid idiot!"

Mr. John took in the scene, but without comment. Instead, he walked to the wagon and began picking up items one by one, examining them, nodding his head now and then. It was a strange sight, the clown and the treasure. I felt a bit of a chill.

Some men I had never seen before were moving in now to get a close look at the treasure wagon. Mr. John waved for them to come and join him. They were all well dressed, I noticed. What did I have to lose? I moved in too. Everybody was fingering the bracelets and the tiaras. I did too. The gold and the jewels were such an attraction that nobody took any notice of me.

Mr. John was talking with one of the men, a small dark-faced, wizened cove. They were talking about ingots and bars and carrots. Mr. John was nodding. Another man, one of the prosperous looking characters, was asking a question. The little bloke and Mr. John were shaking their heads at him and looking as if his question was silly.

A hand grasped my arm. It was Millie's. She looked scared and puzzled. "What's going on, Ned?" she asked.

"It's a long story," I said, "but put it in a nutshell and it's like this. A Spanish treasure ship got blown into the Thames by a storm a long time ago and sank. Lots of people have looked for it, but now, somebody's found it."

"But what has this got to do with us?"

"Nothing, really," I said, trying to sound as breezy as I could. "We're just innocent bystanders, like they say in the papers. Anyway, what are you doing here?"

"Ivor saw Mrs. Radcliffe and some others leave. He got a cab and we followed." She hesitated. "Ivor's had a bit too much to drink."

He was still standing where Millie had left him. He swayed a bit, and his eyes were only half open. I looked for Dorothy and saw her talking and laughing with a skinny bloke with an aristocratic face.

Mr. John was beckoning. Was it to us? Yes, it was, and Millie held on to my arm as we went up to him. He left the other blokes. They had been joined by a couple more people, and

242

they were all having a good chinwag.

Mr. John asked Millie, "Aren't they beautiful, my dear?" He didn't have that little black box that had changed his voice when he had talked to me at the Gaiety Theatre. I supposed he was using his normal voice now. Did it have a vaguely familiar sound to it?

Millie nodded. For some reason, she had regained her usual confidence and no longer seemed nervous. "Yes, they are. You were right when you said you'd have a big surprise for me." She saw my questioning look. "We talked on the stage earlier this evening," she explained to me. I had a sinking feeling in the stomach. That meant that Mr. John had planned for her to be here. But why?

"I was telling Millie about our celebration, Ned. It's true, I did refer to a big surprise. It is, isn't it? Well worth the great effort that has been put into finding these attractive baubles and bringing them out from their resting place of centuries. Wouldn't you agree, Ned?"

Yes, but not worth human lives, I wanted to say. Unfortunately, I was having doubts about being here at all. I didn't like the way the evening was going. Even worse, I didn't know what to do about it. A nod was the wisest reply.

"Quite an achievement for a clown, don't you think?" he asked.

I gave him the nod.

"You have probably wondered who all these people are. Each one has contributed in some measure to the success of this venture. The two there—" He motioned to two of the prosperous looking blokes. "—they are both on the city council and have been very helpful in keeping everything moving along, more or less smoothly. One of them is on the London transport committee, and he has been able to push through legislation to have work stopped on this station so that we could continue uninterrupted." The clown mask concealed Mr. John's face, but the voice gave away the smirking satisfaction in his words.

"The other is the Council's liaison with the police department. He informed us of an intention to send an investigation team down here to see what was behind the stories of ghost trains, giant frogs and so on. We were able to get the platform restored to normal long enough to allow them to do the inspection and conclude that all was satisfactory."

He turned, surveying the platform. "Oh, and there's Martin Gresham." He indicated a small man with a big head and a lot of hair. "He's the supervisor of the digging team. I was inclined to have him permanently removed, but I learned that he had a severe financial problem due to a gambling habit. Dorothy persuaded him to come to the Doll's House and, do you know, he lost even more! We offered him a lifeline—just money, but it saved his life, although he never knew it."

He looked past the gambler. "The lean gentleman there." He pointed to the skinny bloke with Dorothy. "He's on Her Gracious Majesty's Commission for Combating Crime and Corruption. He's been very helpful to us." He sighed. "He's expensive, but he is helpful."

Millie was frowning, confused by all this. I hoped she was going to keep her mouth shut. The future looked grim enough as it was without some out-of-place remark from her.

"The small, dark-faced gentleman is prominent on the metals exchange," Mr. John went on, determined to make the most of his hour of triumph. "He will be handling the bulkier, heavier items, the gold and silver ingots—"

"Aren't you putting everything in a museum?" Millie blurted out. She could have said something worse.

The mask hid an obvious smile. "We will have to see which treasures will go to a museum and which might be saleable. You will understand that I have had significant expenditures in putting this business enterprise together. Naturally, I intend to recover those expenses if I can."

I'm sure you will, I thought. If one small diamond finds its way into a museum, I'll eat my shirt. Millie was nodding, a little dazed. I hoped she stayed that way.

Mr. John pulled at the collar of his outfit with a finger. "Warm down here," he said. "It's this costume."

He peeled off the mask and pulled away the tunic.

I gaped at his face.

CHAPTER 27

He smiled, amused. "Now you see why I kept my identity from you," he said.

I did.

Millie said, "You know him?"

"Oh, yes. It's not the first time I've seen his face."

"I think Ivor needs you," Mr. John said to Millie. Ivor certainly needed someone—to hold him up. Millie looked uncertain, then ran to him. Mr. John nodded, smiling.

"Charming young lady," he said.

"What do you intend to do with her?"

He didn't answer.

"She doesn't know what any of this is about," I said.

"But unfortunately, you do," he said. His red, well-fed face had the same expression it had when he had presided over the meeting of the Hearing Committee of Her Majesty's Home Office. The one where our petition for starting a trade union for cab drivers had been denied.

One of the prosperous-looking blokes came to us. "Sir George, the gold ingots. What do you intend to—"

"I'll be with you in a moment," Mr. John said in a tone of sharp dismissal.

The bloke nodded and left.

"He called you Sir George," I said.

"Sir George Willoughby, yes."

"You're the bloke who donated the candlesticks to the

churches." I could hardly believe it.

"That's right. Then I was obliged to have them stolen back." My bewilderment must have been obvious to him. "Oh, you didn't work out this part? You see, I donated the candlesticks—a quixotic gesture, but it's the kind of thing I liked to do. It's so good for the image. It was then that I learned about the galleon. It wouldn't do for me to be associated with the candlesticks once people began finding out about the galleon, so I simply had them stolen."

"The hallmarks would have given them away."

"Ah, you know about those, do you?"

He beamed at a couple who had come to marvel at the jewels, then he went on.

"The Bishop of Vauxhall sent his nephew, that fellow Paul Worth, to find out who had taken them. He was getting too close for comfort and I had to . . . well, you know about that."

"Luke Marston and Dickie Drew knew too much too, I suppose."

"They did. And they got greedy. They reasoned—correctly—that after their digging machine had cut into the *Nuestra Senora,* once they had found the two candlesticks, there must be more where they came from and they wanted a share of it."

"The professor," I said. "Did he get greedy too?"

He smiled and shook his head. "Not at all. The professor wasn't interested in jewels or gold or money. He wanted to be known as the man who told the whole exciting story to the world. Well, I mean, I couldn't allow that, could I?"

I looked up and down the platform. "You have a lot of people involved in this now. Aren't you afraid one of them will—"

He puffed his lips out. "It doesn't matter now. The treasure is out, and tonight Doll and I'll be on my boat with it and heading off to . . . well, you don't need to know."

"Doll?"

"Dorothy. I call her Doll. When I bought her that place, I named it after her."

"Doll's House?"

"Of course." He laughed at my expression. "There's a lot you don't know after all, isn't there? You realize, of course, that I told her to get you drunk the night before your hearing? She didn't make a good enough job of it. Still, you did look awful. Anyway, it didn't matter. I had fixed you as a bookie runner just to be sure."

"You did that too?"

"Yes, and both of your colleagues had criminal records so it made it easy."

"We deserve a union!" I blazed at him. "And they're not criminals!"

He ignored that. "One more fact you don't know. At the hearing, I told you that the London bus service is expanding from seven hundred buses and adding twelve hundred more. I don't want any competition from a cab service strengthened by a union."

"Buses?" Another light came on. "You own the Willoughby Bus Line!"

"Of course. You're probably wondering why I'm leaving it all and going to a foreign country. Well, I've had enough of it all. Time to take it easy and roll in real luxury. In . . . well, in a certain European country."

"Is Dorothy—Doll—going with you?"

"Certainly. Got a fancy for her, have you? A lot of men have. She's good at what she does, isn't she?"

I could see her talking and waving her hands. She looked wonderful and had three men around her, all listening. I should have known she had no real interest in me. Ned, I said to myself, you have a lot to learn about women.

Sir George's well-fed face and all these particulars were annoying me more and more. He saw it, and a movement of his hand brought one of his bruisers up behind me.

"So what about Millie?" I wasn't sure I wanted to know, but I had to ask.

"I haven't decided yet," he said, as if Millie wasn't important. He looked me in the eye. "I had Dorothy tell Ivor Dunstan to bring her here in case I need her as a hostage to keep you in line. Worth was an annoyance, Marston and Drew were nuisances, the professor was a problem, but you have been far more exasperating. Too bad you are so inquisitive."

"I'm glad," I said. "I wish I could have been more inquisitive."

He shrugged. "I suppose so. Ah, well, too late now. Goodbye, Ned. Time for you to join all the others." He nodded to the bruiser behind me who had moved so close that I could feel his breath. He was a lot bigger and heavier than me. He twisted my right arm up behind my back and pinned my other arm to my side. The agony was intense, and I knew that if I resisted, he could easily break my arm.

He took me along the platform. We probably looked like two pals, arm in arm.

A discussion was being held over the treasure wagon, and more people had joined in. It got a lot more attention than my plight. I stumbled up the steps and tried to trip deliberately, but the bruiser twisted my arm tighter.

Every step was painful but we finally reached the top. It wasn't far to the river where too many men had ended up already.

A ghostly white fog drifted in from the street. It was cold and damp as we stepped into it. It must have only just sprung up and was patchy. One second we could see nothing, and the next we could see across the street. My arms were aching and painful, and when he suddenly released me, it was a shock.

"Make a run for it," the bloke said in a low voice. "Quick!"

I was rubbing my arms, trying to get the circulation back. "What?" I asked, baffled. "Why?"

"I'm one of the colonel's men. I do as Mr. John tells me so I can tell the colonel, but I'm not going to nobble a bloke for him."

"The colonel told me he wanted to get a man into Mr. John's gang—" I started to say, but he hissed, "Get going!"

As he said it, another figure came out of the fog. A voice grated, "You letting this bloke go? What's the idea? You—"

The next second, the two of them were at grips with each other, but the newcomer had the advantage. I saw the flash of a knife, and the chap who had turned me loose gave a horrible gasp and collapsed on the pavement.

It all happened so fast, I had no chance to move. The bloke reached out for me with one hand, the other holding the knife out. It was big and ugly looking. Was it the knife that had caused all those nasty wounds I had seen in police morgues?

"You'd better come with me, mate," he said.

I shrank instinctively from the knife, and he made another grab for me. I sidestepped and realized that we were still at the top of the long stairway. As he came again, I gave him a swift kick on the shin. It caught him right on the bone and he yelped in pain, but I didn't wait for that. I may not be much of a fighter, but I'm fast. I gave him a push sideways. Off balance, his foot missed the top step and he went tumbling down.

Thump, thump, thump, he bumped down the steps. I couldn't see him, but I could hear him. Sooner or later, someone down there would hear him too, and I had no time to waste. I bent for a fast look at the bloke who had saved me, but the knife man had known his business, and the poor bloke was dead.

I raced off into the fog. My arms still ached, but there was nothing wrong with my legs. Through the clear patches in the fog, I could see the lights up at London Bridge, and I kept going towards them. A great black shape rumbled past me, but I couldn't see it clearly. Some kind of vehicle, I supposed, but it was going the opposite way, so it was no help.

I pounded on. My breath was coming in gulps but I kept going. The fog was thicker as I got nearer the Thames, but I didn't mind that. If anybody was behind me, it would be harder to see me. At last I reached London Bridge. Some traffic was coming off it on to Tooley Street, and I had to stop at the curb. A wagon, then a late-night bus went by, and I was just about to set off across the street when a wonderful sight came towards me.

A hansom cab! From its casual speed, it had no fare. I jumped off the pavement, waving my arms.

"Sorry, guv!" called out a cheery voice. "Done for the day, off home!"

I kept on waving and started shouting, too. The cab slowed and stopped. Well, it had to, so as not to run over me. "Blimey, guv, be careful! I nearly—"

I knew that voice. "Titch, stop!" I shouted. "Titch, it's me, Ned Parker!"

"Strewth!" The driver leaned out. Titch Rodgers is a little bloke. That's why they call him Titch. "Ned? Whatcher doin' out here?"

I pulled open the cab door and scrambled in. "Drive!" I yelled.

He was still staring at me, confused. "Drive! Just drive!" I shouted again, and he cracked his whip and we shot off into the fog.

He was only a few years older than me, was Titch. He'd been a tearaway as a kid and got into all kinds of trouble. Then his mother died of pneumonia and it changed him. He worked hard shoveling coal at one of the depots on the river, then got a job cabbying. He was lucky because his master was a nice bloke and treated him well. He didn't really know London at first, but he was a smart kid and a fast learner.

Titch had sensed right away that I was in some kind of trouble. He drove for a couple of minutes to get out of the area, then he slowed down and pulled in at the side of Tooley Street. An occasional wagon rumbled through the fog.

"What's goin' on, Ned? Coppers after you?"

"Quite the reverse," I said. I had heard Leo use that expression once. "Some rampsmen are after me and I *want* the coppers!"

"Criminy!" he said. "That's a turn-up for the book!"

"Not only that, Titch, but I need your cab."

"Godstruth! 'Ere, Ned, I don't know as how I—"

"No time to explain, but it's a matter of life and death."

"Whose?" Titch wanted to know.

"Mine. And you know I wouldn't ask if I wasn't desperate."

He hesitated, then—bless him—said, "All right, Ned, seeing as it's you. Can't think what sort of trouble you've got yourself into. But all right. Just one favor though. I was goin' home. I just live over on Tanner Street. Can you let me off there?"

"Where's the nearest blue lamp?"

"It's at the end of Tanner Street, but—"

"I'll leave you off there. Tell the coppers there to get hold of Detective Sergeant Jackson. Tell Jacko to get some men and go to Sir George Willoughby's private boat. It's called *Lady of Gloucester*. Where would it be, Titch? You'd know. It's not far, that's all I can tell you."

"Surrey Docks," Titch said promptly. "A few private boats there, next to the sufferance wharves. Nowhere else till you get way out to Erith."

"Right, tell him that. And tell him Mr. John and his gang are getting away with a treasure—"

" 'Odsblood!"

"—as well as several murders." Another thought struck me. "Any cabbies live near you?"

"Edgar. Pal of mine. Lives a few doors down."

"Roust him out. Tell him the story and have him tell it to Stanley Havers at the Silver Vaults by the London Wall."

"I don't know if—"

"Get going, Titch!"

After I had left Titch off, I cracked the whip over Esmee's head. I don't know how he could get away with calling her that. I knew it wasn't his wife's name. She was a young horse and a bit frisky, but she was strong. Breezes were blowing to and fro across the river, and the fog swirled, sometimes thick, so I couldn't go too fast. I headed east and on to Jamaica Road.

It's a bad area with all manner of ruffians, but I was fairly safe in a cab. Anyway, I had no choice. This was the only way to the Surrey Docks. Now that I was on my way, I had time to think. Just what was I going to do when I got there? Worst that could happen was that the coppers either wouldn't come or it would take too long for them to get there. Stanley and his security people at the Silver Vaults might not get the message. Did that place stay open at night? I didn't know, but I thought a watchman at least would be there.

The best I could do was keep an eye on the boat once I found it and hope somebody would to come. The more I thought about that, the crazier it sounded. Still, I was committed now, and I kept Esmee trotting at a steady pace.

A loud noise sounded behind me and then a great black monster came racing up and began to overhaul me. Esmee quivered and neighed and edged over.

It was a hearse, the biggest I had ever seen, an enormous vehicle.

At this time of night? Going at that speed?

As it passed me, I glanced over. Two men were sitting up on the driving seats. I recognized their faces as belonging to a couple of the bruisers I had seen on the platform.

I also recognized the vehicle as the one that had passed me when I was making my escape. It had been going in the wrong direction. Otherwise I might have waved it down. Good thing I hadn't, or they might have been able to really use it as a hearse.

I held my breath and kept Esmee on a steady track. The monster went on past me and into the fog, and I let out my breath.

Well, I would have no problem finding the boat! Follow that hearse, was all I had to do!

CHAPTER 28

A hearse was a clever idea for getting the treasure of the *Nuestra Senora* to Sir George's boat. It was big enough, and nobody would question it. The way they were driving it now might raise a few eyebrows, but it was after hours and they were lucky, as the fog was hiding it. Folks were out on Jamaica Road despite the late hour. They always were, but there wasn't much traffic.

Here came more wheels. Though. I could hear a vehicle much heavier than my hansom coming up on me fast. I eased back on the reins and Esmee obliged. It was a brougham and it looked like . . . It was. It was the same one I had been in with Dorothy.

In it was a man and a woman. It was too dark to see their faces, but I had no doubt they were Dorothy and Sir George.

I kept my face turned away, just in case. The brougham gained and as it did, we both went into some really thick fog. I slowed Esmee some more and pulled as far over as I dared, holding my breath. When we came out of the fog, the brougham had passed me and was pulling away fast.

I kept a good distance behind as we rolled along Jamaica Road. I breathed again.

A pub had lots of lights. I could see the name, The Cat and the Fiddle, and a yellow and red sign hung out in front. I knew it, a very popular place. We went on, Jamaica Road widening. People were still out, a fair number of them probably not wanting the law to know what they were up to. The wind was blustery, sending the fog swirling.

Esmee trotted along, keeping a good pace. Titch had a good horse here. She could hit up a rattling pace when she was pushed, and responded even to me, a stranger to her.

See, the thing is, a proper cab horse becomes close to its driver. It knows his touch, and the two of them become close, they can almost read each other's mind. When a newcomer's touch on the reins and the whip shows up, a horse will react one of two ways. It will either refuse completely to do what the driver's signals tell it to do, or it will realize that the new driver has had a nod to go ahead from its own driver, and it will then do as it's told. Esmee was smart enough to agree that my touch was that of a driver approved by Titch.

Lucky for me; otherwise she could have just dug in her heels—well, her hooves—and not budged an inch. Instead, we were sailing along Jamaica Road, slipping in and out of fog banks, and once in a while catching a glance of the brougham ahead. We were able to stay far enough behind that we were not likely to be seen. I was just feeling pleased with myself when I got a nasty shock.

Esmee slackened her pace and edged a bit closer to the pavement on the left. Why did she do that? was the immediate question on my mind. The answer came at once.

Another brougham was about to overtake us.

In the darkness and the fog I couldn't be certain, but it looked just like the vehicle that was in front of us. Or was it? Had it somehow given us the slip, pulled off to let us go by, and was now coming up on us?

I was still trying to work out the answer to that when the driver must have used his whip. His vehicle put on a burst of speed and came racing past us. It was close, less than a foot away, and I had time to get a quick view of the driver. He was a man I didn't recognize. But I did recognize the man sitting alongside him. It was Blinker, Mr. John's head bruiser. Both were staring ahead into the fog.

The rumble of the brougham's wheels were a dull thunder, and then the vehicle was pulling past us. Esmee was smart enough to drop her speed, lacking any other instruction from me, and the brougham shot ahead into a thick grayish white cloud. It was moving fast, but not so fact that I wasn't able to catch a lightning look into the carriage of the brougham. It was packed full of human shapes. As Blinker was sitting up front with the driver, it wasn't difficult to reach the conclusion that the brougham's load was at least a half dozen of Mr. John's bruisers.

I was still worried about Millie. My main hope was that Mr. John had a lot of more important problems than her, but I hadn't liked the way he'd said that he had talked to her on the stage at the New Vaudeville. He hadn't made it clear whether he had planned for her to be brought to the underground station or not. I could only trust in Ivor to take care of her, and I wasn't too happy about that. I hadn't had that good a look in any of the vehicles that had passed me, but I hadn't seen any sign of her, although that might be because of the fog and the darkness.

Warehouses lined both sides of the road as went farther into the heart of dockland.

We must be passing Wapping now, on the other side of the river. We would be at the Surrey Docks within the next ten minutes. I waited until we came into another clear patch, then I urged Esmee into a gallop. The rear of a brougham loomed up just visible ahead, and I slowed her back to a canter, satisfied that we hadn't lost the parade. I didn't know where in the Surrey Docks we would find the *Lady of Gloucester* and would have to rely on the vehicles ahead leading me there.

I wondered if I would be there all alone. My messages to Detective Sergeant Jackson and to Stanley Havers at the Silver

Vaults might not reach them in time. Still, I thought, I don't even know what I can do when I get there anyway. If Millie was there, would I dash in and rescue her, just like one of the heroes in the penny dreadfuls? Ha, ha.

Esmee knew when we had arrived sooner than I did. Her horse sense told her. She probably smelled all those other horses ahead. She slowed her canter to a walk, then she stopped. I got down from the cab. The air was chilly, though the fog patches were fainter here, and it was just a heavy mist. A slight drizzle of rain was trying to fall. It was quiet.

We had stopped near a gate in a wire fence. The gate had been opened, and I led Esmee in by hand, taking it very slowly, one pace at a time. I could feel the breeze off the river, and I went in that direction. A tall lamp standard held an oil lamp that cast the least amount of light to be able to see. Coils of heavy rope were piled up in stacks by a shed with a rusting roof. A couple of heavy wheelbarrows stood near the shed, and I tied Esmee to one of them.

Then I saw the broughams and the hearse. They were pulled up close together, and men were starting to get out of them. They must have only just got here. The bruisers came out first and stood in a cluster, waiting to be told what to do. Sir George—or Mr. John—got out too, and so did Dorothy. Sir George called Blinker over and the two of them talked.

I could hear the sound, but I wasn't close enough to hear what they were saying. I kept well back so that I wouldn't be seen. My fear was that Esmee would let out a whinny of greeting to the other horses, but I didn't know how Titch told her to hold her tongue.

The mist thinned out, and I had to move back hastily. I did get a glimpse of the river though, and I could see a handsome boat tied up there. It was big and long and looked like it could cruise round the world if her owner wanted it to. I couldn't see the name, but I had no doubt it was the *Lady of Gloucester.*

Sir George and Blinker were still talking. Someone else was getting out of the first brougham. My heart sank. it looked like Ivor. Another figure was coming down the step. Yes, it was Millie.

I watched, unable to do anything for her, feeling completely helpless. I had the urge to shout to her, to tell her to come so that we could jump into Titch's hansom and race off into the night.

I knew it wouldn't work. Mr. John's bruisers were much closer to her than I was, and they would grab her first and then come after me. I realized I was going to have to take chances, but that wasn't a good one. Mr. John and Blinker ended their conversation. Mr. John added a few words and Blinker went to the hearse.

The rear doors opened and two men began to drag a large coffin out. Blinker shouted an order, and two more men separated themselves from the group and went to help. They found the weight too much for them, and Blinker hastily got four more men. All of them staggering, they got the coffin to the boat. One unfastened a section of rail, then suddenly a huge light, like the ones they use in the theatre as spotlights, cut through the darkness like a great knife. It came from the boat and a voice called out, "Put that coffin on the forward deck, then step back. Do as you're told, and no one will get hurt."

The words came through a megaphone and were loud and clear. I recognized the voice. It belonged to the colonel.

CHAPTER 29

The man the colonel had planted inside Mr. John's organization had done a good job. Unfortunately, it had cost him his life. It had certainly brought everything to a standstill now. I could see the figures of Mr. John's men, outlined against the white mist like they were painted on a white canvas. The huge hearse was a big black shape too, and the broughams looked small beside it.

I could just hear Mr. John's voice as he spoke quietly to the men near him, but I couldn't make out his words. The men who had brought the coffin walked slowly around it and put out their hands to push it on to the deck. Mr. John snapped out an order, and a rattle of gunshots shattered the misty silence.

They were using the coffin as a shield, and Mr. John was calling out more orders. Other men, farther away, pulled out guns and opened fire too. On board the *Lady of Gloucester,* the rattle of breaking glass mixed with the crunch of bullets striking wood. Mr. John must be furious at the damage being done to his beautiful boat. Good, I thought, serve him right. At the same time, I was dismayed by his single-mindedness. He had immediately ordered his men to fire on his own boat. Most men would have hesitated, but he was ruthless enough to decide that the treasure was more valuable than the boat. He could probably buy a dozen boats with the proceeds from the contents of the coffin.

I tried to spot Millie. In all this turmoil, perhaps I could grab her and sneak her away. But I when saw her, two men were with her and Ivor, pulling them back towards the hearse.

A stray bullet whizzed over my head. The colonel's men were returning the fire. Another came, closer this time. Blimey, this was getting dangerous. I wanted to get away, but I knew I couldn't. I had to stay and see this through.

Where was Detective Sergeant Jackson when I needed him? And the security blokes from the Silver Vaults, what about them? Didn't they have a night shift?

I wondered if there was a harbormaster, or at least a customs office somewhere near. With a lot of expensive private boats in the Surrey Docks, they must have protection. Where was it?

I had a lot of questions but no answers. Another thought came to me. A police station couldn't be too far away. Was it too much to hope that someone had reported gunfire?

Waiting is not one of my strong points. I had to go and do . . . what? Perhaps I could find a police station or get a passerby to do it.

The breeze had strengthened, and the mist was thinning. A weak moon was trying to squeeze between some straggling clouds. If it did, someone would soon see me. If I were to go and look for help, now was the best time to do it. I worked my way back to the gate.

The gun battle was still raging on, and the odd bullet still whizzed past. They'd never notice me. I hurried to the gate; heard footsteps behind me. A rough voice called, out but a volley of shots drowned out the words. As I was reaching the gate, a man moved out of the gloom and into the gateway. I stopped and the other man came from behind.

They marched me back, an iron grip on each arm, back into the battle zone. They had moved one of the broughams and were using it as a shelter. Mr. John was there, and when he saw me, he smiled like a cat that has seen a canary. Dorothy stood, stone faced. Millie and Ivor were there too, both looking scared to death.

"Hello, Millie," I said, and went to move to her, but one of the blokes holding me pulled a hand out of his pocket to show he had a pistol in it. I stayed where I was. A couple more bullets whistled overhead. A third tore into the roof of the brougham, sending splinters flying.

Millie gave me a weak smile. Ivor glared at me as if this was all my fault.

"So you've come back to us, Ned," said Mr. John, "I thought you might, one way or another. I suppose you are responsible for the colonel knowing where and when to find me."

I hadn't expected that. I shook my head firmly. "Not me, no, I—"

"Just like your father, aren't you? Selling tidbits of information to both sides."

"I didn't. I—"

"That was what killed him. You know that, don't you?"

I said nothing. I had heard these stories before and didn't believe them.

He must have seen the disbelief in my face.

"It's true." He was enjoying rubbing it in. "He did a thorough job of nosing out Nathan Zimmerman's jewelry store. Found out about the alarms, the times of the guards' patrols, when the store had built up its biggest inventory—everything. I got together a crew of real professionals . . ."

His voice was getting what the penny dreadfuls call *menacing*. "They did what they were supposed to do, and they did it well. Only you know what happened?"

I thought it safer not to answer.

"Your dad told the coppers. They were waiting, inside, outside . . . Two of my best men were shot dead. One lasted only a week in hospital. The others are still doing time."

His red, prosperous-looking face was more like a snarling wolf-man now. "And now, here you are, playing the crooked cross just like him, blowing to the colonel."

I wanted to shout that I hadn't done that. I wanted to yell that the colonel had threatened me, but that I hadn't snitched to him. I wanted to tell Mr. John that the colonel had held me in Smithfield Meat Market amid all the bleeding corpses of animals as an example of what he could do to me if I didn't pass on to him what I knew, and still I had told him nothing.

I didn't say any of that because my mental protests were overshadowed by the realization that I was being forced to accept a truth. It was a truth I had always denied. And the truth was that my old dad had played both sides against the middle. He had told the ruffians how to crack a crib, and he had told the coppers what the ruffians were doing.

It wasn't an easy truth to swallow, and it was choking me. But it must be true. This wasn't the first time I had heard the story. The colonel had said it, Jacko had said it. I just hadn't believed it. It couldn't be true, I had told myself. But I couldn't fight it any longer.

I shook my head. I suppose Mr. John thought I was protesting to save myself, but really I was saying, "No, my old dad wouldn't do that," yet knowing in my heart that's what he did.

Gunshots crackled again, a real barrage, all of them coming from the boat. One bullet ripped into the brougham, another flew low just past it. Mr. John's men behind the coffin crouched low, holding their fire. No wonder. They were so close that if they poked their heads up, they would get them shot off. Then the shooting stopped. The silence was scary. A couple of seabirds, flying low up the river, squawked, and then there was silence again.

Several of Mr. John's men looked at him, waiting for orders. Then one man shouted, "Look! They're going! See?"

He was pointing out past the boat. Sure enough, a couple of dinghies were nearly halfway across the Thames, men at the oars heaving for all they were worth. The colonel had decided to call it a day. That last volley of shots had provided cover for them. A few of Mr. John's men took aim and fired at the boats, but they were pulling out of range.

"Right!" Mr. John shouted. "Let's get this on board!"

The coffin was a big, awkward shape to push. The tide must be in, too, for the deck of the *Lady of Gloucester* was about two feet higher than the dock. That meant a big lifting effort, and the men strained and grunted. Mr. John waved more men forward, and those around the brougham went to help. Too many cooks spoil the broth, they always say.

That was the case here. Blokes were getting in each other's way, trying to get a handhold, some lifting, some pushing. It would have made a good sketch for the music hall.

Mr. John climbed on board the boat and disappeared inside. Right away, smoke started to puff out of the stack. For the moment, we were forgotten, Millie and Ivor and me. I caught Millie's eye and motioned her to come to me. She looked doubtful but before she could make up her mind, I was amazed to see three hansom cabs coming pounding in through the gate.

They came to a standstill, and men began spilling out. Leading them was Stanley Havers, a gun in his hand. "Come on," I called to Millie, and we ran to Stanley, me waving my arms so he didn't shoot me.

"They're trying to get away," I panted. "The treasure's in the coffin."

"They won't get far," said Stanley. "Look!"

The moon had slid out of the clouds and was bathing everything in a weak light.

Out on the Thames and coming in fast were three police launches, all filled with men.

"Sergeant Jackson got your message, and I was able to have a word with him before he gathered his armada," said Stanley.

Mr. John's blokes weren't putting up much resistance. A couple of shots came our way, but then they saw the police launches and knew they were trapped and outnumbered. Without Mr. John to give them orders, some ran, some just threw their hands in the air.

CHAPTER 30

Why do the police always want a statement? Don't they know what happened, or is it that they can't remember? But I always try to oblige Her Majesty's minions, so I presented myself at the Pimlico Police Station as requested.

After the hectic events at the Surrey Docks, it was late morning before the police let me go. Jacko was at his most official, but I suppose he had to be, what with a senior magistrate being involved and a lot of other prominent persons being named. Not having had a wink of sleep, by the time I had got back home and fed Perseus, I was out on my feet. I slept the rest of the day and night and appeared to give my statement at nine a.m. on the morning of the next day.

Jacko was putting on one of his best performances. Outwardly, it was his "Oh, this is all part of the average day in a busy detective's life," but inwardly, I knew he was gloating. Yes, that was the word, gloating. He could see a possible promotion or, at the very least, a commendation from the commissioner.

After half an hour of questioning, he had me sign the statement. Then he sat back in his uncomfortable chair. "You're telling me a lot of information now that you have been withholding, Parker."

"I wasn't exactly withholding any of it," I explained. "Mr. John—well, Sir George as we know he is—threatened to nobble me if I spilled as much as one bean. As for the colonel—" I gave him a description, detail by detail, of our meeting in the Smithfield Meat Market. "He made sure that I saw every drop of blood coming from those dripping carcasses," I said, laying it on with a trowel. "He told me that I'd be hanging on one of those hooks—that it would be my blood trickling down those drain holes if—"

"All right, all right," Jacko interrupted. "You don't have to go on. I only just had my breakfast."

"Then there was Millie. They threatened her and—"

"Yes, well, we might be able to drop any charges of withholding information, I suppose," he grumbled. "Now, this sailor at the Admiralty. He'd better corroborate your story."

"If you mean he should say the same as me, he will. His name's Lieutenant Waverley. Ask him anything you want."

He wrote the name down. "Why'd you bring in those chaps from the Silver Vaults?" He sounded a bit testy on this point. "This was a job for the police, there was no reason for—"

"I didn't know the word would get through to you. I mean late at night, you could have been at the opera—"

He gave me his glare.

"—or somewhere like that. I didn't want to be all alone out there at the docks. I wanted help from somebody."

I didn't think it necessary to tell him that I had considered summoning the Admiralty too. If I had known how to get in touch with Lieutenant Waverley, I would have had him bring a squad of sailors. Blimey, what a party that would have been!

Jacko grunted. "Now let's go through this business in the London Bridge Underground Station. It all sounds a bit theatrical to me."

"Well, it would be, wouldn't it? Sir George had a lot of money invested in theatres, and besides, his lady friend, Dorothy Radcliffe, put on the shows. Life must have been a big spectacular production to them. Lots of money and people to push around. They were like puppeteers in a way, and enjoying it."

"You're sure about all these important people who were there? If I go pulling them in, I've got to be sure I can nail them. Otherwise, I'm liable to find myself up to the kneecaps in lawyers waving writs and telling me to cease and desist."

"Getting evidence is your job. I can only tell you who they were and why Sir George used them. He had to have work stopped on the station once he found that the only way to get at the treasure was from the platform, so he needed the cove from the transport committee. Zimmerman, the one who was going to handle the ingots and the bullion stuff too heavy for Sir George to take on the yacht—"

"Zimmerman," muttered Jacko, scribbling away. "Yes, I've seen his name before. There was a nasty business at the Mint last year and he—well, nabbing him should make a few people on the Metals Exchange happy."

"The one who's on the Police Commission for Combating Crime and Corruption," I said innocently. "He must be playing both sides against the middle."

"You're apt to find a bad apple in any sack of good ones," said Jacko sanctimoniously. "What about this Dunstan chap? What's he been up to?"

"He was drunk while all this was going on," I said. Now I'm not what they call malicious, but I'm only human. Nobody could blame me for getting in a dig or two that might keep Mr. Ivor Dunstan, singer, actor and comedian, out of my way for a time. "Still," I added, "being in a lot of Sir George and Dorothy Radcliffe's shows, he could have picked up some chaunt. If you lean on him, he might sing to you."

Eventually, Jacko had all the names down and checked them twice to get the spellings right. I said, "You've been asking me a lot of questions. Let me ask you one. Three of us cabbies went to the city offices to present a petition for a trades union. They turned us down. But the chief bloke was Sir George. He owns the Willoughby Bus Line, and they've got hundreds more buses coming on the streets. Naturally, he voted against us. And now, he's exposed as Mr. John, a known gangster. Don't you think we should be able to present our petition again and get three straight coves to hear our case?"

"I'm no lawyer," Jacko said, "but I'd think you've got an excellent case."

I nodded, filing that away in my mind. It would be a useful one to quote if we needed a bit of help.

"Any more questions?" asked Jacko, feeling full of himself now that he had all these juicy tidbits on his writing pad.

"Just one. Did my old dad really sell information to you, the police, and turn around and sell it to the ruffians too?"

Jacko ruffled the sheets of paper in the pad. "It's water under the bridge."

"I think I deserve the truth," I said, hoity-toity.

He still hesitated.

"That's what Mr. John told me," I added. "I don't think he was getting at me. It sounded like—well, it sounded like that's the way it was."

"Influenza was what the doctor put on the death certificate," said Jacko.

"His face was all bashed up and he—"

"He'd been beaten real bad—and by expert punishers. He wouldn't have lived anyway, but he was so weak that the 'flu finished him off right away."

"Did he give information to both sides?" I asked again.

"Persistent, aren't you?"

"I want to know."

"It's past and gone. It—"

"He did, didn't he?"

Jacko gave the slightest of half nods. "No reason to tell you before. Like father, like son is a bad saying. I wish people wouldn't use it. It's not that way at all. I didn't want to see you going the same way."

"It's that why you've always kept a sharp eye on me?" I grinned.

Jacko pretended to be studying his notes.

" 'Course not, I keep a sharp eye on every cabby in London. They're right there in the thick of things, have a finger on the pulse. They're in a position to do a lot of good—or a lot of the other stuff. Good thing they're not all as inquisitive as you though."

"Maybe you wish they were," I said. "Make your job easier, wouldn't it?"

"It's Ned Parker, isn't it? Should be Nosy Parker. That's what they should call you. Perhaps after this, they will. Perhaps anybody who is nosy will be called a Nosy Parker." He pulled the pad towards him. "Now, you'd better get back to that cab of yours. It looks like rain today, should be plenty of fares."

"Yes, sergeant." I gave him a mock salute and headed for the door. "You know, you're not a bad bloke—"

I saved the rest until I had the door open.

"—for a copper," I said, and went out fast.

After I'd unhitched Perseus, I turned him in the direction of Clapham. Young James was in school and Cecilia was cleaning the windows. She looked at me suspiciously, put down her bucket and rags, and brought me into the living room.

"It's not even lunchtime yet. What are you doing here?"

"I wanted to tell you all the news."

Her face changed. "News! You weren't mixed up in that terrible business down at Surrey Docks, were you? It was in the papers this morning, said something about cab drivers—"

I told her the whole story. Well, almost the whole story. I left out a lot about Dorothy Radcliffe.

Cecilia listened with an open mouth. "You did all that?" she asked at the end.

"Oh, I didn't do that much," I said, looking down at my boots and shuffling them.

"They should have put your name in the papers! Helping to catch all those villains!"

"Better they didn't. Some of them might come after me. One or two might have got away."

"And fancy that Sir George Willoughby turning out to be a gang leader! Good job he drowned trying to get away. He was the one you and Mr. Meecham were talking about that day at Saint Mary-in-the-Fields, wasn't he?"

"That's right."

"Then there's that Dorothy Radcliffe, who puts on all those shows! She was his lady friend, it said. Think she'll go to trial when she gets out of hospital?"

"She might."

Cecilia wanted a lot more detail: how close did bullets come to me, how glad I must have been to see the Silver Vaults security people and the police boats coming. I told her nearly all she wanted to know, and she gave me an admiring look. "You're quite a celebrity, Ned—or least you should be. Pity everybody doesn't know about it."

"Just as well," I said.

"What about Millie? I'm amazed at her being mixed up in it."

"She wasn't, really. More of an innocent bystander. She's at home, recovering."

"Can you stay and have something to eat?"

"No, I have to make up for some lost time. Now, what about you? Doing all right?"

"Managing. That nice man at the Admiralty didn't say how long it would take for me to get some of Jack's pay, did he?"

"No. Is it getting tight?"

"Yes, it is." She made a face. "It's going to be a struggle, but surely the navy will be sending me some money soon."

"In the meantime," I said, "why don't you think about opening a little business."

"A business? Me?"

"What about a milliner's shop? You know, ribbons and laces. Or what about hats?"

She gave a little laugh. "Have you any idea of how much it costs to open a shop like that?"

"No," I said, "but it shouldn't be a problem." I put my hand in my pocket, held it out and opened it.

Her eyes got big as soup plates.

She was looking at a ring with an emerald the size of a plover's egg.

"Is . . . is it real?"

" 'Course it is."

"Where did you get it?"

"Well, you might say it fell off the back of a hearse—"

"What!"

"Only in a manner of speaking," I explained.

She gave that sigh she often does when she says I exasperate her.

"What are you doing with it?"

I told her how Sir George had invited everybody on the platform to come and look at the treasure wagon, and how they'd all sifted their hands through the treasures. "I could see Sir George sort of keeping an eye on them to make sure their hands were empty when they took them out. Well, see, my hand was empty too—except I pushed a finger into this beauty here so that only the band showed, and you could hardly see that."

She was still looking at the big green stone, mesmerized. "But what would I do with it?" she wondered.

I thought about that. "I might be able to help you there, sis. See, I know a place on the Finchley Road . . ."

ABOUT THE AUTHOR

Peter King sold his first story at the age of seven and has been writing ever since. He sold 150 articles and short stories to magazines and newspapers in England and the U.S. and has had twenty-five books published—mysteries, teenage adventures, books on mining, metallurgy and space travel.

He owned and operated a tungsten mine in Death Valley, worked in the Amazon basin and led the team that built the engines to put the first man on the moon.